Sign up for our newsletter to hear
about new and upcoming releases.

www.ylva-publishing.com

PRINCIPLE—
—DECISIONS

Thea Belmont

ACKNOWLEDGMENTS

There are so many people who made this book happen. First, I wouldn't be here without Lee Winter, my editor. This manuscript wasn't a diamond in the rough; it was a lump of carbon you took and made into a polished diamond. Thank you so very much for your never-ending patience with me and my self-consciousness, and for all of your skills in making this story something amazing.

Thank you to Astrid and Ylva for taking a chance on me. I can never repay the joy you brought to me with this opportunity, but I hope that I can prove myself as a right choice.

Thanks to Ellie, who brought the finishing touches to Principal Rothschild and taught me the Jewish holidays between September and October with such passion and enthusiasm.

And thank you so very much to Sage, Leslie, Dee, Em, Cherry, Gabie, Abbi, Caity, and, of course, Sophie. I expect my terrible typos will be appearing on social media again soon!

DEDICATION

For the Principle Decisions group chat. Without you all, this would be nothing but a work in progress, abandoned after six chapters.

CHAPTER 1
DOMINATRIX

Professor Vivienne Carter leaned back in her chair and stared at the embossed black lettering on the bright red business card:

Selene
Dominatrix

On the reverse side was a phone number and email address.

The card had slipped out of the book she had just purchased as a favor to her sister, Hattie, who worked at the bookstore. If Hattie wasn't so awkward around any mention of sex, Vivienne might have suspected her of having slipped the card into the book. No, the woman advertising her services had likely decided that the newest racy bestseller would be an excellent place to advertise her business.

It had been some time since Vivienne had engaged in any sexual relationship. Since her brother, Robert, and his wife had died, Vivienne's life was consumed with raising her niece, Claudia. Hattie coparented by making sure the home was clean and the family had a meal to gather around, but the bulk of Claudia's upbringing rested on Vivienne's shoulders. Between that and a full teaching and publishing workload at the university, she had little time to date.

And the few times she had dated, she'd inevitably found herself frustrated by the changes to her routine. It was easier to end things before they became complicated.

At least if she engaged a dominatrix, she wouldn't have to manage the emotional baggage of a lengthy relationship. She'd have her needs taken care of without having to consider someone else's.

Someone knocked at her office door, pulling her from her thoughts.

"One moment," Vivienne said and stuffed the card into her desk drawer. She should throw it away, but not just yet. "Come in."

The door opened. Her sixteen-year-old niece stood leaning against the doorframe, school bag slung over her shoulder. She was the very picture of her brother, with her round face and hazel eyes, though she had her mother's golden hair. Robert, like Vivienne, had had red hair. "Are you ready to head home?"

"In a moment," Vivienne said and closed her laptop. "How was school?"

"Fine."

"Nothing happened today?"

"Well," Claudia began, bouncing on her toes, "Principal Rothschild went on a warpath against Coach Myers. That was pretty cool."

"Rothschild? Isn't Mitchells your principal?"

"No, he left over the summer. It was in the news bulletin."

"Oh." Vivienne didn't usually read the news bulletins. That was Hattie's area. Parent-teacher meetings were hers. "Why did your new principal go on this alleged warpath?" she asked as she packed up her day planner and ungraded papers.

"Coach Myers told Luca that he couldn't join the football team. So Bec and I complained to Principal Rothschild, and she told him off in the middle of tryouts. It was pretty awesome that she did that."

Luca was one of Claudia's oldest friends. He had recently come out as a trans boy. He'd always been athletic, so Vivienne suspected the reason the coach had barred him from the team had nothing to do with a lack of skill. "It's definitely a way to make enemies," Vivienne said. "Take it from me, Claudia. Public humiliation may force someone to obey for a moment, but they'll look for opportunities to take revenge."

Claudia pressed her lips shut, her excitement fading. "I thought it was cool that she called him out for his transphobia."

PRINCIPLE DECISIONS

"And the best place to do that is in a formal setting," Vivienne said as the two of them stepped into the hall. Vivienne switched off the light, then shut and locked the door. "In a position of leadership, especially one so newly forged, it's better to think about the long-term goals for a stable work environment. Sowing discord will only turn the other teachers against her."

"Well, the students love her," Claudia said.

Vivienne sighed. Her niece had missed the point entirely. But she was only sixteen and thought the world revolved around her. She didn't understand that students would come and go, but the teachers remained, and if Principal Rothschild wanted to keep her job, it would be in her interest to have their support.

"How did your classes go?" she asked, shifting to a safer topic as they walked to the parking lot.

Claudia began discussing her recent grades in English and history, described the study group she'd formed, then fell silent.

"Did you not receive your French essay results today?"

Claudia flushed and fiddled with her bag. "I...passed."

Vivienne stopped to look at her niece. "Define 'passed.'"

"C-plus?"

Vivienne pressed her lips together, biting back her anger, and watched Claudia squirm under her scrutiny. "Perhaps I should switch to speaking French at home, then?"

"No, I hate it when you do that. Look, this essay doesn't count much towards anything. I'll bring up my grade with the next essay at the end of the month, and then I'll be back to being an A-minus student."

"Yes, well, unless you want your allowance to drop—"

"Come on! That's not fair. It's not like we live in France. I don't even see the point of taking this stupid class."

"Language is important, Claudia. When you travel, you can't just assume everyone speaks English. By the time I was your age, I already spoke Italian and French fluently and I could read and understand Latin. By my twenties, I'd learned Mandarin and German."

"I know, but...I don't even know if I want to travel."

"Of course you do," Vivienne said. "Everyone travels, or they end up like your Aunt Hattie, working in a bookstore with no idea of how the world works."

Claudia fell silent. When they arrived at the car, she climbed into the passenger seat, set her bag on her lap, and buckled her seatbelt, her face a stony mask.

Vivienne sighed. Claudia had always been fond of Hattie, defending her anytime Vivienne criticized her. Only last night, the three of them had argued after Hattie announced that she would be working full-time at the bookstore and not just helping out. Hattie had a bachelor's degree; how could she be content with a retail position?

They drove in silence, Claudia's bad mood taking up space in the car. As soon as they arrived home, Claudia unbuckled her seatbelt and fled without waiting for Vivienne to turn off the engine, racing up the steps to the porch and into the house.

Vivienne watched her disappear. Her niece would likely remain in her room until dinner. She considered following to explain how disrespectful her actions were, but it had already been a long day. She didn't want another argument with her family.

Vivienne climbed the porch steps. Hattie sat in a rocking chair with a book on her lap, sipping a glass of iced tea. She greeted her sister with a smile that accentuated the wrinkles on her face. "Evening, Viv. How was your day?"

"Busy," she said, her tone sharp.

Hattie looked away, a flush rising to her cheeks.

Vivienne softened, thinking to apologize, but the thought was snuffed out when a door slammed upstairs.

She walked through the kitchen to her home office, set her bag down, and pulled out her laptop and the student papers, preparing for the evening's work. Midway through her preparations, she looked at the clock. Nearly dinnertime.

She pushed back her chair and went out to the kitchen. Hattie had come in from the porch and was at the stove, sautéing onions. A pot of vegetables simmered on another burner.

"Shall I set the table?" Vivienne asked. Usually, it was Claudia's job to set the table for dinner, but she could do the dishes afterwards instead, given her sullen mood.

"Oh!" Hattie looked back at Vivienne, startled. "I didn't hear you come in."

"And yet you knew I was home, so I don't understand why you jump all the time."

"Oh, well…" Hattie returned her attention to the cooking. "So what did you think of Jonathan's bookstore? Quite the business, hmm? And the café has been so busy lately!"

Vivienne set down the plates to keep from saying what she really thought. "It's…good that you're happy."

Hattie glanced at Vivienne over her shoulder and smiled.

Vivienne smiled in return, and it was enough to release the knot in her chest. Perhaps they could make it through dinner without another argument.

"Have you started reading *In Her Control* yet? People are saying it's a real page-turner."

Vivienne tucked a wayward curl behind her ear. She'd only gotten as far as the first page when the card had fallen onto her desk. *Dominatrix*. Something about that embossed lettering sparked an almost-forgotten flame inside her. She shivered, remembering how it felt to have rope twisting around her wrists, remembering the various forms of BDSM she had engaged in with different partners, both on the receiving and giving end.

It had been at least two years since she'd done anything other than masturbation. The dating pool in the Oakdale area was so small that, inevitably, everyone knew everyone else. And given her position, casual sex would only lead to complications. But a dominatrix would be discreet. And it would just be scratching an itch, after all.

"Viv?"

She looked up.

Her sister was looking at her quizzically.

"Pardon?"

"I asked if you had started the book."

"Oh. Only the first few pages or so. I'll get to it on the weekend," Vivienne said.

Hattie stepped forward, her hand raised toward Vivienne's forehead. "You're looking a little flushed. You're not coming down with the flu, are you? You're always working yourself ragged."

"I'm fine," she said, waving her sister's hand away. "I'll go tell Claudia to wash up, shall I?"

"I suppose. Dinner will be ready in a moment."

CHAPTER 2
GROUND RULES

THE WEEK'S CLASSES WERE EXHAUSTING. Teaching first-year undergrads reminded Vivienne why she'd avoided teaching them for the past two years. Many students failed to attend classes or, worse, reeked of cheap vodka and pot as they sat in the back of the room wearing sunglasses—as if she didn't know what that meant. *Please.*

If she was going to teach, Vivienne wanted engaged students, responding to questions rather than staring blankly at her. Third-year students were used to her method of teaching, having completed her prerequisite courses. They knew how to conduct themselves, reminding Vivienne why she continued to teach.

She sat rigidly at her desk, hands curled into fists. Never again, she vowed. Even if Elijah threatened to cut her third-year courses entirely, it would be an empty threat because Janice usually taught the first-years, leaving Vivienne to unteach them everything in their second year.

Perhaps educating the first-year students herself was the lesser of two evils.

She needed a drink.

No, she needed a cigarette, but she'd have to leave her office for that, and she still had fifteen minutes of office hours left. Although usually, the only students who came through her office doors were there to beg for extra credit because they were failing.

Fuck it. She needed a cigarette.

Opening her desk drawer, she reached in to pull out her cigarette case. She stopped at the sight of the red business card.

Selene

Vivienne picked it up.

What she needed was relief. It didn't have to be sex; it just had to be *something*.

Last night, she'd drained the batteries of her favorite vibrator, and despite rolling through three orgasms, desire still prickled under her skin.

Before she could change her mind, she picked up her phone and dialed the number. If the dominatrix was someone she knew, she'd end the call immediately. Her office line was private—they wouldn't be able to call her back.

With the first ring, Vivienne's heart pounded in her chest. Was it a good idea to engage the services of a dominatrix? Wouldn't it be better to stop at the store and pick up some…

"Good afternoon. How can I be of service?"

Vivienne hesitated, her mouth suddenly dry. The husky voice was that of an older woman. Firm. Confident. And no one she knew.

"Hello?"

"I"—Vivienne bit her lip—"found your business card."

"Oh? And which business card is that?"

Which business card? Perhaps the town didn't have enough clientele to sustain the services of a dominatrix, and the woman had a primary job that paid the bills. "The red card."

"Mm. Remind me of the services listed on that card," the woman said in a voice that was almost a purr.

Vivienne shivered, glancing at the door of her office to make sure it was closed. "You know perfectly well."

"I do, but you need to say it."

"Why do I need to say it?"

"If you want this service, you need to say the word."

Vivienne adjusted herself in the chair, tugging nervously at her skirt.

"Go on and say it, and I promise to stop teasing."

Vivienne gulped and shut her eyes. "Dominatrix," she whispered.

As soon as she said the word, she was filled with panic. She shouldn't have done this from her office. Any student wandering the hall might overhear. She should have called the woman from her car or from home. Or not at all. What did she need a dominatrix for anyway? She should have picked up new batteries instead.

"Good girl. You've called the right woman. My name is Selene. I have an opening for tomorrow evening. Say…six o'clock?"

"Six?"

"And do be on time. Tardiness will be punished."

Vivienne scoffed. She had never been late in her life. "I'll be on time."

"Good. Now, I'll need a name for the booking."

"A name?" Of course she needed a name.

"Just a first name. Don't worry. I promise absolute discretion."

"Vivienne," she answered, her heart beating faster. She should have chosen a pseudonym, but it was too late now.

"Vivienne." The woman breathed out her name. "Do you know the address?"

"No, I do not."

Selene gave her the address with instructions to use the back entrance. "The session will be forty-five minutes. However, we'll need to run through some housekeeping matters first, so expect to be there for an hour."

"What sort of housekeeping matters?"

"Just a few ground rules. This needs to be enjoyable for both of us. The first rule is no alcohol beforehand. It tends to dull the senses, and I need you aware of your tolerances."

"That's the only rule?"

"Well, I expect you to be showered before arriving; that's common courtesy. I do have facilities, however, in case you need to clean up before you leave."

Vivienne squeezed her thighs together, anticipation growing inside her. The woman was having an effect on her already. "Fine."

"Mm. Well, I need to run, but I look forward to meeting you tomorrow, Vivienne. I can't wait to play with you." And she hung up.

Vivienne looked down at the phone. It was booked. She was booked for tomorrow.

What the fuck was she doing?

She began to agonize over her choice of clothes. Should she wear something formal or informal? Should she dress up in leather and lace? Did it even matter what she wore, so long as her lingerie was acceptable? Did that even matter?

Vivienne had never engaged a sex worker. She'd been to informally organized orgies and attended a few sex parties, but this was different. It had been a long time since she'd felt butterflies in her stomach.

From the moment Vivienne had her coffee at eight on Saturday morning, the clock on the wall ever-so-slowly ticked the hours away. At last it was four o'clock. Time to change into appropriate evening wear.

"A rather late meeting," Hattie said as Vivienne slid her coat on. "You know, if it's a date, you can tell me."

"It most certainly is not a date," Vivienne said firmly. The last thing she needed was her sister's curiosity piqued. "I'll be home after seven."

"All right. Shall I have dinner ready for seven thirty, then?"

"If you wish." She checked her appearance one last time before picking up her handbag from the table. It held only her phone, wallet, and makeup, in case the woman left marks. "But don't wait for me."

She passed Claudia in the foyer and paused.

Her niece shifted her dreamy expression to neutral. "You're going out?" Claudia asked.

"A meeting regarding some funding, I'm afraid. I'll be home for dinner."

Claudia nodded but didn't move. She tapped her fingers at her sides as she shifted her weight.

"Was there something else?" Vivienne asked. She loathed it when Claudia danced around a topic.

"Bec and Luca are having a sleepover tomorrow night. Could I stay over at Bec's? Mr. Walter will take us to school the next day."

Vivienne pursed her lips. She suspected that her niece was planning to wander off and see young Henry Riley. Not that that was so unusual for a girl her age. Vivienne had often snuck out when she was sixteen. "If you have your homework done by then."

Claudia beamed. "I will," she agreed. "Thank you."

Vivienne waved her off. She considered gently reminding her niece to take protection, then decided against it. Vivienne had given Claudia a pack of condoms when she began dating Henry (much to Claudia's embarrassment) and had revisited the sex talk, making sure Claudia understood consent and equality in sex. Claudia knew she could ask for advice. But more importantly, she had a good head on her shoulders.

"I'll see you later tonight," Vivienne said.

"Enjoy your meeting." Claudia bounced away.

After Vivienne got in her car, she sat for a minute to consider the night ahead. Her stomach fluttered as she buckled her seatbelt and started the engine. The address that Selene gave her was in the business district.

As she pulled into the dark alley, she became briefly concerned that she was being conned somehow. At the same time, she doubted the longevity of such a con—it was far easier to rob someone at an ATM.

The building was a two-story brick house with ivy climbing its walls, nestled between an auto repair shop and a mattress store, both closed for the night. The top-floor lights were on. A shadow moved behind the window curtain, as if someone were walking around in the room.

She was fifteen minutes early. She parked, then looked into the rearview mirror to fix her hair before she stepped out, locking the car behind her. As she reached the door at the top of the stairs, she hesitated. What the hell was she doing? Was this why she had pulled out enough cash for two weeks' worth of groceries? Yet, as she stood at the door of the house, her spine prickled with anticipation.

She rang the doorbell before she could change her mind.

There was the sound of steps walking downstairs, then a shadow shifted through the window's opaque curtain. An outside light flickered on, and the door opened.

The woman—Selene?—looked Vivienne up and down, a smile breaking out on her red lips. "Oh, aren't you just divine."

Vivienne drew in a sharp breath. The woman was nothing like she had expected. When she thought of a dominatrix, she pictured a plain, pale woman wearing red lipstick and dressed in PVC or leather. But Selene was striking in a burgundy blouse and a pencil skirt. Her thick, wavy hair was dark against the soft brown of her skin, making her blue eyes all the more prominent. The sudden rush of desire made Vivienne want to be kissed by her, to be pinned against the wall, curling her hands into the dark mane of hair.

Selene let out a short laugh, her eyes sparkling, as if she were reading Vivienne's thoughts. "Usually, I would make some snide comment about where my eyes are, but I like you."

Vivienne straightened, reaching into her handbag to mask her embarrassment. "Selene, I take it?" she asked, pulling out the business card. "I found this in a book."

Vivienne had the sudden feeling of being a mouse in the sights of a cat. Selene reached out and dragged her fingers along the edge of the card until she was touching Vivienne's hand.

"I had a feeling someone special would find this. Well…come inside," Selene said, stepping aside and gesturing for Vivienne to enter. "I'll give you a tour."

Selene led her down a hall where several paintings were displayed. Vivienne didn't recognize any of the artists' names scrawled in the corners.

Reaching an open doorway, the woman turned to face Vivienne. "Here we have the kitchen. After a session, you will sit here with a cup of coffee or tea until I'm certain you're able to drive home safely." She turned toward another door and flicked a switch before opening it to reveal a small, well-maintained garden inside high, brick walls. The branches of a large shade tree sheltered a variety of flowers. Grass lined the stone-path walkway. "This is the garden, if you want to do any outdoor sessions. There's an outdoor shower too," she said, pointing to the side of the house.

Vivienne looked around, uncertain if she should mention now that she wasn't comfortable in an outdoor setting. But before she could open her mouth, Selene had turned off the lights and gone back inside.

"Follow me," she said, glancing back at Vivienne with a half smile, and led her up a flight of narrow stairs. At the landing, she turned to face Vivienne. "You need to switch off your phone before we begin."

"Of course." Vivienne pulled out her phone and switched it to airplane mode.

"While I don't mind photo sessions, they need to be negotiated in detail beforehand," Selene said and turned to mount the rest of the stairs.

"I don't think that will be necessary."

Without responding, Selene continued down the hall, pointing out the bathroom, then leading Vivienne to the bedroom. As she opened the door, Vivienne's stomach tightened.

She wasn't sure exactly what she had expected—maybe something like a dungeon with shades of black and red—but the expansive bedroom was warm, almost straight-out-of-a-furniture-catalog nice, and with a feeling of home to it. It had ambient light, a queen-sized four-poster bed, and more paintings on the walls. A dresser of dark red wood was placed under the single window, and a full-length mirror hung in one corner. A sheepskin rug was laid out on the floor by the bed.

If it weren't for the hook hanging from the ceiling and a partially opened wardrobe revealing an array of kink tools, Vivienne would have thought this was the woman's actual home or, at the very least, a midrange bed and breakfast.

"How does this work?" Vivienne asked. "Forgive me for being candid, but this is my first time engaging the services of…this profession."

"No need to ask forgiveness so soon." Selene stepped closer. "First, we'll negotiate what you want versus what I'm comfortable doing. We'll begin after we discuss safety."

Simple enough.

"Do you know what you want?" Selene asked.

Vivienne looked over the room as she considered her response. This was not the time to be coy. "Submission, mostly. I like bondage and"—she thought of the riding crop she'd seen hanging from the wardrobe—"being struck…consensually."

"Impact play." Selene grinned, showing perfect teeth. "Barehanded or with a tool?" She stepped closer until she was mere inches away.

Vivienne swallowed, feeling her nerves inflame. What would it be like to be thrown over Selene's lap?

"I have a selection of devices that we can play with," Selene continued. "Given that you're the client, how we do this is entirely up to you."

"I'm not sure." The words stuck in her throat. The idea of laying things out for selection seemed too…clinical.

"Do you want me to lead you in a scene so you're not quite sure what will happen?"

Vivienne nodded, heat crawling up her chest. "That would be…satisfactory."

"Satisfactory," Selene repeated teasingly. She walked around Vivienne in a circle, close enough that Vivienne could reach out and touch her if she wanted. "I'll demand the utmost obedience if you want submission. Are you prepared to obey?"

A shiver ran down Vivienne's spine, and she drew herself taller as the woman came to stand before her again. Close enough to kiss. "If you're as good as you seem to believe."

Selene laughed. "I think we're both going to enjoy this." She looked Vivienne up and down, then drew her gaze back up to meet Vivienne's eyes. "If we're to do some domination with impact play, is there anything off-limits?"

"What do you mean?"

"I keep to all the lovely fleshy areas and away from anything that might do any serious damage. But…some areas fit that description that some people aren't comfortable with."

Vivienne cleared her throat nervously. "I don't mind."

Selene studied Vivienne closely. "This is very new for you, isn't it?"

Vivienne folded her arms. "I've engaged in plenty of BDSM in my time. I'm hardly some twenty-year-old virgin looking to get their cherry popped."

"Oh, I'm sure you have. I'm sure you've played with spanking and handcuffs and thought they were delightful. It's where we all begin." She smiled at Vivienne disarmingly. "How about if I show you a standard play, and if you find yourself uncomfortable at any time, or if you stop enjoying yourself, we'll stop."

"That sounds reasonable."

"Good. Before we begin, let's run through a few things."

"Housekeeping?" Vivienne asked, cocking an eyebrow.

"Ah, so you do listen. That'll make things easier. I'll be direct. I don't engage in sex in the first session, no matter how lovely the client is." Selene paused, drinking her in again. "I'll need you to get tested before there's any sex."

"Tested? I assure you—"

"Assurances are well and good, but I don't know you, and you don't know me. We don't have to engage in sex, if you don't wish to be tested, but those are my rules if you do."

"And how will I know about your history?"

"I'll show you mine if you show me yours." Selene gave Vivienne a mischievous grin.

Vivienne nodded. She didn't even know if she wanted to engage in sex or if she would do a repeat session, so it wasn't worth discussing further.

"Now, is there anything I should know? Any triggers, fears, or concerns that I should be mindful of?"

"No," Vivienne said honestly. There was nothing worth bringing up.

"Any injuries to be mindful of?"

"No."

"Do you know your limits?"

"I do."

Selene's eyes narrowed as she crossed her arms against her chest. "And what's your safe word?"

Vivienne frowned. "'Stop' isn't sufficient?"

"No. And don't choose 'mercy' either. I quite enjoy begging, and you'll enjoy doing it on your knees."

Vivienne sucked in a breath. Begging? She had never begged for a single thing in her life.

Selene grinned, and Vivienne felt arousal tightening low in her belly, making her aware of the lace she wore under her garter belt.

"I recommend a word that's two or three syllables long that you can say through a gag—so avoid plosives and fricative consonants. And you might want to choose something jarring that can be said during role-play."

Vivienne raised her eyebrows, pleased that the woman understood *something* of language. "Fine. What about 'music box'?"

"Suitable choice," Selene said. Then her expression softened. "Final question: what are you hoping to get out of this?"

Vivienne opened her mouth to speak, but whatever lie she had prepared didn't come out. Instead, she looked into the depths of Selene's blue eyes. "To let go."

Selene nodded. "I'll need you to remain honest with me about your current state. You need to let me know whenever you feel unwell or you stop enjoying the scene."

She walked over to the dresser and withdrew a length of rope and a blindfold from one of the drawers. Then she went to the closet and opened it wide enough for Vivienne to see. Selene drew her hands over different items, fingering various tools and toys before she paused over the riding crop.

Vivienne held her breath, but Selene moved on to the next item. She sighed, trying not to be disappointed. This woman was clearly well-versed in her own play; Vivienne would have to trust her.

Selene shut the closet door and placed several items on the bed. She held the riding crop in her hand.

Vivienne tingled with anticipated pleasure.

"Do you have any questions or concerns before we begin?" Selene asked.

"You will be discreet, won't you? This won't come back on me?"

"So long as you assure me of the same, I will never speak a word of what happens between us to another soul."

"Good, because I have excellent lawyers."

Selene laughed. "As do I." She took a step back, gazing over Vivienne again. And then her visage changed, and she seemed to grow taller in her heels. She turned to lift the lid of an ottoman bench. "You can place your bag, jacket, and dress here."

"My dress?"

Selene stared at her, as if daring Vivienne to say something more. Perhaps protest.

Instead, Vivienne drew a breath and stepped forward, placing her bag inside. Then she removed her coat and placed that in the ottoman too. All that was left to remove was her dress. She hesitated.

Selene stepped closer and pulled Vivienne's hair over her shoulder, then unclasped the top of the dress and slowly drew the zipper.

Cool air brushed over Vivienne's skin. The dress slid down her arms, her waist, and her hips. Vivienne stepped out of it and stood in her slip and lingerie.

"*Oh*," Selene commented, brushing her fingers over where the garter clasps hooked onto her stockings. "Did you dress up for me?"

"No," Vivienne said. "I like to match."

"Yes, I understand that. But the garter belt?"

"I don't like pantyhose." She picked up her dress and placed it into the ottoman.

"It suits you," Selene said as she closed the lid.

Now there was nothing between them except silence.

Vivienne glanced at the items on the bed, her heart racing.

Selene settled herself on the bed next to the items and crossed her legs. "Stand here." She pointed at the space in front of her.

Vivienne obeyed. So far, it seemed to be nothing more than a game of patience. She wished Selene would get to it.

"On your knees," she said as if she were a schoolteacher asking the class to sit in their seats.

Vivienne bent her knees to kneel before her. She clenched her hands into fists, then stretched out her fingers.

Selene watched, her eyes boring deep into Vivienne's.

"And now?" Vivienne asked.

"And now, until I say otherwise, you may only speak when spoken to. You are my servant, and I am your queen. You will obey me implicitly." She paused, cocking her head, as if daring Vivienne to protest. "Do you understand?"

"Yes."

Selene corrected her. "Yes, my queen."

"Yes, my queen." Vivienne wasn't sure how she felt about calling Selene "my queen," but it came easier than "mistress."

"Hands forward."

Vivienne held out her hands, palms upward.

Selene turned Vivienne's arms so the wrists faced each other a few inches apart. She took the length of rope and began coiling it over one forearm.

Then, like a parlor trick, Selene knotted and twisted the rope, binding her wrists in an elegant knot before Vivienne could even think about squirming away. Selene slid her fingers between the bindings, making sure they were tight against the skin. "Does it pinch?" she asked.

"No, my queen," Vivienne answered, then dropped her bound wrists.

The riding crop struck her bare shoulder.

Vivienne looked up, surprised at how fast Selene had picked up the crop and confused about what the hit had been for.

"Did I tell you that you could drop your hands?"

"No." Vivienne lifted her hands again.

The crop hit her on the other shoulder.

Vivienne sucked in her breath, the pleasure of the pain rushing through her.

"Do you know what you did wrong that time?"

Vivienne blinked, still reeling from the hit. "No," she whispered hoarsely.

Selene placed the riding crop on the bed, then touched the mark on Vivienne's shoulder.

With a shiver, Vivienne leaned into it.

"When I ask you a question, I expect you to answer 'yes, my queen' or 'no, my queen' every time, without hesitation or question. Can you do that for me?"

Vivienne gritted her teeth at the condescension in Selene's voice. "Yes."

Selene reached for the crop.

"My queen," Vivienne quickly added.

"Good girl," she purred.

Selene fingered the leather handle thoughtfully, then pulled her hand away and picked up the blindfold instead.

Vivienne shut her eyes as Selene placed the blindfold around them, tying it in place. She felt Selene moving around her, and then her fingers were combing her hair. At last, Selene settled her hands on Vivienne's shoulders.

Vivienne waited, her arms growing tired from holding her wrists up.

A warm breath tickled her ear, and Vivienne gasped. Then Selene whispered, "Move forward until you feel the bed press against you here." She stroked Vivienne's body until her fingers rested under her ribs, holding her firmly before slipping away.

Vivienne slowly moved forward on her knees until her hands touched the mattress, then shifted a little more until the frame pressed against her stomach. She waited, anticipating the riding crop hitting her.

Instead she heard the sound of a drawer opening and closing. Her heart beat faster. Had Selene chosen another tool, perhaps a cane? Or maybe a gag to keep her quiet?

"Look at you, keeping perfectly still," Selene said, coming up behind her, fingers stroking her shoulders, her nails running down Vivienne's forearms as she pressed against her back. "So obedient."

Vivienne clenched her jaw, bristling at the comment, but she kept quiet.

"I can't wait to watch you come undone." Selene drew Vivienne's arms above her head.

Vivienne felt Selene set her heels on either side of her calves, her skirt brushing against the back of Vivienne's head. Then there was movement above her.

Something metal was clicking. Selene was fiddling with the rope bindings. Vibrations went through the fibers, then the rope was tugged upward, hoisting Vivienne's arms up until they were reaching above her head, forcing her torso to stretch toward the ceiling.

Selene drew her hands down Vivienne's forearms again. Her fingers were warm against the cool air, her nails blunt as they slid under the rope to check the tension. It was strangely intimate and made Vivienne more aware of her state of undress.

"Do you remember your safe word?" Selene asked as she again drew her fingers through Vivienne's hair, brushing it over her shoulder and off her back. It was gentle and soothing, and Vivienne wanted to press against her hands.

"Yes, my queen," she said, feeling a flutter low in her belly.

"And what's your safe word?"

"Music box...my queen."

Selene stepped away but Vivienne had no sense of where she went. In the quiet pressing over her, Vivienne's chest rose and fell. Her heart pounded loudly in her ears as she stretched her fingers in the restraints.

Then, something cold touched her between the shoulder blades, sliding down the bare skin and over the slip, passing the length of her spine before lifting away.

That was her warning.

The crop snapped against one of her shoulder blades. Vivienne gasped, arching against it. The pain rippled over her flesh even as endorphins flooded her bloodstream. A second strike came, and then a third just as quick on the other side. Vivienne breathed out in relief.

Selene brushed her fingers along Vivienne's shoulders, stroking where she had struck. Perfume filled her senses as Selene stepped in closer behind her, the crop dragging low against her backside.

"Are you enjoying yourself?"

"Mm."

A short thwack against her ass made Vivienne jolt in the restraints. Wetness seeped between her thighs.

"I expect you to use your words."

"Yes."

Another thwack against the other cheek, harder this time, and Vivienne suppressed the moan. "Yes, my queen."

"Good girl."

There was quiet again, except for the sound of floorboards creaking beneath Selene's footsteps. Vivienne's arms and shoulders ached in the restraints. If she squeezed her muscles, the rope drew tighter.

Every strike stung with fresh relief. She wanted it. The suspense and uncertainty between each strike. The brief touch against her skin that both soothed and teased before the next hard and fast strike.

And then the excitement turned to relief, and Vivienne's emotions twisted. It was like the brick walls she had built around herself had turned to glass, and each strike left a crack.

Finally, one strike hit her high across the shoulder blades, and it wasn't a gasp but a sob that broke through.

And then Selene was there, her body pressed against Vivienne's, arms around her. "Are you ready to stop?"

Vivienne nodded, clamping her jaw shut because she refused to cry. She didn't know why she wanted to cry, but the words she needed to say weren't coming out, and she knew she needed to say those fucking words, but if she did, she was going to sob, and she couldn't sob, and—

Selene pressed her hand firmly under Vivienne's chest and over her ribs, tugging at something. And then Vivienne's arms dropped, and she was sagging back against Selene, drawing in a tight breath.

"Lift your arms," Selene said, her voice soft and soothing.

Vivienne did, and the ropes untangled. Her arms fell to her sides.

Selene removed the blindfold and splayed her hand over Vivienne's chest, holding her steady, breathing slow and deep behind her.

She took a breath, once, twice—pressing her tongue against the roof of her mouth until her breath became more even and the need to cry ebbed away. "I'm fine," she said at last, though she trembled and the words caught in her throat.

"You are," Selene agreed, then pressed her lips against Vivienne's bare shoulder.

Vivienne squeezed her eyes shut, again willing herself not to cry as she drew in one breath, then another, and then…the hand released, and Selene moved away.

Vivienne opened her eyes and blinked away the blur.

A hand appeared in front of her. Vivienne looked at it for several seconds before realizing that Selene was offering to help her stand. Taking the hand, she pushed onto her heels, standing awkwardly until the world steadied.

Selene reached her arm around until she was holding Vivienne by her waist.

Vivienne wanted to crumble against her, collapse from the exertion of it all. Instead, she took another breath and straightened herself, holding her shoulders back.

"You don't need to do that," Selene said, her arm steady on Vivienne's waist, the other hand still holding hers. "You're allowed to let go."

"I'm fine," Vivienne said and looked at Selene.

"You are," she agreed, "but you're also allowed to take a moment. There's no one else here."

Vivienne looked away. "I should get dressed." She pulled her hand away. Her skin felt as if Selene had woken every nerve ending.

"Before you do, I need to check over the marks."

Vivienne nodded and allowed herself to be turned around.

Selene touched her back gently, examining her shoulders, drawing the hem of her slip up to look at the marks on her hips and thighs. Vivienne wobbled on her heels, her muscles twitching as Selene softly touched each welt.

"They'll be down by morning." Selene readjusted the slip. "I can put cream on them, if you like."

Vivienne cleared her throat, knowing that if Selene so much as stroked a thumb over her cheekbone, she would burst into tears. "No, thank you," she said firmly. "I can manage that at home."

"As you wish. I'm going to make a pot of coffee. Or would you prefer tea?"

"Coffee's fine," Vivienne said, her voice thick. Her skin burned where Selene's fingers had touched her.

"I'll zip up your dress when you're ready."

"Thank you."

Selene left the room, closing the door behind her.

Vivienne dressed carefully, doing up half of the zipper anyway before giving up when she couldn't stop her arms from shaking. She stood before the mirror. Her face was flushed. Her hair was a tangled mess, but it was nothing that a quick comb through couldn't fix. Pulling out her makeup, she touched up her lips and eyes.

As she made her way downstairs, she heard liquid being poured into cups. For a moment, she considered leaving, embarrassed by what had occurred.

Except…she hadn't paid.

Raising her chin, she stepped into the kitchen.

Selene was putting milk and sugar on the table. She looked up and smiled. "Do you need help?" She pointed to Vivienne's dress.

"Yes, please."

Selene brushed Vivienne's hair over one shoulder, then zipped up the dress. She smoothed down the back of the dress and rearranged Vivienne's hair, her fingers grazing her shoulders.

Vivienne shivered as her touch brushed against the tender marks.

"I wasn't sure how you liked your coffee."

Vivienne sat across from Selene. She didn't feel like crying anymore, but she felt a heaviness, like she could sleep for hours. She hadn't felt this tired since she was working on her doctorate.

"How do you feel?" Selene asked. "And don't say 'fine.'"

"Exhausted," Vivienne said honestly.

"That's to be expected. You took a good number of hits." Selene sipped her coffee. "More importantly, did you find the relief you were after?"

Vivienne considered. She wanted to say she did not. Despite the intended intimacy of the situation, nearly crying in front of a stranger soured whatever pleasure she might have taken from it. But the truth was, all the frustration she'd been feeling that week was gone. Her back was sore, but she felt lighter. "I did," she answered.

Selene smiled. "I'm very good at what I do."

"And arrogant."

"Comes with the territory."

Vivienne brought the cup to her mouth, trying to suppress a smile.

The coffee was decent. It soothed her as she sipped it. Vivienne considered how much money had been invested in the interior of the home to give it such elegance. It was nothing like the dungeon fantasy that one might associate with a dominatrix.

It suited Selene, and it also made Vivienne aware that she still hadn't asked for payment. Was she supposed to broach that?

"Careful. You'll wind yourself right back up with thoughts like that."

Vivienne set her cup down. "I beg your pardon?"

Selene grinned. "You're overthinking something. I can see you stiffening to avoid saying whatever's on your mind, perhaps because of some…social propriety. Whatever it is, just say it."

The woman seemed to read her like an open book. "I was thinking about how payment worked."

"Cash or card," Selene said frankly. "If you use your credit card, the payment will show up as a clothing boutique."

"Do you run a clothes store?"

"That's a story for another time." Selene poured herself more coffee. "Now, cash or card?"

Vivienne pulled out her wallet, withdrawing several bills.

Selene accepted the money with a smile and set it on the table. Then she got up and went to a cupboard, where she pulled out an invoice book and a pen. She scribbled on the page and ripped it off, handing it to Vivienne. "You know by now I'm the type of woman who likes to keep her books in order. My website is at the bottom of the invoice. If you go to the Services Offered tab, you can explore other interests you might have. If you don't find something on the list, we can talk about it the next time you visit."

Vivienne took the invoice and studied it. Selene had written "for services rendered" in one column with the amount of time in the next column. At the bottom was the total. It was all very professional. Vivienne looked up at Selene. Was this merely a business, or was it as much a leisure pursuit for Selene as it was for her clients?

"And why do you think there'll be a next time?" Vivienne asked.

"Because you're going to go home and shower and think of me as you touch each mark."

"Excuse me?"

"And then you'll wait a few days, but you're going to dig up that invoice, find the website, and scroll through the services I offer until something clicks. Then I'll have the delight of hearing your voice on my phone again."

"I certainly will not."

Selene laughed. "Suit yourself, but do check out the services page first. I'm sure you'll find a few things to pique your interest."

Vivienne stared at the woman. She wanted to storm off or snap back, but she didn't. She was glued to her seat, fury and—more importantly—excitement building.

She was excited in a way she couldn't remember feeling since she was a twentysomething, getting up to mischief because she could. Because it made her feel—

Ah. That was it.

She felt alive.

CHAPTER 3
THE GIRLFRIEND EXPERIENCE

Vivienne showered when she got home. Her skin stung, the pain coming to life in the back of her skull, and she could no longer tell if the sensation was pain or pleasure. She closed her eyes, drawing in a deep breath. All she could think about was Selene looking at her and promising that Vivienne would return home and think of her.

As the hot water burned over her back, she held the shower spray over a particularly painful welt and buried her fingers between her legs. As the water stung her back, she trembled, gasping at the orgasm striking through her as she recalled the swish of the riding crop and Selene purring "good girl" in her ear.

Vivienne hated that the woman was right.

She finished her shower, slipping a robe over her pajamas, then went downstairs to dinner.

Hattie set a bowl of roasted vegetables on the trivet. Beside it, meatloaf cooled on a platter that had served many a roast dinner during her childhood.

"How was your meeting?" Hattie asked.

"Perfectly adequate, though I doubt anything will come from it." The lie slipped out easily. The spine of the chair pressed against a welt, causing the pain to flare, and Vivienne bit her tongue. Selene had said the welts would be gone by morning. Vivienne very much doubted that.

Claudia quirked an eyebrow at her, but Vivienne avoided her eyes and poured a glass of water.

"You look different," Claudia commented.

Vivienne nearly dropped the pitcher. She looked at her niece, wondering if her gown had slipped from her shoulder to reveal a welt.

"Relaxed," Claudia said.

"I finished grading the most recent essays from the first-year students," she said, which was truthful enough.

"You're never in a good mood until the end of the year."

Vivienne frowned. "And what, pray tell, do you consider a good mood?"

"You came home smiling." Claudia popped a small potato into her mouth. "I think you went on a date."

"Ridiculous." Vivienne rolled her eyes. "When would I have time to find myself a date? Between my work and my students, not to mention looking after this family, I barely have a moment to go shopping for myself."

Claudia frowned. "Well, you seem happy."

Vivienne glared at her, considering whether to scold Claudia for the petulant tone. Before she could decide, Hattie began talking about her morning shift at the bookstore.

Vivienne listened to Claudia eagerly inquiring about the changes at Hattie's work, as if a bookstore café were some new and revolutionary idea. Neither Claudia nor Hattie had taken half as much interest in her work. It was something shiny and new, she supposed. It would pass. Eventually, it would be a job like any other, and they would find new things to be excited about.

Just as her desire to hire a dominatrix was shiny and new.

And yet, when Vivienne went to bed that evening, she replayed the encounter repeatedly, reliving each strike and tease, remembering how it felt to have her hands coiled and knotted so beautifully in rope and how Selene's nails had raked across her skin.

The relief at the end, when she'd…

No, she couldn't admit that. Submission and impact play was one thing, but nearly crying? Vivienne couldn't honestly find relief from someone hitting her hard enough and long enough that she cried, could she? It went against her very nature. The only reason she'd become so adept at sneaking out of the house as a teenager was to avoid that same punishment.

But then…that was different.

She thought of the way Selene's hand had splayed against her ribs. How she'd known just when her limit was met and undid everything so effortlessly, then held her until the urge to sob had ceased.

Vivienne turned over in bed, pushing the thought away. No, she didn't want to think about it any longer. She couldn't allow herself to indulge in that fantasy anymore.

The next morning, Vivienne found Claudia alone at the breakfast table, one leg bouncing as she paged through the Sunday paper.

Vivienne made herself a cup of coffee and joined her at the table. "What time are you going to Rebecca's?" she asked.

"Luca's," Claudia corrected, although Vivienne was certain it had been Rebecca's yesterday. "Could you drop me off by ten?"

"Of course." Whether it was Luca's or Rebecca's didn't really matter. Claudia's friends were always polite, making small talk when they came to the house, but she was especially fond of Luca. Perhaps it was because Luca was Claudia's first friend in grade school. Or maybe it was because she saw elements of herself in the boy. "And you've finished your homework?"

"I've got one more thing to do, but I was going to do it with Luca and Bec."

"Is it a group project?"

Claudia shrugged but didn't look up from the paper. "Sort of."

"Claudia, we agreed that if you went to a sleepover, you would finish your homework first."

Claudia glanced up at Vivienne with a flash of teenage rebellion in her eyes. "It's just a small project for biology. If we work together, it will be faster."

Vivienne pressed her lips together and held Claudia's gaze. "If you don't honor the agreements you've made, people will stop offering them to you. Finish your homework, or you'll be calling your friends to tell them that you will not be able to make it today."

Claudia slapped the newspaper shut and pushed her chair back. "Fine. I'll go finish it." And she stormed up to her bedroom and slammed the door.

Vivienne closed her eyes, suppressing the urge to go upstairs and tell her off. Claudia's mood swings were becoming worse. Robert used to get into foul moods as a teenager, but Claudia's seemed to be explosive—though she preferred it over Hattie's teary outbursts.

"In a mood, is she?" Hattie asked as she came down the stairs. Her sister was still in her nightgown, curlers in her hair. She bustled around the kitchen.

"We had an agreement that if she finished her homework, she could sleep over with her friends, but it seems she's decided to blow it off."

Vivienne sipped her coffee, then opened the newspaper. She read about the local Denton family scandal, then about a new highway set to open next year, before she turned to the personals section.

Selene had no ad listed. Not that it mattered; Vivienne wasn't interested in pursuing her services again.

"I thought I'd work out in the garden today. Do you have any plans?" Hattie asked.

"Just work, Hattie." Vivienne closed the newspaper. She had a journal article to write, and she intended to have the first draft finished by the end of the semester.

She finished her coffee and took her mug to the sink, then went to her office and shut the door behind her. A long time ago, the office had been her father's, and many of his law books remained on the shelves. Working at the heavy desk was a familiar comfort to her.

After her parents passed and Robert had married, he moved into the house while Vivienne, after some years of travel, had settled in the city and built a career at the university.

And then when the plane crashed, leaving Claudia without her parents, Vivienne returned home. Hattie moved in to help with arrangements and never left. Vivienne was grateful, though she would never admit it. She was perfectly capable of raising Claudia by herself—and had for the most part—but the house was big, and Hattie helped fill it.

She switched on the computer and pulled up her article. After reading through the last section she had written, she sighed and opened a browser, typing Selene's website into the address bar.

The website, like the house's interior, was elegantly designed with a vibrant use of red. It had the usual tabs, including a blurb about the dominatrix with detailed, tantalizing information. Photos disguised her face while showing her in a range of outfits with different devices. Most of the photos were tame, with Selene holding the familiar riding crop. In others, leather and rubber were prominently displayed.

Vivienne clicked on the Take a Tour section, which showed the house in daylight with a view of the garden area.

Finally, Vivienne clicked on Services.

She glanced through bondage, domination/submission, impact play, medical play, mistress/pet, and other standard kinks that Vivienne had heard of or experienced herself. She was intrigued by a few, disregarded several as not her thing, and then stopped, intrigued, when she saw:

Girlfriend Experience, Deluxe
Includes everything in the Girlfriend Experience package, plus a few bonuses. Discuss with Selene to have this tailored* experience to your liking.

Recommended for weekend bookings.

You must be a repeat client to experience the full benefit.

Vivienne closed the browser. Warmth spread across her face. She knew very well what the Girlfriend Experience was, yet the idea of a tailored encounter sent a shiver down her spine.

Was that where she was with her life? So lonely that she wanted to fall into the arms of a sex worker and play pretend?

No, that was absurd. Vivienne didn't need to see the woman again. She'd had her fun, and even if she went to see Selene again, it wouldn't be for something like that.

Besides, it'd be far cheaper to pick someone up at the bar if she craved that kind of experience. She could drive up to the city, go to a cocktail lounge, and choose from among a sea of people. But then there was the hassle of the conversation dance, making sure the other person used protection, and figuring out how experienced they were. Assuming she could even find someone she *wanted* to have sex with.

Vivienne closed her eyes and leaned back in the creaky old office chair. Maybe she should see if one of her old flames was in the area.

No, she thought and returned to work. She had just finished reading through her most recently written paragraph when someone knocked.

Without waiting for a response. Claudia pushed the door open, crossed her arms over her chest, and leaned against the doorframe.

Vivienne glanced at the clock on her monitor. How long had she spent scrolling through Selene's website?

"Have you finished your homework?" Vivienne asked gently. The last thing she wanted was a screaming match.

"I did," Claudia said. Then she sighed and dropped her arms. "I'm sorry. You were right. I promised to finish my homework, and I should keep my promises."

If it wasn't a sincere apology, at least it was something. If Claudia was admitting fault to get what she wanted, she'd at least done what Vivienne had asked.

"Thank you," she said, pushing up from the chair. "You said you were staying at Luca's tonight?"

Claudia nodded and smiled. "Popcorn and horror movies."

"Will Henry be there?"

"Not to stay over, if that's what you're concerned about."

Hardly, Vivienne wanted to say. Once Luca became comfortable with his identity, it seemed ridiculous to bring in a no-boys rule, given all the previous times he had stayed over before transitioning. To draw a line now and forbid Claudia from attending a sleepover because Henry would be there seemed hypocritical and, frankly, disrespectful.

Something was going on, and if it wasn't Claudia sneaking off to have sex with Henry, what else could it be? "Have you got everything you need?" Vivienne asked.

Claudia gestured to the overnight bag in the hallway. It looked crammed full, and Vivienne wondered why until she reminded herself that her niece should be allowed some secrets.

If the teenagers were pilfering alcohol from the liquor cabinet, they would have fun and nurse a hangover tomorrow. If that was the case, a hangover would be punishment enough.

"Is your phone charged?"

"It is."

Vivienne nodded, then picked up her handbag and keys. When she told Hattie where they were going, Hattie asked, "Oh, could you pick up some milk and eggs on your way back? I used the last of them on breakfast this morning."

"It's not exactly on my way, but if you can't do it yourself... Is there anything else you need?"

"Never mind. I can always cook something else or run out myself—"

"No, you've already asked. No point in both of us leaving the house today," Vivienne said.

By the time Vivienne got to the car, Claudia was waiting in the passenger seat, her bag on the floor.

"And you're sure that you have everything?" Vivienne asked.

"Absolutely."

On the drive over, Claudia tuned in to her favorite station and hummed to the music. Her bad mood seemed to have evaporated.

As they pulled up to the Fitzgerald farm, Vivienne adjusted her sunglasses. She considered asking if Joe had noticed any strange behavior with his son.

But as soon as the car stopped, Claudia jumped out of the car with a quick goodbye, then ran up the steps, not even giving her a chance to speak with Mr. Fitzgerald.

So be it. The door opened, and Claudia hugged Luca and Rebecca as if it had been months since she'd seen them rather than a little over a day. If they were up to no good, Vivienne would find out soon enough.

Vivienne headed into town to pick milk and eggs from the local grocery store.

It was a simple enough task, except for the fact that she ran into Selene at the dairy case. Selene placed an item in her cart, then turned, coming face-to-face with Vivienne. She wore a black raincoat over a red dress. Her hair spilled down her back.

Despite being in this town for over fifteen years, Vivienne had never once seen the woman. She had to fight the urge to run her fingers through her hair.

Selene raised her eyebrows and stared at her, as if to suggest it was her move.

"Excuse me," Vivienne said politely, stepping around her. She could feel the woman staring after her as she made her way to the milk. She grabbed the closest carton before moving to the eggs and taking out a dozen. Then she hurried to the cashier.

Except it was the local Oakdale Market, which meant there were only ever two cashiers working at one time, and one was dealing with a customer who seemed to be doing her monthly shopping. The other cashier had two people in line. Selene was the second.

She turned to glance at Vivienne, then smiled and looked away.

All Vivienne could think about was the photo of Selene posed in lingerie on the Girlfriend Experience, Deluxe, webpage, a paddle in her hand and a raincoat like the one she was wearing, opened suggestively.

Vivienne got in line behind her, pride refusing to let her walk away. The cashier was checking out an older man, who was very slowly counting out his money.

The other cashier was still scanning through a hundred items. Vivienne looked back at the gentleman, who was now arguing over a coupon.

It was as though the universe was tormenting her.

Selene laughed softly as she shifted the basket in her hand, and Vivienne felt her cheeks burn. Perhaps she should step away, say something vague about needing something else, and return after Selene had left.

"Do you often huff like that behind strangers, or is there something I can help you with?" Selene asked, half turning to look at Vivienne, her eyes sparkling. "You seem wound up about something."

Vivienne's chest tightened at the sight of Selene's face. She pictured the woman's mouth falling open as she leaned forward to—

"Well?" Selene pressed. "Did you need something?"

"I'm fine," Vivienne responded and looked from the man ahead of them, who was now requesting a manager, to the woman in the other line, still only halfway through checking out her groceries.

"I didn't ask if you were fine," Selene said, low enough that only Vivienne could hear. It was the same tone she'd used last night. "I asked if you needed something. You're making a lot of noise for someone simply standing in line." A look of amusement broke over her face.

"What do you think you're doing?" Vivienne asked.

"Making small talk. What do you think you're doing?"

"Waiting to purchase my groceries."

Selene glanced down at Vivienne's basket and then back up again. "I see. Had a chance to peruse my services yet?"

A jumble of words piled up in the back of Vivienne's throat. She was saved from responding when the manager finally showed up.

"Oh, you have. And you've found something you like, haven't you?"

Vivienne averted her eyes, refusing to respond. If Selene wanted to rile her up, that was fine. She would just look for another dominatrix to—

No, she wouldn't. She wasn't going to look for a new sex worker because she didn't need that service.

Selene turned away to check out, still chuckling. Vivienne pretended not to hear her small talk with the cashier, though she watched Selene from the corner of her eye until she left.

Only then did Vivienne let out a breath.

───※───

Vivienne drove home to Claudia's music playing in the background, unable to calm the turmoil in her belly. When she arrived and set the grocery items on the table, Hattie opened the carton of eggs. Two of them were cracked.

"Oh, that's all right," Hattie said as she took them out. "I'll just toss them into the compost."

Annoyed with herself, Vivienne said nothing and returned to her office to work on her journal article. But instead, she booked an appointment with her gynecologist. She was overdue for a checkup anyway. It had nothing to do with Selene because there was no way that she would engage the woman for any further services, least of all sexual services.

She scrolled through her article, trying not to think about Selene's hungry expression when she'd looked her up and down, as if she could undress Vivienne right then and there and take her on the spot.

She closed the document, shut off the computer, and went upstairs.

CHAPTER 4
ROPE

Abigail knocked on the doorframe of Vivienne's work office. "Professor? We were scheduled for eleven."

Vivienne motioned her in. She gestured to the chair in front of her and put down her pen. "What can I help with you, Abigail?"

"I was hoping you might have a TA position available."

Vivienne frowned. Despite her best efforts, the department head was unwilling to provide her with the funding for a teaching assistant. "There's nothing paid," she said.

"I don't need a paid position. There's an opportunity to go to Greece next year with Professor Haddon, all expenses paid, but I need some TA experience to apply."

Vivienne was familiar with the program. "I can give you a recommendation and place a good word with Professor Haddon, if that's what you need."

"It is."

"And I could use the extra help. It would be after hours on top of your workload, and I'd still expect you to make your grades. If I don't think you're handling it, I'll terminate you immediately."

"I can handle it," Abigail said confidently.

"In that case"—Vivienne reached into her file drawer and pulled out a form—"fill this out, and bring it back to me tomorrow."

Abigail brightened. "Thank you, Professor. I appreciate your help." She picked up her bag and left.

Vivienne had just begun making a list of Abigail's duties when someone else knocked and opened the door without waiting.

"Vivienne?" Elijah, the department head, stepped in.

Vivienne smiled tightly.

"Janice has gone on leave unexpectedly for a few weeks. I understand a family member is in palliative care, and she needs to spend time with them." He cleared his throat. "I need you to cover her classes."

Vivienne narrowed her eyes at him. "She teaches religious studies."

"You double-majored in language and religion," Elijah pointed out. "Wasn't your most recent article on original Hebrew texts during the Second Temple period?"

That was an oversimplification of her last article. It had been about the evolution of the Hebrew language into Mishnaic Hebrew, but she didn't bother to correct him. She leaned back in her chair and stared at Elijah. It was true she was educated in certain religious studies, but it wasn't an area she enjoyed teaching.

"Is there no one else?" she asked. "I already have a full schedule."

"I've checked your roster, and you have room on Monday and Friday. You don't even need to change your office hours."

Maybe not, but she used her non-teaching days for grading student papers and administrative work. "How long is it for?"

"Six weeks at most."

Six weeks! Vivienne bit her tongue to stop from snapping back. "I'll need funding for a TA until she returns, then."

Elijah smiled and nodded. "I can find some funding."

Well, that would help Abigail, anyway. Vivienne might be able to use her to help with the overflowing work. "Thank you, Elijah. Send over what you have from Janice, and I'll prepare a lesson plan for next week."

"I...need you to start this Friday."

Vivienne felt her shoulders tense. She studied the wood grain on her desk.

Ever since her session with Selene, she'd been more relaxed than ever. But now she could feel frustration returning, like an itch under her skin she couldn't quite scratch. She wanted to scream and hit something.

She forced a smile at Elijah and agreed to teach the class she only had four days to prepare for. It would eventually lead to further career advancement, she reminded herself.

Besides, if she managed to show the students what a proper education looked like, Janice might find herself out of a job, leaving her and other competent academics to teach the up-and-coming minds of Oakdale University.

"Thank you, Vivienne." Elijah turned away, leaving her office door wide open. Annoyed, Vivienne got up and closed it, then returned to her desk. She drummed her nails on the surface as she rolled her shoulders and neck, trying not to remember how the crop had stung against her skin. She didn't want to book another appointment, especially not so soon, and especially not after running into Selene in the grocery store.

No, she needed to wait.

Vivienne reached into her drawer and pulled out her pack of cigarettes. She opened the window and, lighting one, blew the smoke outside, watching it curl away into the air.

Six weeks wasn't that long. A month and two weeks. She could handle the pressure of that many classes, despite the anticipated headaches.

Friday arrived sooner than seemed possible. Abigail eagerly took to the position of TA and was pleased when Vivienne told her she'd found some funding.

That gave Vivienne time to work on the new lesson plan. It also meant she spent long days and evenings at work and missed out on Claudia's first time cheerleading for the high school. It wasn't a small sacrifice. She promised her niece that she would attend the school's charity event in two weeks. And there would be other games.

Janice's class was a second-year subject, and Vivienne had difficulty understanding the information Elijah sent over. Although she understood the general framework, she had no idea what points Janice was trying to convey or discuss with the class. She prepped as best she could, but when it was time for class, Vivienne had a knot in her stomach.

She walked into the classroom and wrote her name on the whiteboard, said "Good morning," and looked over the class. There were more students than Vivienne had expected. "I'm taking over for Professor Whitler for the next six weeks. Can anyone tell me where she left off?"

Several students spoke up to explain where they were, and Vivienne felt the knot in her chest ease. The students listened. They were invested in the material.

She finished the class, satisfied that she'd managed to teach what Janice intended in the way she intended, but she had a sour taste in her mouth.

Was Janice Whitler a better teacher than her? Or did religious studies simply attract more students than language did? Was that why her third-year classes were so small?

Perhaps she had gone about teaching the wrong way. Pushed when she should have nurtured. Not that Janice was nurturing by any means, but she must be doing something right if her classes were as popular as they were.

Vivienne seethed, jealousy gnawing at her as she returned to her office and collected her work for the evening. She had planned to stay later to keep away from Hattie's bustling and to avoid Claudia picking a fight, but she was suddenly raw with deep-seated feelings she thought she'd left behind.

Her body ached and itched with nervous energy under her skin.

And she wanted to call Selene, desperately wanted to call and see if she had an opening. She wished she didn't want it, didn't want to come off as needy.

But...it was a service like any other, and if Vivienne could have found relief from a spa, she would not feel so conflicted about booking a new appointment.

Vivienne had spent the last few evenings trying to avoid thinking about the woman, and yet with every masturbation, she inevitably daydreamed about the riding crop on her back, Selene's hand splayed over her chest; or she fantasized about running into her and being shoved against the nearest available surface and—

The sound of shoes clicking on the polished floor outside her office door made her look up.

She cleared her throat, her cheeks burning, as if she had spoken her thoughts out loud.

Sex. Vivienne needed sex. Casual sex, no strings attached. She flicked through names in her head, trying to think of someone, but any ex-lovers she trusted for casual sex were now either monogamous or out of state.

After two years, Vivienne should have learned to push her needs away and redirect that desire into something productive. And if she really needed to scratch an itch, there was more than one vibrator by her bed.

Vivienne packed up her paperwork. She had every intention of going home, working on her article, and then having a sit-down meal with her sister without thinking about Selene.

At least that was the plan.

She walked confidently to her car, bag in hand. All she had to do was get into the vehicle and drive home. But as soon as she got in and closed the door, she pulled out her phone and dialed the familiar number.

"Good afternoon." Too late, Vivienne realized she'd called from her personal phone. Now the woman had her number. Even if she hung up, Selene could call back. If she didn't answer, her voicemail identified her. There was no point in pretending. "Good evening."

"Vivienne," the woman purred. "I thought it was you."

"And why would you think that?"

"You've been on my mind. How can I be of service?"

Vivienne drew in a breath. "I—" She hesitated. "I was curious about your services."

"And which services are you curious about?"

Vivienne struggled to control her breathing. "The same services."

"You'll have to refresh my memory."

Vivienne gripped the phone tighter. "Dominatrix services."

"You need to be more specific. Many things fall under that particular umbrella."

"Honestly," Vivienne said, exasperated. "Must you needlessly tease me?"

"Always. And you're in luck. I have something available in about two hours, if that suits."

It seemed too good to be true. And yet…the ache filled her. She wanted it more than she wanted anything else at that moment. "It does."

"I look forward to seeing you. Think about how long you want the session to run. I have a few ideas of what we can do." And then the call ended, leaving Vivienne with Selene's words swimming around her head.

A few ideas. What on earth could that mean?

Vivienne closed her eyes and sank into the seat. Her gynecologist appointment wasn't until tomorrow, and her results would likely not be in for another week. But the idea of feeling that crop against her skin again sent a shiver down her spine.

Vivienne arrived fifteen minutes early and sat in her car, gripping the steering wheel as she tried to understand how she had gotten there.

She was outside a dominatrix's business house, wearing slinky lingerie and a new dress. She had put more effort into how she looked for this appointment than when she went to work. Was this her life now? Driving out into the middle of nowhere to get spanked?

Apparently so, because as she looked in the rearview mirror to fix her lipstick, a blush spread across her cheeks.

She got out of the car, walked up to the building, and rang the doorbell. She counted her racing heartbeats until she heard the sound of Selene's heels on the hardwood floor.

A shadow appeared behind the door just before the dominatrix opened it. Her hair looked as though she had only recently run her fingers through it. She leaned against the doorframe with an eyebrow cocked and waited for Vivienne to speak—just as she had at the grocery store. Damn her.

Vivienne's breath caught. She was torn between shrinking away and pushing forward to assert her own dominance. "Evening," she managed to say.

"Evening." Selene appraised Vivienne's body, and she took in a slow, noticeable breath, as if she couldn't wait to devour her.

"Well?"

"Hmm?" Selene returned her gaze to Vivienne's eyes.

"Are you going to let me in, or should I recall some password?"

"Oh, I like the idea of a secret password. What do you think it is?"

Vivienne crossed her arms, considering whether to turn around and leave. But before she could act on the half-formed thought, Selene laughed, pushed off from the doorframe, and stepped aside.

Vivienne glared at her to make sure she knew how unimpressed she was. She stepped inside the warm hallway and removed her coat. Suddenly, she felt overdressed.

Selene closed the door and stepped around in front of her. Vivienne held her ground, refusing to step away.

"You look well," Selene commented. "Less…frightened."

Anger flared inside Vivienne. "I beg your pardon. I was not frightened."

"At the grocery store you certainly were. I could have said 'boo,' and you would have run away screaming…or maybe just melted in a puddle on the floor." She stared at Vivienne's mouth as she spoke. "Difficult to say."

Vivienne swallowed hard.

"Have anything for me?" Selene asked, stepping forward again.

Vivienne took a step back. "I—have an appointment tomorrow," she said.

Selene smiled wider. "You won't regret it, and personally, I'm looking forward to it." She turned around, and Vivienne followed her up the stairs and into the bedroom. Selene turned to face her. "Do you know what you want?"

Vivienne's heart pounded. She wanted the same as last time: to forget about the world and feel alive. "I trust you," she said.

Selene nodded. "I have an idea."

"And what is that?" Vivienne asked.

"I've been thinking about you." Selene opened a dresser drawer. "I know exactly what you want, Vivienne." She drew out two lengths of red rope and a blindfold, then turned to face Vivienne again. "You want the illusion of lost control."

She dropped the items in the center of the room.

Vivienne looked at them, both relieved and disappointed to see there wasn't a riding crop on the floor.

"Take off your dress," Selene said.

Vivienne obeyed, reaching behind to unzip, then rolling the dress down to the floor and stepping out of it.

"That is to come off too," she said, pointing to the slip.

Vivienne felt a quiver low in her belly as she shimmied out of it.

Selene looked Vivienne over and again smiled broadly. "You will need more patience this time. Put your clothes away, heels too, and then we'll begin."

Vivienne bit her lip as she picked her clothes up off the floor and set them neatly into the ottoman. She hated how the woman made her feel like a child.

"Do you remember your safe word from last time?"

"I do."

"What is it?"

"Music box." Vivienne felt ridiculous as she said it, but the point of a safe word was to be jarring enough that both of them knew it needed to end.

"I'm going to tie you up," Selene said, "and then we'll see where you're at. If you're still comfortable, I'll blindfold you and engage in some light impact play. At any stage, you can tell me to slow down. If it gets to be too much, say your safe word, and if you forget it, you can let me know you've forgotten it."

Vivienne nodded.

Without warning, Selene sharpened her expression. "On your knees."

Vivienne felt the command slip over her like a burlap bag as she fell to her knees on the hardwood floor.

Selene pulled up a wooden stool and sat on it, looking far more elegant than anybody had a right to on such a small seat. "If you ever want to learn to do this, I can teach you," Selene said and held out her hand.

Vivienne placed her hand face-up into Selene's palm and watched her toss the length of rope over her wrist.

"When I lived in New York, I ran a workshop with other dominatrices." She held her hand out again. "I've been doing rope since I was…oh, a young girl, I suppose."

"May I speak?" Vivienne asked, unsure if the game had begun.

"You may speak. We're still setting up." Selene tied a knot on Vivienne's other hand. "You'll know when we've begun."

Selene wove the ropes in a spiderweb pattern up and down Vivienne's arms while explaining about the different knots she was tying and the safety precautions she had in place so that, anytime Vivienne needed to get out, Selene could release her quickly.

It was fascinating to watch the knots being tied and adjusted. Selene moved expertly, as if she had been tying knots for years, which she probably had, tying up herself and others.

"Are you doing this because of the last session?" Vivienne asked as Selene began drawing the rope over her waist.

"Not for the reasons you think," Selene said. "You were relaxed when I tied you up before. Most people panic at being unable to move, but you seemed entirely at ease." She brushed her fingers over Vivienne's stomach as she slipped and weaved the rope, keeping one end in her lap. "I thought I might indulge the rope bunny in you."

And then she dragged her fingers along Vivienne's skin, stroking her ribs. Vivienne drew in a breath, trying to focus on the feeling of the rope.

"Turn around."

Vivienne scooted around on her knees until her back was to Selene, who drew Vivienne's hair over her shoulder before resuming the rope pattern. A shiver shot down Vivienne's spine as Selene tightened a knot.

Vivienne cleared her throat. "So you've used ropes from the beginning. But what about everything else?"

"You'll have to be more specific." Selene rested her hands just below Vivienne's bra. She could easily undo it if she wanted to, and Vivienne could do nothing to stop her.

"When did you decide to be a dominatrix?"

"It's not as interesting as you might think," she said, resuming her work with the rope. "Girl meets boy, boy wants to try things with girl, girl is much better at it than boy, boy becomes sulky, so girl leaves. It's a tale as old as time."

Vivienne scoffed. "Sounds like most men."

"Oh yes," Selene said. Without warning, Vivienne felt a breath brush over her shoulder, a nail tracing a pattern on her skin. "Don't worry. If you're interested in domination, I'll play with you. I'm very good on my knees."

Vivienne closed her eyes, heat flickering low in her belly. She was starting to get an idea of what Selene had been getting at before.

"There." Selene pressed a kiss against Vivienne's shoulder. "Now, lie on your back."

Vivienne shifted as much as she could on her own, then Selene's hand was on her, helping ease her down to the floor.

Selene stood up, picked up her stool, and sat down by Vivienne's feet. She began unraveling the second piece of rope.

"You're not done?" Vivienne asked.

"I told you. This is about patience. Don't worry. There will be plenty of time to play with whatever toy you want."

Selene lifted Vivienne's foot from the floor and began tying it.

In her state of undress, tied up and lying on the ground, she watched Selene lift one leg onto her lap and then the other, binding her ankles together. And she didn't stop there. Vivienne's thoughts reeled in fantasies.

She slipped the rope up Vivienne's leg, slipping it over calves and thighs in loops like a fishnet. Vivienne looked away as she felt the rope slip over the highest part of her thigh.

"There are certain knots you can tie," she said, lacing the rope around Vivienne's inner thigh, "that can induce arousal while the occupant squirms in their bindings."

"I'm aware," Vivienne said, her voice heavy with desire. "Is that what you're doing?"

"I can, if you want," Selene said. "I can also do it so you'll have no relief from it."

Vivienne imagined herself bound and squirming, the rope rubbing between her legs, close but not touching. She bit her lip. "And how much would you need to change for either of those?"

"To make you squirm, I'd need to adjust it. But I could get you off as it is."

Vivienne laughed. "I'm sure you could, considering how quick your hands work."

"Oh no, you misunderstand. I could make you come without my hands ever touching your clit."

Vivienne raised her eyebrows. Selene might be talented, but it would take more than a well-placed rope to bring her to ecstasy. "You can try, but it won't work."

"Is that so?" Selene gently lowered Vivienne's legs to the ground. "That sounds like a challenge."

Vivienne looked at her legs. Only one leg had rope all the way up; the other was bound only at the ankle. The higher rope was knotted so that, if she twisted, she might be able to rub herself against it, but that wasn't something she planned on doing. She looked at Selene as if to ask, *Is this your worst?*

Selene smiled down at her. "If you like, I can take a photo. I have a Polaroid camera."

"Absolutely not!"

"I wouldn't show your face, just the ropes."

"No," Vivienne said, then added, "thank you."

Selene took in Vivienne's body. "All the things I could do to you, and you'd be begging for me not to stop."

Vivienne felt the words tremble through her. The idea of being at the complete mercy of the woman filled her with longing. She ached for Selene's fingers pressing against her.

"You won't, though," Vivienne said. "I don't have test results yet."

Selene grinned. "There are plenty of things I could do to you that don't involve taking your underwear off," she said. "All you have to do is ask."

What things, she wanted to ask but bit back the words. "What are you planning on doing?" she asked instead, hoping she didn't sound as aroused as she felt.

Selene crouched beside her and picked up the blindfold. "First, I'm going to blindfold you."

The idea of being bound and blindfolded, relying only on her other senses, made Vivienne shiver.

"And then…I'm going to watch you squirm."

Selene placed the blindfold over Vivienne's eyes, then combed her fingers through Vivienne's hair. "One more time: do you remember your safe word?"

"I do."

"Good girl," Selene said.

Vivienne heard the click of Selene's heels as she walked away, and then a creak of the wardrobe door, before a drawer was opened. A pause followed until she spoke.

"You're mine now, Vivienne. Ask politely for anything you want."

Which meant: *answer correctly or you'll be disciplined.* She swallowed.

In the silence, Vivienne sat taller, waiting for the woman to punish her with the riding crop, cane, or paddle.

Or her bare hand.

Vivienne pressed her thighs together. The rope rubbed on her bare leg, touching just below her sex. She was tempted to see if she could move the rope a little higher, but the last thing she needed was for Selene to see her rutting against a piece of rope.

Something soft slid slowly over her bare leg and down. And then disappeared.

Vivienne hadn't even heard the woman approach. Had Selene taken off her heels?

Then a weight settled on Vivienne's hips, and the woman stroked up her sides, drawing her hands slowly over her ribs. Vivienne arched against the rope, her bound hands splaying out as she tried to lean forward to find her.

"Relax," Selene said. "I won't do anything to you."

Of course, because I haven't been tested yet.

"Unless you ask me to."

Vivienne caught herself before she moaned, clenching her jaw shut. No way would she let Selene know the effect she was having on her.

And yet, as Selene caressed her neck, Vivienne wondered what it would be like to feel the woman's hand around her throat as she—

Too late, she realized that her hips had rolled and she had pressed herself against where the woman was straddling her.

"Ask me nicely to do unspeakable things to you," she whispered, brushing her hand across Vivienne's cheek. "Ask me nicely."

Vivienne choked, the words tight in her chest, building up in her throat. *Please, my queen.*

How could she beg for such a thing?

Selene's fingers were so close to her mouth, Vivienne could almost taste her.

How close was she? Was she hovering just above her face? Was she sitting upright, smirking, watching with interest? Was Selene about to kiss her?

Vivienne breathed in her perfume. Her mouth parted, hoping to receive Selene's kiss, but Selene only shifted her weight, keeping one hand on Vivienne's face. The other hand slid up her waist until it cupped just under her breast. Vivienne's nipples hardened, aching to be touched.

Selene pressed her fingers against the underwire of her bra. The hand on her cheek tilted Vivienne's head up.

Vivienne no longer cared which part of Selene's lips touched her as long as she felt them. But the woman held her in suspense, as if daring her to beg.

She wouldn't.

"Ah, I see," Selene said at last.

And then she was gone. The only sound was Vivienne's breathing. She ached to push the blindfold off, to see where she was and look at her.

She wanted to plead for Selene to return, but she swallowed her words. For all Vivienne knew, Selene was standing right next to her, watching her shift her shoulders, stretch out her hands, and adjust her feet, feeling for any slack in the ropes.

"My queen?"

"Yes?" She sounded closer than Vivienne had thought.

"What unspeakable things would you do?"

Without warning, Vivienne was tugged into a sitting position. Before she could even gasp, Selene brushed her lips against hers. "Do you want a taste?"

Vivienne relaxed her mouth, her lips parting. "Yes." It was the only thing she wanted.

After a pause that seemed to take a lifetime, Selene's weight was back on her lap, her breath warming her mouth. Their lips met.

Vivienne moaned. Selene was sucking on her lips, curling her fingers into her hair. She would have grabbed Selene, but her hands remained bound and pressed between them, and it was all she could do not to wriggle forward to brush the rope between her thighs.

"Naughty," Selene said and then grazed her mouth down her jaw, down to her neck and across her shoulder.

She tried to remember how long they'd agreed to in this session, but the thought merely flitted through her mind and was quickly erased. All she wanted was Selene rubbing against her thighs and kissing her like the world was running out of time.

Selene slid a hand under the cup of Vivienne's bra while she continued fisting her hair, tugging her head back, all the while biting and sucking at her shoulder.

It would leave a mark, but Vivienne didn't care. She keened as her nerves electrified.

Selene stroked her nipple, tweaking it gently, then pinched it.

Vivienne moaned. The rope on her thigh was pressing against her underwear.

"I told you I could get you off without touching your clit," Selene growled into her ear.

"But you were so naughty that I don't think I will."

"No!"

"No, what?"

"Don't stop, my queen."

"Say 'please.'"

Vivienne clamped her jaw shut as Selene tugged her hair again. Even blindfolded, she could feel Selene's eyes penetrating her, commanding her to say it.

"Please," she breathed.

"Was that so hard?"

Selene squeezed her breast again, and the rope rubbed against her underwear as Selene rocked on her lap, her teeth and tongue still on Vivienne's shoulder, applying just the right amount of tension.

Vivienne felt the pressure build low in her belly, growing with each movement until her hips jerked with the climax and she gave a sudden, strangled gasp.

As she shuddered, she felt Selene's laughter rumbling against her chest. Soon the pressure of the rope became too sensitive, and she jerked her hips away. She trembled with the aftershocks, trying to catch her breath.

Selene relaxed the grip in her hair as she trailed her lips against Vivienne's neck, pressing lightly against the skin. Then she pushed up the blindfold, resting her thumbs against Vivienne's cheekbones, and gazed at her, studying her.

Vivienne pushed up to kiss her, desperate to feel Selene's breath against her mouth, but Selene pulled away.

"How do you feel?" Selene asked.

"Good. I won't doubt you again."

"You and I both know that's a lie."

The endorphins were still flooding Vivienne's bloodstream. She hungered to do it again, to see if Selene could get her off more than once.

But instead Selene began untying her, quickly unraveling the knots.

The moment the ropes were pulled away, Selene seemed to pull on a mask. Perhaps Vivienne had crossed a boundary. "Are you okay?" she asked.

"It's been a while since I tied anyone up like that," she said and looked away.

Vivienne placed her hand on Selene's shoulder.

"I believe *I* should be comforting *you*." She took Vivienne's hand from her shoulder and held it gently. "How do you feel now?"

"Tired," she admitted.

"Mm, that can happen. Come here." She pulled Vivienne into her arms and pressed her head against her shoulder.

Vivienne hated how soothing it was. She pulled back from Selene's touch.

"You can take a shower, if you want," Selene said. "I'll clean up in here and make some coffee."

Vivienne nodded. A shower and coffee would be good.

She retrieved her clothes from the ottoman and shut the bathroom door behind her. She looked at herself in the mirror. There were lines on her back where the rope had pressed as she lay on the floor, but otherwise, the only mark was a single small welt on her shoulder—easily hidden.

She stepped into the shower. The warm water pressure beat down her back, soothing the knots.

Vivienne soaped up and, taking the shower head in hand, rinsed between her thighs. The water massaged her clit, and Vivienne sank briefly into the feeling, her arousal growing at the thought of getting off while the woman was downstairs. But she disregarded the thought, setting the showerhead back in place and standing under the spray until she had her desire under control.

No matter how enjoyable this session had been, it wasn't real. This had been a fantasy seduction service, and Selene was a businesswoman. And while Vivienne wanted to feel her hand relieve the pressure building between her thighs, it was all pretend.

A pleasure service between two consenting adults.

And if she was going to delve further into that service, actually allow the woman to touch her intimately, she needed to keep that in mind.

Vivienne went down to the kitchen where Selene was making coffee and sat at the table to wait.

She wanted to apologize. She wasn't sure what for, though. Perhaps for kissing her or not doing the right thing, or whatever it was. But instead, she sipped from the cup that Selene placed before her.

Something had shifted between them.

"Did you enjoy yourself?" Selene asked politely.

"I did," Vivienne said. "Did you?"

"Always," Selene said, but her tone was brusque.

"I…" Vivienne began, then looked away. "I think we should stick to what we did in the first session…if this is to continue."

"You're the client. Whatever service you want, I'm happy to provide."

Vivienne looked away. She was a client, only a client. Selene surely had a dozen more just like her.

Setting her cup down and reaching for her purse, she asked, "How much for the session?"

CHAPTER 5
BACKSEAT PRIVACY

Vivienne sat at the dining table, flipping through the morning paper while Hattie served Claudia breakfast, then sat down at her place. Her niece was ignoring her this morning.

As Vivienne folded up the newspaper, she noticed her sister and Claudia exchanging glances. Finally, she asked, "Will somebody tell me what's going on?"

Claudia dropped her fork dramatically, pushed away from the table, and went upstairs.

Vivienne looked at her sister. "What on earth was that about?"

"Well, you, um, missed another one of Claudia's cheerleading shows. She's been feeling…neglected because of the time you've been putting into your students over her."

Vivienne frowned. "It's early in the school year. I couldn't have missed—"

"No, you haven't missed the big events, but you didn't go to the fundraising event you volunteered for, the one you promised to attend two weeks ago."

"Has that happened already?"

"It was yesterday. You were off at a meeting."

Vivienne sighed. Yesterday she had had a meeting with Abigail to show her how to grade essays for one of her classes. Looking back, though, she could see how it might come across as neglectful to Claudia, especially since she had promised to go.

"I'll speak to her," she said.

"She'd appreciate it more if you attended something. There's a game next Friday; perhaps you could go."

The idea of sitting on the bleachers and watching a game she didn't care about as Claudia danced around in a skimpy uniform was not in her top ten list of things she wanted to do. "I'll clear my calendar for next Friday evening."

Vivienne rescheduled her next meeting with Abigail. If it was that important to Claudia that she attend the game, she would make time.

When she told Claudia her plans, her niece made a snide comment, that she doubted Vivienne would ever leave her work undone.

It was rather hurtful, but it was not entirely untrue. Lately, she had been more focused on her work than her family.

By the time Friday rolled around, Claudia had warmed to her again. She talked about the importance of the upcoming match and shared details about her classes.

The tension eased, and Vivienne thought the worst was over. There were only three more weeks until Janice returned, giving her plenty of time to get back onto her own schedule.

They arrived early and parked close to the stadium. The three of them made their way to the bleachers with a picnic basket and a blanket. Claudia ran off to join her squad. Vivienne and Hattie found seats with a clear view of the cheerleaders.

"It's good that you came," Hattie said as she opened the picnic basket and took out cups and a thermos of hot chocolate. "You seem to be running yourself ragged lately."

"I've taken on a class for one of my colleagues," she reminded Hattie. "Thankfully, Janice will return soon."

"Didn't you get a TA?" Hattie asked. "Abigail?"

"Yes, and she is doing surprisingly well," Vivienne said. In truth, Abigail was responsible for the fact that she was sleeping at all. The girl had taken to the job and surpassed her expectations. Elijah, as promised, had managed to wrangle some funding, which gave Abigail a nice stipend.

But the fact was, she used her work as an escape. The Carter household was loud and raucous at times, and Claudia's foul moods mixed with Hattie's need to incessantly process whether or not she was going to move out gave Vivienne an excuse to hide in her office.

"Oh, there's the new principal," Hattie said, waving across the bleachers to a sea of people. "Claudia's quite taken by her. Girl power and all that. She's a bit scary in the PTA, though; won't let any of the parents walk over her. Reminds me of you, actually."

"Fascinating." Vivienne said with a sigh and looked over to where her niece was warming up with the cheerleading squad. "When does Claudia's part finish?"

"When the game is over," Hattie said, pointing to the scoreboard.

Vivienne looked to where she had pointed. The timer had not even started counting down. Just as she was about to ask when the game would begin, the players came onto the field and the crowd began to cheer. Claudia and the other cheerleaders performed a routine. *At last.*

The game began. Vivienne wasn't sure what the point of the game was, so she simply clapped when Hattie clapped and yelled when Hattie yelled, hoping that it was the right thing to do.

After about an hour, Hattie said, "Why don't you go stretch your legs? It's almost halftime, and you can use the bathroom before there's a line."

Vivienne agreed, though there was no way in hell that she would use the school's public bathroom.

She climbed down from the bleachers and headed toward the car to get her cigarettes. As she leaned against the car to light up, Selene entered her field of vision.

Vivienne felt her heart pound.

"Vivienne," Selene said, blinking. "I didn't take you for someone interested in school sports."

"I'm not normally, but my niece thinks I'm ignoring her," she explained, still holding her unlit cigarette and lighter in her hands. "I…" She was about to say that she hadn't expected Selene to be there either when she realized with a start that the woman was likely there because she was a parent.

"Well, we do what we can for those in our care," Selene said, "even if we don't have any interest in the event." She said it flippantly, but Vivienne noticed her shoulders tighten.

Guilt overtook her. It had been two weeks since she had last visited Selene, yet every time she considered calling, she thought of how the woman had pulled away at the end of their last meeting.

"I'm sorry," she finally said, "if I made you feel uncomfortable."

Selene frowned. "What do you mean?"

"The last session," she said.

Selene tilted her head. "What do you think happened?"

"We..." Vivienne hesitated, looking around to see if anyone was within earshot. She stepped closer. "We engaged in the services I asked for, but at the end of the session, you seemed to withdraw, as if I had gone too far. What I'm trying to say is that we don't have to have sex, if you're not...interested."

Selene smiled brightly. "Oh no, I quite enjoyed it. I'm sorry if you thought otherwise."

"Are you sure? I'm fine with continuing the previous services or..."

"Vivienne." Selene stepped back and looked her up and down. "Believe me, the idea of fucking you against the nearest surface is never far from my mind. Let me formally apologize for misleading you."

Now Vivienne smiled. "And how would you do that?"

Selene turned and, taking Vivienne's hand, led her deeper into the parking lot.

They walked past a dozen cars, finally arriving at a black sedan. Selene pulled a key fob from her pocket and clicked the doors unlocked. "In you get," she said, opening the back door.

Vivienne hesitated.

"No one's around." She motioned around the parking lot. "And the windows are tinted, so no one can see inside." She raised her eyebrows.

Vivienne's heart pounded so loud, she was surprised Selene couldn't hear it. But she wasn't about to leave, so she climbed into the backseat and slid across, leaving room for Selene to climb in beside her. As soon as the door was shut, the interior light switched off.

"And now what?" Vivienne asked.

"And now"—Selene reached up and curled her hand behind Vivienne's neck—"I make reparations."

Selene pressed her lips to hers, and Vivienne shivered as she leaned back. The woman climbed on top of her, teasing, tugging, and sucking Vivienne's mouth. Then she slid her hand up Vivienne's thigh and underneath her skirt while pressing her hips purposely against Vivienne's.

"This is your apology?" Vivienne gasped as Selene kissed her again.

Selene laughed. Vivienne slipped back against the leather seat, one foot pressing against the door, the other pressing against the floor as Selene kissed her deeply, her tongue exploring Vivienne's mouth while she stroked her thigh with one hand and undid Vivienne's jacket with the other.

"I saw the doctor," Vivienne gasped between kisses.

"Good girl," Selene said. "I assume it was good news?"

Vivienne nodded, and the woman covered her throat with nips and kisses.

"Do you have a copy of the results for me?" she asked, sliding her hand from her thigh over Vivienne's underwear.

It had been so long since anyone had kissed her like this, like they wanted all of her. It might be unethical to engage with a sex worker at your niece's cheerleading event, but it was hardly a cardinal sin.

"Mm-hmm," she managed, then reached into her jacket pocket and pulled out her phone. She quickly pulled up the report and showed it to Selene.

The woman glanced at the screen, and her face lit up. "I'm going to enjoy ravaging you." Selene pinned Vivienne onto the backseat and tugged the jacket out of the way, then began stroking between Vivienne's legs.

Her long, slow movements had Vivienne gasping, desperate for more. She was dizzy from her touch.

Selene smiled slyly and pulled back. "Something the matter?"

"Selene," Vivienne said, panting, "if you don't stop teas—" She gasped as Selene slid her fingers over the edges of her underwear.

"If I don't what? What will you do?" Selene asked, stroking over the silk seam until she reached Vivienne's clit. "You're mine now."

Vivienne moaned and nodded.

Selene pushed Vivienne's underwear aside and gently stroked between her lips. "Do you want me to fuck you?" she asked. "Or should I leave you like this?"

"For fuck's sake, just fuck me."

Selene pressed her lips against Vivienne's mouth again, kissing and biting. Then she paused. "Say 'please.'"

Vivienne pulled Selene closer, her nails digging into her back as Selene stroked her again, pressing firmly against her entrance. The other woman tried to pull away, but Vivienne thrust her hips up against her.

"Please," she said.

"Please what?"

"Please fuck me.'

"If you insist." And then Selene was kissing her again while she stroked her clit and slid her fingers around the labia.

Vivienne gasped as Selene pushed two fingers into her with a firm thrust. She squeezed her muscles around her fingers, moaning into Selene's mouth.

It had been so long since she had been fucked, truly fucked, and it took her breath away.

Selene thrust her fingers in and out, her thumb drawing over the clit.

Vivienne squeezed her thighs, trying to press closer. "Selene," she gasped, "stop teasing."

"Oh no. This is *my* apology. I can do it however I want."

"Do it fast, or I swear I'll take over."

"Such a spoilsport," Selene said and sighed melodramatically. Then she returned to kissing Vivienne, increasing the thrusts of her fingers.

Vivienne rocked in rhythm with the thrusts, moaning and begging Selene to get her off. She squeezed her eyes shut, riding closer and closer to the moment.

Please, please, please let me—

And then she was arching, every muscle clenched, and Selene kissed her again as she cried out, wetness dripping against her thighs, making her slide on the leather seats.

Vivienne clung to Selene as she felt the rush come crashing down.

Selene slid her fingers out, snapped Vivienne's underwear back in place, and dragged her thumb over the seam one last time before sitting back in the seat.

Vivienne jerked at the touch.

"There," Selene said. "Now you see that I would be very pleased to fuck you, should you ever wish to engage in that side of my services."

Still trying to catch her breath, Vivienne said nothing.

Selene reached into the center console and pulled out some tissues to clean her hand. She grinned down at Vivienne. "At a loss for words?"

Vivienne pushed herself into a sitting position. "I...can see why..." She trailed off, unable to piece the sentence together. "Yes," she finally answered.

Selene leaned back against the door. "My demeanor the other day had nothing to do with you," she said, handing Vivienne a tissue.

Vivienne wiped the tissue between her thighs, cleaning up the wetness as best she could. "It just seemed to happen after we engaged in...whatever you call that form of rope use," Vivienne said.

"It was situational. It had nothing to do with you." Selene looked at her thoughtfully. "If I have a problem with you or any services you want to engage in, I'll be up front. I don't have a problem saying no, even to clients who look as lovely as you do while you're gasping my name."

Vivienne flushed, tasting Selene's name on her tongue. She wanted to press close against her again, but instead she asked, "Is it even your name?"

Selene smiled. "You haven't worked it out yet."

"Haven't worked what out?"

Selene shook her head. "Gone are the days when I could blend into a city, never seeing a client outside of sessions."

"Why have a service here at all, then?"

"Why engage my services when you live here?" Selene shot the question back at her. "Because you want to."

Vivienne glanced away from the intensity of Selene's stare. She didn't like how easily the woman seemed to read her while remaining an enigma herself.

Besides, she'd been away from the game for too long. Hattie was likely to come and search for her, and this was not something she wanted to explain to anyone.

"Thank you for your honesty," Vivienne said, then wondered if Selene required payment for services rendered. She tried to think how to bring it up without sounding awkward.

"You can return to your family now," Selene said. "If I come to you, like today, I don't expect payment. But if you come to me, I think it's fair to say you're requesting a paid service."

"Am I to expect a repeat performance?"

Selene leaned forward and, pulling another tissue, wiped Vivienne's mouth, cleaning off the ruined makeup. "Here," she said, reaching into the center console to pull out a lipstick. "It's not the exact shade you wore, but I doubt anyone will notice."

But before Vivienne could take it, Selene uncapped the lid. Holding Vivienne's jaw steady with one hand, she used the other to apply the lipstick, focusing on Vivienne's mouth. Then she fixed the line with her thumb.

She looked up to meet Vivienne's eyes and smiled as she capped the lipstick, then combed her fingers through Vivienne's hair. "There. Now you look less like you were fucked in the backseat of a car and more like you were wind tussled."

"Thank you." Vivienne nodded. "I'll…see you another time."

"I look forward to our next session."

Vivienne scoffed. "Who said there was going to be a next session?"

Selene laughed. "Of course there's going to be a next session." Then she shooed Vivienne out of the car.

Vivienne opened the door, looked around to make sure no one was around, then stepped out of the car, fixing her skirt as she closed the door, and walked back to the stadium.

She returned to where Hattie was sitting, adjusting her jacket as she took her seat. If she smelled of sex, Hattie didn't seem to notice.

All Vivienne could smell was Selene's perfume, light and intoxicating, as if it had permeated her skin.

She pulled out the thermos from the picnic basket and poured herself a cup of hot chocolate, then tried to focus on the game, watching the players move from one side of the field to the other.

Before long, the endorphins faded, and boredom returned. Only the cheerleaders—and Claudia—held Vivienne's interest.

When the game was over, Claudia rejoined Vivienne and Hattie, bouncing excitedly, talking about how happy she was for Luca. Apparently, he had either managed to kick a goal or block a goal kick. Vivienne was pleased to see Claudia's excitement.

"We're going to go get pizza," Claudia said as Henry and Rebecca came up beside her. "Luca's gone to get changed, and then Henry will drive us to the pizza place."

Vivienne nodded. "Do you need us to pick you up later?"

"No, Henry will drop us off. I'll be home before midnight," Claudia said, then ran off with her friends. Whatever reason Claudia had had for being surly earlier in the week seemed to have disappeared.

She turned to Hattie. "Shall we?"

They returned to the car. Vivienne glanced at the black sedan.

"Everything okay, Viv?" Hattie asked. "You seem distracted."

Vivienne snapped back to the present and nodded.

On the drive home, Hattie chatted about the night's match, then segued to the upcoming PTA meeting, where they were planning how to raise money for the football team. Finally, Hattie seemed to notice that Vivienne wasn't responding. "Viv? You haven't said anything since the game."

"I'm not sure what to say," she admitted. "Claudia looked happy, and it's good to see her expanding her group of friends."

They drove in silence for a few minutes, then Vivienne asked, "The PTA meeting. Are all guardians welcome?"

"Are you going to get involved?"

Vivienne considered. Realistically, she could not take on another commitment with her current schedule. "I suppose not," she said. "I happened to run into one of the parents when I went down to the car, and thought it…"

"Ooh, a single father? You should ask him out the next time you see him. Or was it a single mother? I can't imagine any of the men would interest you enough to get involved."

Vivienne sighed. "No, nothing like that," she said, feeling the heat rise in her cheeks. The idea of dating someone was overwhelming. Even Selene.

She wasn't sure Hattie believed her. From the corner of her eye, she saw her sister glance her way, her eyebrows raised.

Vivienne was sorry she had asked. It was better to stay away from the PTA to respect Selene's privacy, no matter how curious she was about her personal life. Plus, she didn't have time to organize bake sales and God knew what else to raise money. Better to open her wallet and donate.

Hattie switched to chatting about moving out; now that she was full-time, she was able to save up. Vivienne listened anxiously. In fairness, Hattie probably could afford to move out, given the inheritance from their parents and the proceeds from the sale of their business. But even with these funds supplementing her income, it would be difficult to save for retirement. The cost of living in Oakdale was high.

"Viv?"

Vivienne glanced at her sister.

"The turnoff was back there."

She had indeed passed their turn, and now they were driving across the bridge to the other side of the river. She turned the car around, embarrassed that she had been distracted.

After they arrived home, Hattie headed for the kitchen while Vivienne headed upstairs and took a quick shower. Thinking of the encounter with Selene made her body hum again, and a rolling hunger grew inside her once more.

She'd thought that by having sex with Selene, that hunger would drop away and she'd be able to manage herself. Instead, the flames were fanned, and all Vivienne wanted was to kiss between the woman's thighs until she called out her name.

Vivienne shook off the image.

Selene hadn't really explained her withdrawal. She could have been remembering a client or thinking about an ex-lover—or she could be lying.

Vivienne doubted it was a lie. Although this was Selene's business, she seemed genuinely eager to draw Vivienne to new heights of passion.

She thought guiltily of the evening's encounter as she dressed again. She shouldn't have succumbed in such a public space. If they'd been caught, not only would it have reflected poorly on her, given her prominent position at the university, but it would have affected Claudia as well.

She went down to the living room, fixed herself a whiskey, and sank into her armchair.

A few minutes later, Hattie came in and said, "You're allowed to date."

Vivienne looked at her. "What makes you think I want to?"

"Well, it's just been so long since I've seen you happy with someone. You don't need to protect Claudia from your romantic interests. You're allowed to date."

Vivienne sipped her whiskey. "My being single has nothing to do with my status as a guardian. I simply don't have time to date."

"I'm not saying you should find someone and settle down. But life is more than just work."

"My work is important to me." Vivienne had spent decades building her career, authoring papers, journal articles, and even a few books. There was no way she would give it up for someone, no matter how good the sex was.

She sipped her whiskey in silence until her sister returned to the kitchen with a tray that held two servings of leftover corned beef and salad.

"I'll need to go food shopping tomorrow," Hattie said.

The mention of food shopping reminded Vivienne of meeting Selene in the grocery store. She flashed on being pinned in the cereal aisle while the woman had her way with her.

Vivienne ignored the image, returning to eating her dinner while Hattie filled the silence with talk of Claudia and the fundraising event the PTA would need to organize.

Claudia arrived home around eleven, her cheeks flushed. She set her bag down, all the while babbling excitedly about her evening.

Vivienne was hit with a wave of exhaustion. It had been a long day.

In the privacy of her bedroom, her thoughts returned to Selene, and she pulled out her vibrator to quell the growing desire.

CHAPTER 6
SUSPENSION

"Vivienne." Elijah entered her office, oblivious to the fact that she was in the middle of a discussion with a student about her recent essay that was thirty percent of the semester's grade.

She smiled apologetically at the student. "Yes, Elijah?"

"Unfortunately, Janice won't be returning as expected. She's requested additional time off. I'll need you to continue teaching her classes until she returns."

It had already been a month since Vivienne had taken over Janice's classes. Her time was stretched, and she was stressed trying to plan lessons for her own classes, never mind Janice's second-year students. Abigail was a much-needed help, but there were some things she couldn't leave with her.

The journal article she was writing was behind schedule. She barely saw her family outside of dinner, and she was getting less than five hours' sleep a night. She had been counting on Janice's return.

"I'll require further funding for my TA," she said, making no effort to disguise her reluctance. "But that's no issue, right, Elijah?"

"Of course," he said. "Thank you, Vivienne."

Vivienne returned her attention to Maddison. The girl was staring wide-eyed, as if she had just witnessed something she shouldn't have.

"Where were we?" Vivienne asked.

"You were telling me how to earn extra credit," Maddison said, "so I don't lose my scholarship."

Vivienne nodded and reviewed Maddison's grades so far. It was only the most recent essay that had dragged down her overall grade. "Before you take on an extra-credit project, why don't you rewrite it? Perhaps you can dig a little deeper into the subject matter."

Maddison audibly sucked in a breath, a pinched expression on her face. It clearly wasn't the response she was looking for.

She sighed. "I can do that. When do you want it by?"

"Two weeks."

Maddison nodded, picked up her things, and left.

Vivienne watched her go. She had probably been too lenient with the deadline, but the truth was she was too exhausted to care. She was working hours of unpaid overtime just to keep her classes and Janice's caught up and had been pushing herself to attend Claudia's sporting events, given that she couldn't find the time to take Claudia to and from school.

She considered eating dinner in her office to get an extra hour of work in, but she and her sister had agreed when Claudia first learned to walk that they would eat dinner together as a family, no matter what.

Her sleep schedule was the only area she could afford to cut. But the tension was building up. With so little time for herself, she would snap if she didn't do something. She needed an hour or two.

Vivienne picked up the phone.

"Vivienne. I thought you'd forgotten about me."

"I've been busy. Do you have time for an appointment this week?"

"Hmm. Let me see."

Vivienne closed her eyes and tried to slow the pounding of her heart. Maybe Selene would have time this afternoon.

"How long were you looking for?"

Vivienne opened her planner. "What do you have available?" she asked as if they were scheduling a business meeting.

"Saturday morning. You can have me from nine until twelve."

Vivienne closed her eyes at the choice of words. *You can have me.* Oh, she would so enjoy having her.

"Three hours?"

"Let's say from nine until eleven, and I promise not to watch the clock," Selene said. "I like the idea of you in my garden. But there are many things we could play with."

"And just what were you thinking I would enjoy in your garden?" Vivienne asked, trying to maintain some semblance of control.

"We'll discuss that once you're here. I would enjoy hearing what you would like to do."

"I'll see you Saturday," she said, her mind filling with various fantasies.

At least now she had something to look forward to.

Vivienne spent the next few days going from meeting to meeting, from class to office. It was an especially busy time as students started to realize that unless they did something soon, they wouldn't make the grades they needed. She went home, ate, then shut herself in her home office for lesson planning until late at night.

Twice, Hattie had commented on how tired she looked, asking if she was eating enough, and each time Vivienne had snapped back that she was perfectly fine and had only recently seen her doctor.

At breakfast Friday morning, Vivienne drank an extra cup of coffee, trying to ease her headache. She was giving a test this afternoon in one of her classes that would give her a better idea of whether to reevaluate her lesson plans. If it weren't for that, she would succumb to her headache and call in sick.

"Auntie?" Claudia's soft voice broke through the haze. "Can I ask you something?"

Vivienne set her cup down.

"Luca's having trouble with some of the boys on the team. They're not letting him use his locker. I've tried talking to Coach Myers, but ever since Principal Rothschild told him off, he doesn't seem to care. And I'm worried that if I go over his head again, he'll make things worse for Luca."

Vivienne paused to consider the question. "I can speak to the boys' parents, if you think that will help." It really wasn't her place to do so; it really should be Luca's father.

"No, that will make it worse."

Vivienne couldn't argue that. "Honestly, Claudia, there's very little you or Luca can do about bullies. It may be in his best interest to quit the team."

"But he wants to be a part of it! It's not fair that they can take away his enjoyment of it."

"It's not," Vivienne agreed. "But there are some fights you need to walk away from. That is, unfortunately, how the world works. Luca's unhappiness is not your responsibility. Perhaps he could find a team that's more open to having a trans player."

Claudia sank back in her chair. "But none of the other teams are open to it."

"Then maybe start a new one. I doubt if Luca's the only one who feels excluded."

"No! Then they get what they want."

Vivienne sighed. "Yes, they do. And it's not fair, and it's not right, and I'm really sorry. If we could wave a magic wand and teach them all a lesson, we would. This fight may not be worth it. Sometimes it's better to walk away and create your own happiness."

"Is that what you did?"

Vivienne frowned. "Pardon?"

"Aunt Hattie told me that things were hard for you when you started at the university. That the others—"

"Your Aunt Hattie is repeating gossip. No, my situation was entirely different. I wasn't berated like young Luca. It was just some minor office gossip, nothing I couldn't rise above."

"Maybe I should speak to Principal Rothschild."

"You could," Vivienne agreed. "And then she'll speak to the coach. And then what? I don't mean to discourage you. What you want to do is admirable. But perhaps you should think about what's actually fair for Luca rather than seeking justice."

"That's what I'm doing," Claudia said.

"Are you certain?"

Claudia wrinkled her nose. "It *is* about Luca. He's getting bullied by these...these...*dicks*," she finished, spitting out the word.

Vivienne knew that no matter what she said, Claudia would go her own way. She had already decided what she was going to do.

"Speak to Luca," Vivienne urged. "Maybe speak to his coach yourself. But consider what the repercussions might be. The last thing you want is to make life even more difficult for your friend."

"I only want him to be happy."

"And that's not a bad thing to want," Vivienne assured her. "But be sure that this is really about Luca's interest and not about your own hero complex."

"Hero complex? Is that what you think this about?"

It was, but Vivienne didn't want to engage in that argument. Her headache was now a throbbing migraine. She needed to lie down in a dark room with a damp towel over her face. "Do you need me to drop you off at school?"

"Or what, you think my hero complex will have me try to rescue a cat out of some tree?"

Vivienne sighed. "Do you want me to drive you or not?"

"I can walk to Henry's and see if he'll take me."

The way she said it made Vivienne narrow her eyes. "Has something happened between you and Henry?"

Claudia shook her head. "I don't know," she admitted. "It's fine. He's busy. He and his dad are fighting."

Vivienne was familiar with Henry's feelings about his father. Once, Claudia had begged to let Henry move in with them, and although Vivienne wasn't against the idea, the reality would be tricky. Besides, Henry had an older sibling, and Claudia said he often cooled the clashes in the family.

"I'll drop you off. Be ready to leave in five minutes." That would give her enough time to finish her coffee.

A few minutes later, Claudia reappeared. "Ready!"

Vivienne sent her out to the car, then went to her office to pick up her bag and laptop. She reached for her laptop, then stopped. The light wasn't on.

Opening up the computer, she watched the screen flick on…and then off completely. It had worked fine last night.

Vivienne plugged it in and waited. The computer screen flickered.

Panic welled up. The last thing she needed was for her computer to crash with all of her work on it, including her lesson plans. And, yes, although she had backed it up on the cloud, it was inaccessible to her from any of the school's computers. She would have to use her cell phone.

Vivienne unplugged the laptop and shoved it into her bag. If the charging cable was the issue, then all she needed was to get a new one. There was a computer shop in town. She could duck in, confirm if the charging cable was the problem, and pick one up. Vivienne slung the computer bag over her shoulder and closed the door to her office.

"Auntie? Are you okay?"

"Fine," Vivienne said in a tone that suggested she was anything but. "Let's go before we're late."

Vivienne drove to Claudia's school and pulled into the parking lot. Claudia climbed out, wishing Vivienne only a brief goodbye before running off, as if to avoid dealing with her bad mood any further.

Not that Vivienne could blame her.

Just as she pulled out of the parking lot, she noticed a black sedan pull in. Vivienne watched the car pass, catching Selene's image. She couldn't see anyone in the passenger seat, but maybe her child had forgotten something.

Vivienne didn't think on it any further as she drove to the computer shop and walked in just as the sign on the front door flipped to *Open*. Vivienne pulled out her laptop and put it on the counter. "My screen went black, and I need it to be fixed ASAP. I need it for my classes."

"Of course." He plugged it in. The screen flickered, then turned black as before.

"Ah," he said. "It could be an issue with the charging cable, or maybe your screen is burning out. But…have you visited any unsecured websites recently? If you downloaded something from one of them or clicked on an ad…" He glanced at her awkwardly.

Under usual circumstances, Vivienne would be able to say no. But the truth was, she had been searching some websites in order to understand some of the services Selene offered, and there was every possibility that one of them had downloaded a virus onto her laptop.

"Can you fix it?" she asked.

"Oh, definitely. It might wipe out your hard drive, though."

Vivienne blew out her breath. She would lose a lot of resources she had saved for her article, and it would be difficult for her to retrieve them again. "Try to avoid that, if you can."

"I can have it back by Monday. I'll check the cable and the screen first."

"Monday's fine." She'd have to use her phone until then.

"Let me get your contact details."

Vivienne checked the time on her watch. She was going to be late.

Vivienne managed to be on time, and she made it through class without having to use her phone too much. But then she was late to her office hours after she stopped by the library to borrow a laptop.

When she arrived at her office, one of her students was sitting on the ground by her door. "Professor Carter," he said, getting to his feet. "I need an extension for the essay due next week."

Vivienne pulled out her keys and unlocked the door. "Which essay is this?" She pulled the borrowed laptop from her bag, sat at her desk, and opened it. The battery was low. And of course she didn't have a charging cable for it. She closed the computer and looked up at the student. He sat across from her desk and began nervously twisting the hem of his shirt.

"Ah—well, it's...technically Professor Whitler's class. And she's usually fine with giving extensions, so long as..."

Vivienne raised her eyebrows. "So long as...?" she prompted.

"Ah...can I have an extension? Please? I have an exam on the same day, and I just really need..."

Vivienne leaned back in her seat. "Did Professor Whitler give you a schedule for when assignments were due?"

"Yes."

"So you have been aware that your essay and exam would be on the same day since your first week of classes."

"I mean, technically, yes, but I didn't actually realize that until... until this week," he admitted.

"Matthew, isn't it?"

"Or Matty. Most people call me Matty."

"Matthew, I will not grant you an extension. You've had all semester to plan for this. I suggest you go over your schedule for the rest of the semester and modify your plans as needed."

"But Maddison—" He stopped himself.

Vivienne waited to see if he would continue.

He didn't. He mumbled an apology, then bolted from the room.

She changed the setting on her borrowed laptop to Power Save and stared at it. Then, rubbing her head, she opened the desk drawer, looking for Advil.

The drawer was empty. She'd used up the last of it.

At least the day couldn't get any worse.

But just as she was about to eat lunch, her phone rang. "Ms. Carter?"

"Yes. Who's speaking?"

"This is Mrs. Lewis. I'm calling from Oakdale High."

Vivienne lost her appetite.

"Your niece got into a fight this morning. Principal Rothschild would like you to come to her office today. Usually, we'd call Hattie, but she isn't answering her phone."

Claudia had gotten into a fight, and Vivienne suspected she knew the reason for it. "I'll be right in," she said and hung up.

She wolfed down her lunch. She had two hours before her next class. She left a note on the door's whiteboard, advising that office hours were canceled for the day and for students to contact her through email or, if it was urgent, to reach out to Professor Haddon.

Her mother always said that bad things came in threes. Vivienne hoped Claudia's fight was the last of her bad luck.

She considered calling the bookstore and asking Hattie to deal with it. But Hattie would be a pushover and would agree that Claudia needed some kind of punishment. And Vivienne knew perfectly well that Claudia was probably only protecting her friend.

She parked in a teacher's spot, as if challenging them to do something about it, and walked to the principal's office.

Mrs. Lewis, the head administrator, was on the phone. Claudia, Luca, Henry, and Rebecca sat together on a bench with their heads bowed. Bruises were forming on their faces. On the opposite bench were a half dozen boys Vivienne didn't recognize. The door to the principal's inner office was closed, the occupant identified as *Principal Anna S. Rothschild.*

Claudia and her friends all began speaking at once.

She lifted her hand, silencing them. "Have your parents been called?" she asked, looking at Claudia's friends.

"Yes," Rebecca answered. "They're with Principal Rothschild now, except for Henry's dad. Mr. Riley's at work."

Vivienne glanced at Henry, then addressed Mrs. Lewis. "Do I need to sign anything, or may I join the meeting?"

"Oh yes. That would be fine."

Vivienne opened the door. Inside the principal's office were six other parents. She nodded at Claudia's friends' parents, then glanced over at the principal—and froze.

She had engaged in dominatrix services from Claudia's *principal.*

Selene spoke first. "Ms. Carter, I take it?" she asked, tilting her head. "I thought we requested your sister."

"She's unavailable," Vivienne said, closing the door behind her.

"We were just concluding this matter." Selene folded her hands neatly on the desk in front of her.

"And what matter would that be?" she asked. She remained standing in the doorway, afraid that if she took a step, she'd wobble.

"Claudia and her friends were fighting with some other students. Oakdale High has a zero-tolerance policy. Suspension next week for all parties is appropriate."

"Ridiculous," Vivienne countered. "Whatever Claudia's reasons were for fighting, I'm sure they were justified."

Selene rose to her feet, her expression conveying enough authority to silence everyone in the room. "Ms. Carter," she said, her tone clipped, "why don't you take a seat, and you and I can discuss what happened. There's no need for anyone else to stay longer."

Vivienne straightened her shoulders and stepped over to the empty seat but remained standing.

Selene held her gaze. Vivienne waited for her to say something else. But instead, Selene walked around her desk and showed the other parents out. Then she asked Mrs. Lewis to lead the students back to class.

When she returned to the room, she shut the door behind her. "Sit down," she said.

Vivienne felt her knees grow weak. She wanted to obey, but she also wanted to resist.

"You're a principal?" she hissed.

Selene fluttered her eyelids. "In fairness, I hadn't put two and two together until I saw you at the football match the other weekend. And at that point, I thought you had also worked out the truth. Hardly my fault if you came to the wrong conclusion."

"You—"

"—are here to discuss Claudia, not our prior association. Now, sit. Down."

Vivienne scoffed but sat down, crossing her legs. "This is absurd. As I understand it, Claudia was defending her friend against bullies. If anything, she should be rewarded."

"Did she discuss the fight with you?"

"No, but she told me Luca Fitzgerald has had some issues with bullies."

"Yes, well, unfortunately, Oakdale High's policy on fighting is clear."

"Did Claudia start the fight?"

Selene leaned back in her chair. "Some witnesses say she did, and some say she didn't. Apparently, one of the football players made a snide comment, and Claudia retorted. As she was walking away, one of them lunged at her, but Henry struck him first."

"It sounds to me like they started it."

"And if it was just a matter of words, it would be far more straightforward, but it escalated to a physical fight. One of the players was taken to the hospital with a broken leg. His parents would like to see Claudia and her friends expelled. Or at least Luca, who they say started it. But not everyone agrees with that."

Ah. So there were deeper politics at play. Selene's frustration had nothing to do with Vivienne and everything to do with the other parents. Likely Selene—Principal Rothschild—had been dealing with them for quite some time.

"This could ruin Claudia's academic prospects," Vivienne said. "It could ruin all of their prospects if they're suspended. Surely something else could be done."

"Between you and me, I would very much like to separate this issue and deal with what is probably true about Luca being bullied, but unfortunately, I cannot. None of the children has reported anything to me outside of this event. Claudia says she spoke to Coach Myers, but he told me that her version is an overdramatic retelling."

"So you can't do anything because a teacher minimized Claudia's reporting?"

"Oh no," Selene said. "I just have to be careful about what I do." She drummed her nails on the desk. "Suspension is what the parents of the football players want, and, given that it would be for all the students, that seems fair. But you're right. It could affect their academic chances and opportunities for scholarships." She flashed her eyes at Vivienne.

Vivienne felt her cheeks flush. She cleared her throat. "So you'll reduce their punishment?"

"Well, there needs to be punishment. Detention for sure. And I can get creative, maybe find something for the students to do together. Perhaps have them donate their time to a charity to remind them that they need to work together."

It didn't seem fair to Claudia, but Vivienne was willing to concede. "And the other children?" Vivienne asked. "How will you deal with the kids who bully Luca?"

"I will handle it. But if you'd like to take up the issue, our PTA could use your input. Or perhaps you would like to have another meeting." Selene tilted her head, staring at Vivienne brazenly.

Vivienne grunted and ran her hands over her skirt. "We already have a meeting scheduled," she said, keeping her voice low.

"That we do. I shall see you tomorrow, Ms. Carter." Selene stood up and moved to the door. "Perhaps some corporal punishment may be required."

Vivienne sucked in her breath as she pushed up from the chair. She could see herself clearly bending over Selene's desk as, cane in hand, Selene showed her a new kind of punishment. "Maybe," she answered.

As she passed Selene, Vivienne heard her whisper, "I'm looking forward to it."

CHAPTER 7
OUTDOOR EXHIBITION

Vivienne stood at the door of her closet in her robe, looking over her lingerie. She couldn't decide what to wear—unusual for her.

Usually, she'd go for her favorite ivory-and-black set, but Selene had already seen that. She had a ruby set, but Vivienne wasn't sure how it would look with her red hair. Maybe the emerald or the black.

Vivienne sighed. It had been some time since choosing what to wear had made her nervous, a fact which increased her unease about this whole situation. Why did she feel a need to impress the woman? Was it the physical excitement, or was it something deeper?

Perhaps she was so lonely that she had created an entire romantic fantasy around Selene. It wasn't unheard of.

But that didn't help her decide which lingerie to wear.

It wasn't as if she had anyone to ask. She had never really had close friends, aside from her sister. And that hardly counted.

Perhaps that said more about her than she liked. The only person she considered a friend was Florence Haddon, Elijah's wife, and that was only because once, while drunk at a university mixer, Florence had confided to her that everyone there was a coward and Vivienne was the only person she trusted to tell the truth.

But Vivienne couldn't ask her about this.

Scowling, she grabbed the ivory set. It would have to do. It wasn't as if she had never had sex with the woman. She didn't need to impress her. So what did it matter what she wore?

But then she switched to the emerald, slipping on a simple black dress over it.

"Oh, you look nice," Hattie said as Vivienne made her way downstairs. "Where are you off to?"

Vivienne checked the time. It was still early. "The office. My laptop is in the shop, and I have work I need to finish by Monday." Not entirely false. She did plan on going to the campus library that afternoon.

Hattie looked at her curiously. "Well, I'll be going to the bookstore. Do you want me to drop you off?"

"No need. I'll be at work for some time."

"Are you sure? I get off at four. I could pick you up again."

Vivienne pressed her lips shut. "I'm certain. What time are you leaving?"

"Oh, Jonathan's opening, so I'll probably wander off in about fifteen minutes."

Vivienne nodded. She'd leave a little later; otherwise, Hattie would see her driving away from the university, and she didn't need that.

Too late, Vivienne remembered that Saturday mornings were busy with weekend markets. The streets were filled with pedestrians. She was going to be late.

Dreadfully late.

Ten minutes after the hour, she rang the doorbell.

Selene was waiting just inside, and she opened the door, her eyebrows raised. "I warned you that I don't appreciate clients arriving late," she said, blocking the door with her body.

"I forgot about Saturday market traffic. I don't usually drive in this end of town, especially on the weekend."

Selene didn't blink as she said, "Perhaps I should buy you a GPS, and you can check it for traffic. Or shall I have you read the clock on the wall until I'm satisfied that you can tell time?"

Vivienne flushed. "It won't happen again."

"Odds are that it will occur again." Selene pushed open the door. "But you can make it up to me. Come inside before someone sees you, Ms. Carter."

Vivienne stepped into the hallway with a shiver. She waited for Selene to lead her up to the bedroom, but she was shown to the garden instead.

There were businesses on either side of Selene's house that were open. The streets were not that busy, but the auto shop's door was up, and the mattress store had its lights on. She trusted the employees weren't aware of Selene's business, given that the house was unmarked, but even so, Vivienne bubbled with nervousness.

"I have the strangest suspicion that you are an exhibitionist," Selene said as she led Vivienne outside to the garden.

"Exhibitionist?" Vivienne repeated. "I hardly think so."

"Mm. And if I fucked you out here, knowing there are people on either side of the house, you wouldn't get aroused by the idea that you had to keep quiet?"

Vivienne flushed. The sound of hammering on metal drifted over from the auto shop side, along with occasional chatter and laughter, far enough away that she couldn't make out the words.

The idea of having to keep quiet was…tantalizing, to say the least.

"I bet if I told you to get undressed right now, you'd be a quivering mess by the time I had you kneeling on the ground."

Vivienne looked away. She could see what Selene was getting at. "Isn't an exhibitionist someone who likes to be watched?"

"For some people. For others, it's the thrill that they might get caught." Selene's hands slipped around Vivienne's waist, and suddenly, she was backed up against a tree, face-to-face with Selene. Butterflies filled her belly as she imagined what might happen next.

"If you're very, very quiet, no one will know," Selene said. "But if you're loud—and I know you're loud—the men will peek over that great big fence to see what's going on. We don't want that, do we?"

Vivienne glanced at the fence. It was tall and would be difficult to see over. They'd have to have a ladder. Since they worked at an auto repair shop, that wouldn't be difficult.

"Do you think you can be quiet?" Selene asked, tugging up the skirt of Vivienne's dress and stroking her bare skin. "Or will I have to gag you?"

"I can be quiet," Vivienne assured her. "I live in a house with two other people."

Selene played with the lace on Vivienne's hips, then leaned forward and pressed a kiss to her mouth.

There was something about the way Selene kissed. She started out tenderly, then deepened it, drawing out more and more passion. Then she was all teeth and tongue, and Vivienne would drown in rapturous delight.

Selene kissed down Vivienne's neck and shoulders while unzipping her dress and pushing it down her arms until it was bunched around her waist. Then she reached up and drew the bra straps down her shoulders. The cups slipped down over Vivienne's ribs, exposing her breasts.

"Give me your hands," Selene said, then kissed her so hard that Vivienne forgot to ask why.

She quickly found out. Selene slipped leather cuffs onto her wrists, then lifted Vivienne's arms up and linked the cuffs over a branch, leaving her standing awkwardly with her arms in the air.

Selene looked Vivienne up and down. "Much better." Then her mouth found Vivienne's again.

Vivienne's legs were shaking, and she grasped at the branches just for something to hold onto. Next door, the drilling and hammering continued as the men talked and laughed. Vivienne fought the urge to cry out, all too aware of their proximity, yet electrified by the idea that they might catch her and Selene in the act.

Vivienne moaned softly, biting her lip to prevent the sound from becoming louder.

Never moving her hands from Vivienne's breasts, Selene looked up. "I once made someone orgasm from this alone."

"I don't doubt it," Vivienne said breathlessly, then squeezed her eyes shut.

"For once, you didn't argue with me. And here I was, ready to prove my point." Selene dropped her mouth against Vivienne's nipple again, drawing her teeth over it. The sudden spike of desire shot straight between Vivienne's thighs.

"Oh! Selene, I..." She rocked her hips, a low moan at the back of her throat. She was so close, she could barely stand up.

Selene pulled back. "You need to be careful," she warned. "If you can't be quiet, we'll have to find something else to do."

Vivienne nodded.

Selene squeezed her hand on one breast, and with the other, she tugged at where Vivienne's dress was bunched around her waist, pushing it down her legs until it wrapped around her feet. "If you're quiet, I'll give you a reward later."

"What kind of reward, my queen?"

"Be good, and you'll find out." Selene played with her breast and nipple, squeezing with just enough pressure that Vivienne bit her tongue to hold back the whimpers. "Can you be good for me?"

"Mm-hmm," Vivienne managed.

"Good." Selene kissed between Vivienne's breasts, over her ribs, and moved lower.

Vivienne grasped the tree limb as Selene reached for the scrap of emerald material between her thighs. But instead of the underwear being pulled down or pushed to the side, Selene drew her tongue over it as she slid a hand down Vivienne's waist.

Vivienne's shoe fell off, but she didn't care. Didn't care if it got covered with grass stains, not when Selene was doing *that* with her tongue.

Vivienne pressed against the tree, feeling the bark scrape her back as she rocked her hips over Selene's tongue, slick and sliding with every movement.

She wanted the woman's fingers inside her.

Vivienne looked down just as Selene looked up, the corners of her mouth curling up as she slid her tongue over Vivienne's clit.

Vivienne's hips jerked, and she wrapped one leg around Selene, digging her bare heel into Selene's back. A string of curse words escaped from her mouth.

The noise of the mechanics stopped, their laughter dying as they paused in their work.

And then Selene was tugging Vivienne's underwear aside and sliding her tongue over Vivienne's folds, two fingers pressing inside.

Turning her head into the flesh of one arm, she tried her best to muffle the moans. And then she came, biting the flesh and squeezing her vaginal muscles around Selene's fingers. Stars danced behind her eyes…and then Selene slipped away with a final lick.

Selene eased Vivienne's foot onto the ground. "How did that feel?"

Vivienne, still catching her breath, could only manage "Mm."

Selene straightened, then wrapped her arms around Vivienne and kissed her, moving her lips softly until Vivienne felt an ache in her chest. Selene was like a harbor in the storm of her life.

"You almost managed it," Selene said.

"Almost?"

"You got rather noisy right at the end. I suppose I'll give you a passing grade."

"Passing grade! What does that even mean?"

Selene drew circles with her fingers over Vivienne's torso. "It means you're all mine, and I get to inflict all sorts of punishments on you." She cupped her hand under Vivienne's jawline, her thumb resting on her cheek. "Don't worry. I promise you'll enjoy this almost as much as I will."

Vivienne shivered, standing as tall as she could to adjust her grip on the tree. There was nothing she wanted more than to touch Selene, to stroke her skin and run her hands through her hair. But the most she could do was lean against the tree and hope she looked seductive.

The look Selene gave her told Vivienne that she had her, at least for the moment. If she said just the right words, she could do the same things to Selene that Selene had done to her. And right now, the idea of tying Selene up and going down on her until she begged was precisely what Vivienne wanted.

Selene laughed. "Oh, I don't think so. You'll need to say out loud whatever naughty thought you have in your head and ask me very, very nicely."

Vivienne didn't want to ask. She didn't want to demand to be untied, to be the dominant one. She just *wanted*.

"Be a good girl and wait here for me," Selene said, dropping her hand. Then she turned around and made her way down the stone path back to the house.

Vivienne, still tied up, her bra around her waist, her underwear pushed to one side, and her hands still bound to the tree branch, shivered as a breeze brushed through the garden and made her even more aware of her state of undress.

She kicked off her other heel and stood on the balls of her feet until Selene returned carrying tools.

"Don't you look good enough to eat," Selene said, setting the tools aside, blocking them with her body. "No peeking." Bending over the tools, she hummed to herself.

Finally, she picked something up and turned back to face Vivienne, tucking the item in the back of her skirt. Moving closer to Vivienne, she stroked over her hips, moving to the curve of her waist, and then up to her breasts.

"I'm going to turn you around, and then I'm going to mark your back, and you're going to take it like a good girl because you were late. Do you know how many minutes you were late?"

"Ten, my queen."

"Fifteen," Selene corrected. "You should have arrived five minutes before your session."

Vivienne nodded, trembling with anticipation as Selene unbound her wrists, turned her around, and bound them again.

Then she pressed her body against her back.

Vivienne sighed.

"Do you remember your safe word?"

"Music box," Vivienne said.

Selene combed her hand through Vivienne's hair, nails lightly scratching her scalp.

Vivienne leaned into her touch.

"Let's begin, then, shall we?"

Selene's strikes were solid and firm. The leather struck her skin and wrapped around the edges of her nipples. Endorphins flooded Vivienne's bloodstream. She hissed, pushing up on her toes. She counted eight strikes—halfway there.

Selene paused long enough to press kisses down Vivienne's back, then unclasped her bra so that it fell away.

Vivienne's heart beat faster as Selene held her steady, her hand cool and soothing against Vivienne's skin. Her nerves were raw, and pressure was building in her chest.

If she was pushed too far, she would cry again. But part of her wanted that. Needed that.

Work had built to new degrees of stress, and she had so much to do. Her workload had doubled, Elijah was pressuring her, and without her computer, she was hobbled. At home, family dinners felt volatile even on good days.

She would never allow herself to break in front of her family. But Selene wasn't family.

Selene struck her again, and Vivienne gripped the tree limb, holding it firmly as one strike followed another. The strikes, loud and sharp, felt different from those in the bedroom.

At the twelfth strike, she bit her lip, her emotions building.

The sex was fantastic, and the bondage soothing, but…this was a different experience altogether.

Thirteen. Vivienne gasped. The strike hit hard over her shoulder, ringing through her body. Yet her desire grew, and she needed the strikes to be harder. She needed to prove that she could take it. She wanted it more than oxygen.

Fourteen. Vivienne dug her nails into the palm of her hand. One more.

Fifteen.

Selene would be so proud—

Oh.

She stared at the tree, aware of its grooves, aware of the rope, aware of the grass at her feet. She felt every inch of her skin, heard every beat of her heart.

Vivienne knew this feeling.

Selene touched her, and Vivienne trembled. She turned to look at her, the woman she was growing to like too much.

Selene.

Her wrists released from the tree, she fell against her. Selene pushed her back up and turned her around, studying her. "Where did you go?" she asked.

Vivienne opened her mouth to explain, but speech failed her. She needed to get home and wash herself, rid herself of this feeling.

Pulling herself away from Selene, she picked up her clothes and dressed quickly, ignoring her question. Then she ran out of the garden, through the house, and into her car.

Only after she was in her driveway did she allow herself to cry.

She was falling for a fantasy.

It wasn't real.

It couldn't be real.

It had to stop.

CHAPTER 8
FAMILY MATTERS

Vivienne returned home from work that evening more than a little sore. The muscles in her neck and shoulders were tight, which brought her headache back with a vengeance. Opening the door, she was greeted with raised voices.

"—fault! It's not like—"

Vivienne looked up. Her niece was on the stairs, yelling down at Hattie, but she stopped abruptly when she saw Vivienne.

Wonderful.

"What's going on here?" she asked, taking in Claudia's pinched lips and Hattie's dazed expression.

Hattie shook her head.

Vivienne looked back at Claudia. Her niece was in her cheerleading clothes with her bag slung over one shoulder.

"Nothing," Claudia said tightly, giving Hattie a warning look before stomping up the stairs and slamming the door to her bedroom.

Vivienne turned to her sister.

Hattie shook her head. "She brought a letter home. Apparently, she's failing French. She didn't want to tell you because she knew you'd blow up."

"Blow up? I mean, I don't understand how she could fail French." She paused, considering. "Maybe she's spending too much time on cheerleading activities and she needs to focus more on her studies."

Hattie looked away, frowning.

"Spit it out."

PRINCIPLE DECISIONS

She met Vivienne's eyes. "It's not like you're here to help her with French homework. Just because you and Robert had an aptitude for languages doesn't mean she does too. Maybe she's not really interested in learning another language, and there's nothing wrong with that. She's doing well with all her other classes."

"Nonsense. Learning a language is not that difficult, and once she learns one, it'll be easy to pick up others. Not to mention the college benefits of having a second language. Claudia's cheerleading talent is great, but I doubt she'll win a scholarship for that. It'd be better if she pursued an academic scholarship."

"She could get it for cheerleading," Hattie argued. "She's pretty good."

"Because being pretty good is all you need to get a scholarship these days? Honestly, Hattie." Her sister seemed to have no idea how the real world worked. Cheerleading was fine, if Claudia wanted to attend community college. Otherwise, she needed to focus on academics.

She shook her head and went to her office. She plugged in her laptop—newly repaired but at the cost of losing all the journal articles she'd downloaded—and began posting student grades on the university website. No doubt, she'd have a dozen emails by morning, begging for a redo of the assessment or time to complete extra credit. Given how thinly she was spread, she wouldn't have time to grant their requests, nor would Abigail with her workload.

She was halfway through uploading the first-years' grades when Hattie knocked on the door for dinner.

"I'll be right out."

"Vivienne," Hattie said sternly.

Vivienne sighed, pushed herself away from her desk, and followed her sister downstairs. She looked at the empty table. Claudia hadn't come down.

Hattie glanced upstairs before setting down three plates of food.

Vivienne stood up. "I'll call Claudia down." If Vivienne had to interrupt her work to be at family dinner, her niece needed to as well, despite her sour mood.

She knocked on Claudia's door. She heard shuffling, then her niece opened the door and crossed her arms over her chest. "Yes?"

Once upon a time, her niece would have received compliments from her teachers about how well-mannered and polite she was. "I beg your pardon?"

"Beg all you like. I'm not coming down. Why should I come down to dinner when you and Aunt Hattie are just going to argue? I have work to do. I already know that you're going to cut me off from my friends."

"Claudia," Vivienne began, keeping her voice steady, "dinner is something we do as a family. I am asking you to come down and join us."

"Why?"

"Because we're a family, and we eat meals together."

"How can you say we're a family when you're never here?" Claudia said, raising her chin. "And the few times you are home, you're in your office."

"That's why we have family meals."

"You don't even take me to school anymore or pick me up. Henry does! It's like you don't care as long as I bring home good grades. You only got involved when I got into trouble for that fight. Otherwise, you're too busy!" Tears filled her eyes. "You don't care what I have to say or do as long as I'm not failing or in trouble."

Vivienne's throat tightened. "Is that how you feel? That I don't care?"

"Do you?"

"Do you think I'm working twelve hours a day, seven days a week because I want to? I'm doing it because I need to put food on the table and a roof over our heads. I am working to pay for your education and your extracurricular activities, or did you forget who paid for your cheerleading uniform? Nothing's free, Claudia. I work to provide for our family."

"We have an inheritance. You don't need to work this hard!"

Vivienne scoffed. "How much inheritance money do you think we have? We could not have lived off that money all this time, and, yes, while it is more than most families have, it would go very fast if anything happened to your Aunt Hattie or me."

She waited for her niece to respond. When she didn't, Vivienne continued. "You have shown me that you have no idea how money works. I'm cutting you off from your allowance. If you want to go out with your friends, go to the movies, or pay for school excursions, you will pay for it yourself. I expect you to get a job by the holidays."

"You can't do that!"

"I can and will," Vivienne said firmly. "It's time you learned some financial responsibility."

Claudia's face flushed. "I'm still not coming down to dinner."

"Fine. But don't expect the food to be there when you get hungry. If you want to eat, you will sit with your family."

Vivienne turned on her heel and walked away. The door slammed shut behind her.

Claudia's insolence had gone too far this time. It was clear she and Hattie needed to be firm. If her niece thought money was so easy to come by, then she could find out what it was like when she didn't have any.

Vivienne returned to the table. Hattie stared at her plate, pushing food around. She looked up when Vivienne sat down.

"Is Claudia coming down?"

"Does it look like she's coming down? Or did the slammed door make you think we had a peaceful interaction?"

Hattie clamped her jaw shut.

Vivienne picked up her knife and fork and began eating, anger destroying any enjoyment of the food. Maybe she'd been too harsh with Hattie, but it seemed like her sister constantly made her the bad guy. She was the one always saying no to Claudia, drawing lines in the sand, while Hattie got to play nice. Still, something had to be done.

"Claudia needs to learn the value of money," Vivienne said, pushing her plate away, her meal unfinished. "We will no longer pay for her extracurricular activities or social life. If she wants to spend all kinds of money on clothes and dates, she can earn it herself, as we did."

"That's not fair. We hardly worked at all while we were in school. Father only made us work through the holidays."

Vivienne picked up her napkin and wiped her mouth. "Perhaps you did not, but Robert and I both worked at the school. Robert worked with the librarian, if you recall, and I assisted Mr. Rutherglen."

"Assisted," Hattie said, making air quotes.

Vivienne stared at her. "Do you have something you want to say, Hattie? Or do you prefer to make veiled comments?"

"Just that…we all knew…that you and Mr. Rutherglen were…" She trailed off.

"That we were what?" Vivienne asked, her anger rising to the surface. If Hattie continued to dance around the words, she would yell at her.

"Sleeping together! Not that it mattered. I mean, in retrospect, it was inappropriate on his part. He was over a decade older than you. But it wasn't your fault. Just that he…paid for—"

"He certainly did not!" Vivienne snapped. "And we were not sleeping together!"

"Viv, it's fine. I understand. Besides, it was decades ago, and Robert saw—"

"I have no idea what Robert thought he saw, but we were *not* sleeping together. For fuck's sake, Hattie! He was married with a daughter!"

"Because we all know *that's* stopped a man before," she said. "Look, if you say nothing happened, I believe you."

"You do not. Otherwise, you wouldn't have said it." Vivienne took a breath, fighting off a wave of dizziness. "Rutherglen took an interest in me because of my aptitude for language. We were never sexual. In fact, he often told me that he hoped his daughter would grow up to be like me."

Vivienne's chest tightened. She hated that Hattie was tainting the memory of the teacher who had mentored her in languages. She couldn't imagine why Robert thought they had been sleeping together. Rutherglen had always kept a professional distance with her.

Except once, when she had cried about her father striking her.

It didn't matter. It was so long ago, and Robert was dead.

Suddenly nauseated, she pushed herself away from the table. Had Robert honestly thought that she had slept with her teachers for money and extra credit? Hattie apparently did.

She returned to her office, pulled the door shut behind her, and sat at her computer.

What did it matter what a dead brother thought of her? Or what a sister who earned minimum wage thought? Or what others believed, for that matter? Similar rumors had followed her during her undergraduate years. It shouldn't matter.

It didn't matter.

She returned to uploading grades, letting the monotony of the task take over. It was almost midnight when she uploaded the last one.

She went upstairs to bed.

The house was quiet. Both Hattie's light and Claudia's light were off.

She changed into her pajamas, brushed her teeth, and climbed into bed. But, despite her exhaustion, she couldn't stop thinking about the conversations between Robert and Hattie.

Did people at the university think the same thing? Did Janice gossip with the staff about how she had slept her way into her position? Did students?

Vivienne stared into the darkness, discomfort creeping over her. It seemed like the more she had tried to grow and mature, learning to be more polished and sophisticated, the more people seemed to think she was some wanton hussy.

Perhaps they always would, no matter what she did.

Thunder rolled through the skies, threatening a great storm. She longed for Selene, who looked at her with respect. But being with Selene was impossible now. She couldn't even bear to return the voicemail Selene had left to check on her after the last disastrous session.

CHAPTER 9
DRENCHED

It was raining heavily, and Vivienne was willing to push her anger aside long enough to take her niece to school, but she did not come down for breakfast.

As she drank her coffee, Vivienne heard light footsteps as Claudia tiptoed down the stairs, then opened and shut the front door. Vivienne got up from the table to peek out the front window. Henry had his truck parked in their driveway and was opening up an umbrella at their front door.

Even though Henry drove Claudia to school most days, he was still a teenager, and she didn't quite trust him to drive safely on the wet roads. Still, it was sweet of Henry to bring an umbrella so Claudia didn't get wet between the door and the car.

Just as well. Vivienne needed to leave early anyway. She didn't really have time to drop Claudia off at the opposite end of town.

It was still raining heavily as she drove to campus. The roads were overflowing in places. Sometimes with rain like this, the main road flooded, blocking her from getting in. She considered canceling classes for the day, but it would depend on whether the rain continued and how many people lived off-campus.

Vivienne had just sat down at her desk when Abigail appeared. "Professor Carter," she said, "have you read your emails this morning?"

Vivienne opened her laptop. "Not yet. Why?"

"It's just that…um, the grades you put up are wrong."

"How so?"

"You gave Matthew's results to Mo, and Maddison now has James's, which works in her favor, I suppose. But...it's like that for the entire class."

Vivienne's stomach clenched. There were dozens of emails from students questioning their grades. Clicking into the system, she reviewed the grades she had posted Saturday night. How had she made such a mistake? It would take hours to fix, hours that she could not dump on Abigail.

Vivienne combed her fingers through her damp hair, feeling a headache starting behind her eyes. She would also need to write a report explaining the error and how she planned to fix it. She wanted to scream, but she swallowed the frustration and anger.

"Professor?" Abigail asked softly. "Is there anything I can do?"

"This is my mess, Abigail. I will fix it." She rubbed her eyes, trying to figure out what needed to be done, when she heard Abigail clear her throat. She looked up. "Do you mind if we reschedule our morning meeting? I need to fix this as fast as possible before any of the scholarship students are affected."

"Of course. Do you want me to take your first class this morning?"

Vivienne glanced out the window at the heavy rain. "No. I'm going to cancel classes, given the weather. Can you make it back to your dorm safely?"

"I'll probably go to the cafeteria," Abigail responded. "But you have my number if you need me."

Vivienne thanked her, then considered what to do next. Part of her wanted to quit everything—her students, her classes, her academic life—never to be seen again. But that wasn't who she was. Still, she was overwhelmed with the amount of work ahead of her. She'd been stressed before, but fixing this error felt insurmountable.

She took a deep breath and got to work. She began by sending an email to Elijah to let him know what had happened. Then she emailed her students in the affected classes, letting them know she was aware of the error and would rectify it by the end of the day.

After clearing her schedule, Vivienne pulled out her calculator and got to work. She didn't eat lunch, didn't even take a cigarette break.

Instead, she made a pot of coffee and only got up from her desk to use the bathroom.

The rain—it was a full-blown storm now—worked in her favor, giving her a reason to cancel classes.

By the time she finished, it was the end of her office hours. She had accomplished nothing except to rectify her mistake and send half a dozen emails to assure the scholarship students that she would personally fix any issues that arose from her error.

The storm was still raging. Vivienne packed up her laptop, traded her heels for flats, and buttoned up her raincoat. She slogged her way through the rain to her car, feeling as if the entire day had been wasted. She sank into the leather seat, watching sheets of rain run down her windshield.

She wanted to cry, scream, or hit something but didn't have the energy. Instead, she put her seatbelt on, started the ignition, and drove out of the parking lot, straining to see through the rain.

She drove on until she saw flashing lights and barriers ahead, blocking the main road. The river must have overflowed its banks. She would have to take the forest road.

Vivienne had grown up in the forest. She knew the forest roads better than most—sleeping with a forest ranger one summer added to that knowledge. She would find her way home through the rain and the dark on the mud-slicked roads.

Too late, she realized her arrogance when she dropped into a hole in the road. She spun her tires fruitlessly and tried rocking the car out, but it was no use. She was stuck.

Pulling her raincoat tighter around her, she got out of the car to assess the situation. The tire was in a deep, muddy hole. She would need to be towed out.

She climbed back into her car and pulled out her cell phone. No service.

That left her with two options. Option one was to stay in the car and wait for the storm to pass. Then she could go get help. Option two was to go get help now.

Option one was far more practical, but today had already been a waste. The idea of sitting and *waiting* for the storm to pass would make her crazy.

Option two, then. Maybe she was hoping that something else would go wrong so she could scream at the world.

She got out of the car again and snugged deeper into her already wet coat. Then she locked the doors—though it seemed unlikely that anyone else would be out in the middle of nowhere in a rainstorm—and began following the trail to the nearest highway, hoping she could flag down a car.

The flats she had put on were only marginally better than her heels in this weather; the soles were leather, and her feet slipped in the muck of the fire trail. Water gushed along the trail, and soon her shoes were waterlogged, her stockings mud splattered, and her dress soaked, despite her raincoat. She slipped and slid, grabbing at nearby branches to keep from falling into the mud.

She knew she should return to her car to wait for the storm to clear—however long that might take—but she kept stubbornly trudging through the forest, fighting back tears, until she emerged from the woods onto the old highway. Not far away, she saw a flicker of light.

It might be a house. If it was, she could ask to use the phone. If they turned her away, she didn't know what she would do.

The house was part of an old farm. It was set back from the road, no neighbors in sight. But the lights were on, at least.

Vivienne trudged up the wooden steps, shivering in her wet clothes. But she was happy to have cover from the rain at last. She knocked and waited.

When the door opened, Vivienne found herself face-to-face with the last person she expected to see.

"Selene?"

"Vivienne? What are you doing here?"

The warmth of a blazing fire from inside the house washed over her. "My car got stuck. I didn't know you lived here. I just need to use your...your..." She shivered again, her teeth chattering. Selene opened the door wider and ushered her inside, leading her to stand by the fireplace. Water dripped in a puddle around her feet.

"Your car got stuck?"

"The r-river overf-flowed, and they sh-shut down the main road." Vivienne would be embarrassed if not for the fact that she was freezing. She tucked a piece of her wet hair behind her ear.

Selene helped Vivienne strip off her wet coat. "Where did you get stuck? It seems you don't know the roads that well," she muttered.

"F-forest road." She knelt in front of the fire. "I use them w-whenever traffic's b-backed up."

Vivienne's coat and Selene disappeared. When she returned, she began unzipping Vivienne from her dress.

"I'm f-fine," Vivienne insisted. "I just n-need to use your t-telephone."

"Well, the lines are down, and I don't get cell phone service out here," she said. "So you'll have to wait. Stand up and let me undress you."

"I w-wouldn't want that."

"Is that so? Is that why you left our session without explanation?"

Vivienne felt her cheeks flush with heat. Selene was right to be annoyed with her. Since their last session, Vivienne had ignored her attempts at contact; she was too ashamed at how she'd run out.

Selene wrapped a towel around her, then disappeared again with the rest of her clothes.

Vivienne turned toward the fire and let the warmth seep in. The shaking eased somewhat, but she was still chilled and her muscles were tight.

"I've run you a bath," Selene said when she returned. "We can try the phones after you've warmed up."

"I don't n-need a b-bath."

"The fact that you're still shivering tells me otherwise. Now, you either get in the tub, or I bend you over my knee and give you a warm enema to stop you from getting hypothermia," Selene said, raising her eyebrows. "Is that what you want?"

Vivienne scoffed but allowed herself to be shown to the bathroom. The tub was half-full and deep enough to submerge in.

Vivienne pushed her slip down over her hips, then tried to undress, but her hands were shaking, so Selene undressed her, unclipping her garter belt and helping her slide out of her stockings.

It was terribly intimate, and twice Vivienne slapped Selene's hands away. But Selene merely arched a brow and stepped back to let Vivienne to fumble again on her own.

Finally, she climbed into the bath. The warmth permeated her body as she sank deeper into the water.

Selene picked up Vivienne's underclothes. "Don't get up to trouble," she said and disappeared once again.

The warm bath soothed Vivienne's aching muscles and warmed her chilled bones. Being here with Selene, although unplanned, was a fine line between fantasy and nightmare. Here she was in a beautiful woman's house, having arrived cold and wet. Her clothes had disappeared. What was a woman to do?

And yet her guilt prevented her from enjoying herself. Selene was obviously hurt, and she had every right to be.

Vivienne sank deeper into the bath, listening to Selene's footsteps in the hall. What would happen if she apologized and offered to make it up to Selene? What would Selene ask for in return?

Selene reentered the bathroom with two fresh towels, a nightgown, and a robe. "Here. Your clothes were filthy, and your stockings were beyond saving. I've put everything else in the wash. You can wear this for now."

"Thank you," Vivienne said. "You don't need—"

"To stop you from dying? Unfortunately, duty of care is written into the law, and I don't want to be charged with willful neglect. Despite what you may want."

"I was nowhere near death," Vivienne snapped. "I was out in the rain, not a snowstorm."

"You were half-drowned," Selene said. "Now, get out of the tub before you drown."

"I'm not an invalid."

"Aren't you?" Selene asked.

Vivienne stepped out of the bath and allowed Selene to pat her dry. Selene stepped back and watched Vivienne put on the nightgown and robe, then handed her the dry towel for her hair. Then she opened the door and headed down the hallway.

"Are you following?" Selene called back to her, and Vivienne's heart skipped a beat.

Vivienne followed her into the kitchen and sat down at the table. Selene placed a cup of coffee in front of her.

A delicious aroma drifted from a cast-iron pot on the stove. Selene must have been cooking dinner when Vivienne arrived. Her stomach gurgled, and Vivienne flushed.

Selene set out two dishes and placed the cast-iron pot on the table. When the lid was removed, Vivienne recognized the contents as shakshouka.

"I don't need—"

"Don't be rude. Let's eat, and then we can check the phone lines."

Vivienne wanted to check them now, but instead she sat obediently at the table. She was embarrassed at the situation she found herself in and further humiliated by the fact that she was being treated like a temperamental child.

She still wanted to apologize, but like a child, she also wanted to stomp off back to the woods to find her car.

Finally, Vivienne took a bite of the food, tasting paprika, cumin, and hot peppers in the sauce. Selene seemed to like her food the way she liked to punish—quick and searing—and Vivienne was a fan of both.

The food warmed her through better than the bath had and gave her a sense of comfort that only a home-cooked meal could provide. She tried not to show her approval, or Selene would become smug.

"If I didn't know how stubborn you were," Selene said between bites of food, "I would never believe your story about getting stuck on the fire trails. Most people would have waited until the storm passed."

"I'm not most people," Vivienne said defensively. She hated how small she felt with the woman. "The fire roads go by my home, and usually they're fine. I've driven them in the rain before."

"But this time you were unlucky."

"Yes, well, I hit a big hole. I would argue it was man-made, but it could just as easily have been dug out by an animal. And then the heavy rain made it worse."

"And here you are. You're lucky I live here. Not so long ago, this was just an old, decaying house."

Vivienne raised her eyebrows. "So you haven't always lived in Oakdale?

"No. I moved here about…oh, a year ago," she said. "But I was familiar with Oakdale. I used to have a regular client who paid me to visit them here."

"Why?" Vivienne asked.

Selene tilted her head. "Why not?"

Now she'd overstepped, and Vivienne felt even more like she should apologize. "Why would someone need a whole weekend of sex and kink?"

"For many reasons, including the fact that it's not just about sex and kink. You should try it for yourself."

"Is that your sales pitch?"

"It is," Selene said. "Now, explain to me again what happened. You were coming home from work, saw that the main road was cut off, and decided to take the fire roads, despite the heavy rain?"

As if on cue, there was a flash of lightning followed immediately by a peal of thunder.

"Yes," Vivienne said.

"And you had no idea that I lived here?"

Ah. "You think I took the forest road in a storm, intentionally got stuck, and decided to slog through the rain and mud to your house?"

"Your story is that you got stuck. For all I know, your car is parked up the road a little ways."

"Why would I do that?" Vivienne asked. "Do you think I'm so insecure as to create this situation?"

"I'm never certain about these things. It comes with the territory."

Vivienne studied the other woman. If she had to guess, someone had previously come to Selene's private residence under false pretenses. "I have better things to do with my life than chase after a woman."

"And what does such a person do to occupy her time?" Selene asked. "Outside of engaging a dominatrix."

Vivienne frowned. "I work at the university, as you know."

"There's more to it than that."

"Yes. Well, I write and publish journal articles, but I'm behind on my latest at the moment."

"What do you write on?"

"Language. I wrote one on how language shifts, which changes the meaning of religious texts. But my current article is about how language development shapes a culture's view on the world." She sighed, thinking about the work she'd lost to the virus on her laptop.

"Sounds fascinating."

"It is to me," Vivienne said. "Most people find it to be dry. The students I teach have aspirations of working for the United Nations as a translator rather than working in academics, so what I find interesting, they rarely do."

"What did you hope to be when you were first in college?"

Vivienne looked quizzically at Selene. Was she genuinely interested, or was she gathering information to use later? "I had an aptitude for language, and I wanted to travel, so I roamed the world to become proficient in different languages. Then I came home and began working on my PhD."

"Why this town?"

"Because it's home," Vivienne said, but that wasn't quite true. "Because Claudia couldn't live in the city," she admitted. "She deserved to be in a good school and be able to walk home without fear of something happening."

Selene nodded. "Understandable."

"So why did you move here?"

Selene set her fork down and smiled tightly. "Change of scenery."

Vivienne, seeing the crack in Selene's mask, looked down at her plate, unwilling to pry.

When they had finished eating, Vivienne got up to take their dishes to the sink and began to wash up. Selene followed her to the kitchen but made no attempt to help. If Vivienne expected some dance around a guest not having to do the dishes, she was annoyed but not surprised; it was not that unusual for a guest to wash up after the host had cooked.

When the last plate had been put in the dishwasher and the final pot scrubbed, Vivienne turned to face Selene, who was studying her.

"You can try the phone, let your family know you're safe," Selene said. "I suspect you'll need to stay the night."

"And why is that?" Vivienne asked.

"Because the road is washed out, and I highly doubt you want your sister to get stuck on the same fire road you did."

It was a valid argument. Though she knew someone with a truck and a tow line could pull her out, it was far too late to ask for such a favor. And staying the night would provide her with an opportunity to—

She stopped the thought, reminding herself that she had no further need for Selene's services. She walked over to the phone on the wall.

"Carter residence, this is Hattie."

"Hattie, it's Vivienne. I wanted to let you know—"

"Oh, Viv, I was worried when I heard about the roads. I tried your office, but there was no answer."

"Well, I'm safe, but I likely won't be home until tomorrow. I just wanted to let you know that."

"Are you staying with Elijah and his wife?"

Vivienne paused. Should she lie to her sister or admit the truth? Not liking either option, she simply said, "I'll see you tomorrow, Hattie," and hung up.

She turned back to face Selene, who raised her eyebrows. "So, what do you want to do now?"

Vivienne sucked in a breath, a low flutter in her belly. She knew what she wanted, but she would never admit that. "What are the options?"

"I have plenty of books to read. Or we could play a game. Or we could move to the living room."

"And do what?"

Selene smiled coyly, then led her to the living room. She settled into the worn armchair facing the fireplace, crossing her legs seductively on the ottoman. Vivienne stood by the mantel, forcing herself to look around the room instead of at Selene.

The house was in stark contrast to Selene's bright and more modern house in town. The living room was small and sparsely furnished with the armchair and , ottoman, a couch, and a coffee table. The walls were painted in muted colors.

"Is this your home?" she asked.

"As much as any other place I've lived. Why do you ask?"

"The décor doesn't really suit you." Selene had only been living in Oakdale for a brief time, but everything in this house looked old, like it had been here for decades.

Selene laughed. "No, I suppose it doesn't, but it suits me well enough."

"Did you decorate the other place?"

"Yes and no," she answered. "I chose the art and the bed. Everything else was accumulated over time."

In the awkward silence that followed, Vivienne became all too aware of Selene's proximity. Her hands rested gracefully on the armchair, and all Vivienne wanted was to feel them on her.

Selene broke the silence. "Why haven't you booked another appointment with me?"

Vivienne blinked. "I…" The words swelled in her throat.

"Did I push your limit without realizing?"

"No." Vivienne shook her head. "I mean…maybe, but it wasn't that. It was…" She swallowed, trying to sort her thoughts. "I was scared."

"Of me?"

"Of how I feel about you."

"I see," she said, a smile twisting her lips. "You ran away because you like me."

Vivienne felt her face grow hot. "Only you could make it sound so juvenile."

"I'm not the one who ran away from her *feelings*."

Vivienne gritted her teeth. "It's not about my feelings. It's about what happens next. You're either interested in me or you're not. And if you are interested, we'll grow closer until you eventually become frustrated by how I prioritize my life. You'll feel neglected, and then all those good moments will sour between us until there's nothing left but resentment. It hurts to walk away now—you're one of the few good things I had going—but it's *necessary* so those moments aren't tarnished."

"Of course it will end poorly if you've already decided how it ends. Don't I have a say?"

"I've been through it enough times. It never changes." Vivienne softened. "I know it sounds bitter, but there's no place in my world for a partner. I don't know if there ever will be."

"Maybe I don't want a partner," Selene suggested. "We can try different ways of being together to see what works, but we're not there yet. For now we can set some boundaries about what we each need and desire in and out of the bedroom. We can just *be*."

Vivienne shook her head, even as warmth filled her body. "I don't know how to just *be*."

"No, I suppose not." Selene smiled. "But I can show you how, if you'll let me."

Vivienne nodded, her heart pounding, her mind filling with insecurity—and distrust. Why would Selene make such an effort if not for money? "It's been a very long night and a longer day. I can't make any promises."

Selene nodded. "Of course," she said softly. "We don't have to decide anything today."

"Good," she responded, though the word sounded hollow.

"Is that not what you want?"

"No. I—" She cut herself off. "Of course it is."

"Liar. Tell me the truth. What do you want?"

Vivienne considered. "I suppose I want my cake and to eat it too. But I don't want to make any decisions tonight…" She knew how she sounded. She still wanted Selene, and for tonight, at least, she could pretend that the storm had swept them into another world where Vivienne didn't have work or family responsibilities. She could indulge in the pursuit of what she wanted. But that wasn't fair to either of them.

"I see." Selene stood up and moved closer to Vivienne until she stood beside her. She took Vivienne's hand in hers. "How about this: whatever happens tonight, we have no expectations, make no promises. If you want to spend the night talking and then never speak to me again, I'll understand. I'll also understand if you want something else."

Vivienne raised her eyebrows. "Something else?"

Selene smiled. "No strings, no promises for tomorrow," she said, reaching up to touch Vivienne's cheek. "Let tonight be Vegas. Whatever happens here stays here."

"And what happens tomorrow?"

"Tomorrow isn't here yet, and I would very much like to play a game with you."

Vivienne looked at her curiously. "What game would that be?"

"It's where I pretend I'm angry that you ran off without paying, and you play the penniless admirer."

Vivienne froze. She had completely forgotten that she hadn't paid for her last session.

"I'm not upset," Selene assured her. "It's just a game. I won't make you do anything you don't want to."

Vivienne laughed. "I assure you, you will never get me to do something I don't want to do, regardless of how I feel about you." She moved closer until she was only a breath away. "So, *my queen*, however can I make up for such a terrible mistake? Is there anything that would please you?"

Selene looked at her hungrily, and Vivienne felt her desire. "Perhaps a caning, unless you have another idea."

Vivienne shivered and looked away to the fire, not wanting Selene to see how much she would enjoy being bent over a surface and feeling the cane crack over her skin. She became intensely aware of not wearing underwear beneath the nightgown.

"What do you think, Vivienne?" Selene said softly in her ear, her lips gently brushing against her.

"I—" Vivienne said, but her voice was thick with arousal, her face hot. All she could think about was Selene running her hand over the welts, telling her what a good girl she was. "I think you know best."

Selene reached out to cup her face, forcing her to look into the woman's brilliant blue eyes. "You don't need to lie to me," she said. "If you want me to spank you, all you have to do is ask me nicely."

Vivienne held Selene's gaze, afraid that if she blinked, the woman would devour her.

She could smell her perfume, faded but sweet, as Selene curled her fingers around Vivienne's jaw and gently tilted Vivienne's head up. "Ask me nicely," Selene said. She spoke softly, but there was no mistaking the authority.

"And what would nicely look like?"

"You're a clever girl. I'm sure you'll figure it out," Selene said with a grin.

If Selene wanted to play, Vivienne would play along. She'd had enough of being seduced. Selene might have experience exerting authority over others, but Vivienne had never heard a complaint about her own techniques.

"Do I say, 'Please, Principal Rothschild, won't you bend me over your knee?'" She smiled when she saw the woman's smirk falter. Vivienne leaned in closer and felt Selene's fingers slide down to her shoulders. "Or should I just get on my knees and beg?"

Selene caught her breath. "I like the idea of you begging."

"You're going to need to work harder to get me to beg for you. I'm sure you can figure it out."

"Disrespectful," Selene said, still holding Vivienne's shoulders. "You can try to wind me up all you want, but you still need to ask me nicely."

Vivienne sensed she was under Selene's skin. "Please, Principal Rothschild," she purred.

Selene tightened her fingers, then leaned forward as if to kiss her.

Vivienne closed her eyes to receive the kiss, but instead, Selene swung her around and pushed her onto the armchair, climbing onto her lap, one leg on either side, effectively pinning her in place. Only then did Selene kiss her, cupping her jaw in both hands. The kiss started out soft, and then Selene gently sucked and bit on Vivienne's bottom lip.

Vivienne sighed as Selene moved her mouth down her throat and onto her neck, each kiss soft and tender until, without warning, she sank her teeth gently but firmly into her shoulder.

Vivienne moaned into the pain, holding the woman tight against her.

The pain stopped as Selene pulled away to look into Vivienne's eyes. "I'm going to punish you in a way that you're not going to like. It won't be what you want."

"And what, pray tell, do you think I want?"

"I think you want me to bend you over my knee and spank you until you're soaked, and then you want me to fuck you while you squirm in my lap while I tell you what a good girl you were for taking such punishment."

Vivienne bit her tongue to keep herself from making a noise. There was no point in denying it.

"Don't worry. I'm still going to spank you, but you ran out without paying me, and now I need to teach you a lesson." Selene stepped off of Vivienne's lap, then took her hand, tugging her out of the chair, and led her upstairs to her bedroom.

The room was simply furnished with a bed, a bedside table, and a dresser. The bed was made up with a green cover and a thick fur thrown over it. On the bedside table was a stack of books. The dresser held an array of products. It was the only part of the house that looked like Selene's.

Selene shut the bedroom door behind her and looked at Vivienne. "What's your safe word?"

"Music box."

Smiling, Selene ran her fingers over the satin collar of Vivienne's robe, then pushed it off her shoulders. "I'm going to make you beg, Vivienne Carter. You came into my territory, into my home. You're mine now."

"Yours, am I?" Vivienne asked, and her heart fluttered.

Selene played with the straps of Vivienne's nightgown, then pushed it off Vivienne's shoulders as well. It caught at her hips.

Vivienne tugged it the rest of the way down and stood before her, eager and nervous, unsure about whatever came next.

Selene leaned forward and kissed her again. Vivienne softened, her mouth parting to slip her tongue over Selene's.

But Selene pulled away. Tucking her hair behind her ear, she ordered, "On the bed, in the center, please."

Vivienne rolled onto the bed.

"Oh no. Face the head of the bed on all fours."

It would leave her exposed. Very exposed. She could comply, or she could refuse and demand something else.

Vivienne knew without a doubt that if she asked for something else, Selene would switch in a heartbeat.

She didn't want anything else.

She rolled over, got onto her hands and knees, and straightened her back, looking straight ahead.

"That's my girl," Selene said. "Shift back a bit. I'll tell you when to stop."

Vivienne scooted backward awkwardly on the bed.

"Stop."

Vivienne glanced over her shoulder.

"Eyes ahead." Selene's voice was sharp. Vivienne heard her walking around the bed, then felt her hand move down her back and across her backside. "Stay right there. Don't move."

Vivienne shivered as Selene lifted her hand and walked away.

She heard a drawer open and close. A moment later, Selene wrapped something metal around Vivienne's ankle, then pushed her other leg away and cuffed it as well, adjusting what felt like a bar between her legs so her thighs were pushed wide apart.

"A spreader?" she asked.

"Oh yes," Selene confirmed. "It leaves you beautifully exposed."

When she was finished, Vivienne was spread open. Selene would be able to do and see as she pleased.

Selene dropped her hands over Vivienne's waist, scraping her nails down the skin of her backside and thighs. Vivienne calmed as Selene petted her. It was both patronizing and relaxing.

"Now, we should do this in sets of five. Does that sound fair?"

"Yes."

"Yes…?" Selene prompted.

"Yes, Principal Rothschild."

Selene laughed heartily. "I don't think I'll ever get tired of hearing you say that." Then she ran her hands over Vivienne's body again, drawing her nails across the muscles of her lower back. "I believe... fifteen lashes is fair, given the outstanding amount."

"Fifteen?"

"Mm-hmm. Fifteen lashes that we'll do in sets of five."

Vivienne took a deep breath, waiting for the first strike.

It came firmly and without warning against the left cheek. Selene was using a cane. The second strike hit on the other side. Vivienne bit back a sound, digging her hands in the fur throw. The third strike was low, hitting both of her hamstring muscles and stinging enough that Vivienne gasped.

Three strikes. She couldn't remember if she was supposed to be counting.

The fourth strike came across her ass, and heat pulsated across it. The cane gently rested against her. She held her breath. Was that meant to be number five?

And then she saw a shadow flicker, and she braced just as the strike hit hard and true, stinging her just below the buttocks.

She squeezed her eyes shut, breathing through the pain, feeling it throb.

Selene pressed her fingers over the marks, stroking the welts. "You did well."

Vivienne squirmed at her touch, feeling the inside of her thighs become slick. She stared down at the fur throw. As humiliated as she felt, she still wanted to feel Selene stroke her fingers across her legs, mixing plain with pleasure.

"Ready for the second round?"

Vivienne nodded, then cried out when Selene pinched a welt. "Yes, Principal Rothschild."

"Good. You're learning," Selene said and drew her fingertips over Vivienne's thighs. "Let's see. I could be cruel, but I don't think I will be. I think I'll be nice."

Vivienne whimpered.

"I know what you want, but this isn't about that." Selene ran her hand over Vivienne's back, stroking along the curve of her skin.

And then Selene removed her hand, and the next strike came. Vivienne squeezed her eyes shut as the cane cracked over her ass, just missing the back of her vulva. It stung enough that tears moistened her eyes. She curled her fingers into the throw, breathing out hard as she pressed against the spreader between her calves.

It hurt, but it hurt *good*. Pain rolled over her even as endorphins flooded her bloodstream.

"Would you look at that," Selene teased and then slid her fingers over Vivienne's outer labia and spread her cheeks wider.

Vivienne whimpered at the touch.

"My, my, you do enjoy a good spanking, don't you?"

"Yes, Principal Rothschild."

"Perhaps I should get creative. Think of other ways to punish you for your rude behavior. Maybe make you—" A ding sounded downstairs. "Excellent. The washing machine's done. Stay where you are. I won't be happy if I've seen you've moved."

"Yes, Principal Rothschild."

Vivienne held her position. Selene touched her lightly on her back, then combed her fingers through her hair. Then she was gone, the stairs creaking under her weight.

Seconds ticked by, then minutes. The heat and sting on her skin turned cold and then faded to a dull ache. There was only quiet, amplifying her thoughts.

If anyone besides Selene walked in, she would be on full display. Every part of her was naked and exposed. Yet she knew she was safe. It was unlikely that anyone would find the house, be invited inside, and make their way up the stairs to Selene's bedroom.

Despite knowing this, Vivienne had a sense of anticipation. It was improbable but not entirely impossible that someone would come across the lone house and find their way upstairs.

The stairs creaked, and Vivienne felt anticipation break across her skin. She was helpless. What would happen if someone were to—

"Look at that," Selene said, and Vivienne prided herself on not jumping, despite her surprise. "You remained perfectly in position. Aren't you just the most obedient woman."

"Are my clothes—?"

The cane struck low on the side of her thigh, making Vivienne gasp.

"You are to be quiet unless spoken to," Selene reminded her. "Now, where were we?" Vivienne heard Selene walking around the bed. "I think two more lashes should do it."

Vivienne scowled. There should be at least eight more.

Selene touched the welts, and Vivienne hissed at the sensation. Two spots were especially painful, and Selene stroked them, rubbing the nerves raw. The pain was like pins against her emotions, pricking her until she felt like she might cry.

"You've done well," Selene said. "I'm reducing the strikes because your skin's a little more delicate than I expected. But I'm proud of you."

And then Vivienne felt Selene shift away, and she bowed her head.

The first strike was hard and firm, landing on one of the smaller welts. Vivienne moaned as it sparked up her spine. Her eyes filled with tears. She wasn't sure if it was from the strike or hearing the words "I'm proud of you." It was absurd to get worked up over them, and ridiculous to feel them dig into her, sharper than any strike.

Proud of you.

Then the cane struck a final blow, and like a crumbling dam, Vivienne collapsed on the bed. She refused to cry.

Quickly, Selene unbuckled and removed the spreader and then climbed onto the bed, pulling Vivienne into her lap.

And Vivienne hated it, hated how the woman stroked her hair, how she hushed her and ran her hands over her body, pressing kisses to her back and shoulders, whispering about how good she'd been.

Because it hurt, hurt more than it should, and Vivienne wanted it again. She wanted Selene to tell her that she'd done really well, even if it wasn't true. She wanted it so badly.

She closed her eyes. Selene stopped combing, but her hands remained, one on her head, the other on her back, pressing her closer, steadying her. And then, when the pain had passed, Vivienne drew a breath and got off the bed, feeling embarrassment wash over her again, just as it had in their first session.

She licked her lips, trying to think of something to say that would soften what had happened. But when Selene looked into her eyes, the words died in her mouth.

"I'm going to put cream on the welts, since you'll be staying the night."

Vivienne tried to protest, but when Selene pressed against a welt, she winced. "Fine," she agreed. "Only because I won't have access to my own."

Selene went to the dresser and shuffled through the drawers, pulling out a jar of cream and returning to where Vivienne waited. "Lie down for me," she said as she sat on the edge of the bed.

Vivienne obeyed, rolling onto her stomach and resting her arms over the pillow. "Do you do this for your other clients too?"

"I do," Selene answered. "Some, like you, are stubborn, making it harder to provide adequate care. But I usually find a way."

Vivienne hissed as Selene gently but firmly rubbed cream into each welt. She shuddered at the intimacy. Sex and kink were easier than allowing someone to dress wounds. And despite how intimate it was, it didn't feel like foreplay. It felt like what it was: aftercare.

"None of the welts have broken the skin," Selene said as she moved her hands delicately down Vivienne's thighs. "They won't scar, but they'll sting for a few days."

"Wonderful," Vivienne said dryly.

"Oh yes," Selene said. "One of my favorite things is knowing that even after you leave, you're going to think of me." She applied the cream on the other side. "When you get in your car or you're sitting in your office, you're going to feel the pressure and think of me."

"They won't be happy thoughts."

"Oh, but they will be," Selene said. "You're a masochist, Vivienne. You like this."

She wanted to protest. "I thought masochism was self-harm."

"There's a difference," Selene said as she drew her fingers away. "Self-harm is when you're hurting yourself to feel something or to cope with emotional pain. Masochism can also be used to cope with emotional pain, but it's for pleasure."

"I seem to cry most times."

"There's nothing wrong with seeking relief, but I hope you'll tell me if it's more than that."

Vivienne remembered their last interaction in Selene's garden. She had wanted pain. She had wanted badly to hurt, and when she'd felt the tenderness of Selene's touch, it had been overwhelming. "Why does it feel different this time?"

"Because you were searching for relief." Selene looked at her as if she were looking into her soul, and Vivienne felt even more exposed. "I'll play with you on negotiated terms, but I'm not your partner at this stage. I can't be the emotional support you need."

"I'm not asking you to be," Vivienne asserted, then pushed up onto her hands and knees. She winced. The pain of the welts hurt differently this time, a dull ache that throbbed rather than a sharp sting.

She pushed herself off the bed. She was stuck in the woman's house until the storm ended—probably tomorrow. As much as she wanted to seduce Selene, dominate her until she was weak and submissive, she knew that sex was off the table for the moment.

She pulled on the nightgown and robe, then pulled her hair over her shoulder.

Selene, still sitting on the edge of the bed, watched her with interest.

"What time is it?"

"Relatively early," Selene said. "I have some administrative work to do. Would you like some coffee?"

"Please."

Selene took her hand and led her out of the bedroom. When she did, Vivienne's frustration evaporated.

Selene was kind in a way that made Vivienne realize that being in a relationship with her might be doable. But the truth was, she didn't have time. She might never have time.

Despite that, for Selene, she would make time.

CHAPTER 10
MISSED OPPORTUNITIES

Vivienne spent the night on the sofa, restlessly falling in and out of a light sleep. Occasionally she got up to put more wood on the fire. She woke up with the weight of guilt on her chest. Selene's words—*I'm proud of you*—still rang in her ears.

Around the time the morning light peeked through the shades, she heard Selene quietly making her way down the stairs. Vivienne closed her eyes, pretending to be asleep until the movement of dishes in the kitchen was too loud to ignore.

Wrapping a blanket around herself, she drifted into the kitchen and sat at the table. Selene was frying bacon and getting ready to make eggs. Coffee was already dripping through the Keurig.

"Good morning. There's orange juice in the fridge, and the coffee's almost ready."

Vivienne poured herself a glass of juice, then picked up a mug of hot coffee. By the time she sat back down at the table, Selene had finished cooking the bacon and eggs and had set down the plates.

"Sleep well?" Selene asked as she scooted in her chair.

"Well enough," Vivienne lied and cut into the eggs. The soft yolks flooded the plate.

They ate breakfast without further conversation. Vivienne fidgeted in her chair, trying to ease the sting on the back of her thighs.

Selene glanced up, then said, "Your clothes are dry. I set them out for you."

"Thank you," Vivienne said and looked down at her plate again. She felt as strange today as she had yesterday. How could she have known that by taking the forest road she would end up at Selene's house, engage in kink with her, then spend the night on her couch?

Because sleeping in the same bed would have been too intimate.

Except she had spent most of the night thinking about making her way up the stairs and into Selene's bed, sliding between the sheets, pressing her lips to Selene's mouth, and feeling her sigh against her. She wanted to stroke her body and feel her whimper and moan against her. She considered masturbating instead but decided against it. It felt somehow…impolite.

Instead, she'd lain awake thinking about Selene's unspoken invitation. Not acting on it felt like the right decision, despite how she ached for her, how wet she had been after the spanking. But now she regretted it.

She could feel Selene watching her. She had laid out the offer last night. They could be casual sexual partners or continue on as patron and client.

Or she could walk away.

Walking away would be the safest option, but it wasn't what Vivienne wanted. She wanted to be teased until she begged, then feel Selene inside her again. She brought the mug of coffee to her lips, staring into the light brown liquid.

"What are you thinking about?" Selene asked, setting down her knife and fork.

Vivienne looked up. "Nothing of interest."

"Your face is a lovely shade of red, so I highly doubt that's true."

Vivienne looked away. "Don't be absurd." She sipped her coffee, trying to ignore the way Selene looked at her, as if she could have Vivienne on the nearest surface in a matter of seconds.

"Do you have any clients today?" Vivienne asked in a feeble attempt to distract her thoughts.

"I do not," Selene said. "Do you need me to take you home?"

It was still raining, but it was a soft rain that trickled gently down the windows, and it was unlikely to let up anytime soon. Vivienne would need to call a truck to pull her car out of the muck.

She nodded. Even in the best of conditions, she wasn't sure how long it would take her to walk home. "If you wouldn't mind."

"Not at all, but then you would owe me another favor."

Vivienne looked at her, startled.

Selene laughed. "That was a joke, of course."

Too bad, Vivienne thought, looking away. Pain shifted through her. She wouldn't mind owing the elusive Principal Rothschild a favor. The idea of being on her knees had never seemed so attractive.

I'm proud of you.

She wished Selene hadn't said those words.

After breakfast, she brushed her teeth with Selene's spare toothbrush, then tried to tame her tousled hair. She dressed in her now-clean clothes, smoothing the dress gingerly over the welts.

She studied herself in the mirror. It wasn't too late to seduce her, she thought. It wouldn't be difficult to accidentally brush her fingers against the woman and feel her respond. After all, she'd masterfully elicited the spanking last night. How difficult would it be to draw Selene out of her underwear?

She sighed. The moment was past. She gave her hair one last comb-through with her hands and went back downstairs.

Selene was waiting in the foyer, wearing boots and a raincoat. Vivienne followed her outside into the pattering rain. Selene held an umbrella over them both as they walked to her car. She opened the passenger door first to let Vivienne in, then moved around to the driver's side, folding up the umbrella and removing her raincoat before quickly getting in.

They drove in silence to the main road. Then Selene spoke. "I'll need you to give me directions. I know you're on the other side of the forest, but I don't know where."

"Oh, it's… As you drive into town, take a left at the library."

"Easy enough."

Selene drove carefully on the wet roads. Vivienne leaned her head against the window, letting her fatigue drift over her.

After a few minutes, she asked, "What does the Girlfriend Experience involve?" She flushed and looked away, pretending indifference.

"For most clients, it usually involves drinks and dinner, then we return to their hotel room and negotiate from there. Are you asking about the Girlfriend Experience specifically, or are you asking about the Deluxe version?"

"The latter," Vivienne said, pleased at how calm she sounded.

"For you, I would advise booking a weekend in advance. You'd pick me up, we'd drive to the city, get a hotel, and then get drinks and dinner. I would flirt shamelessly with you in public, planning to seduce you later. The next day, we would have breakfast together, then visit the art museum, where I would impress you with my knowledge of the fine arts before seducing you somewhere entirely inappropriate. You wouldn't be allowed to make noise because, if you did, I'd have to gag you."

Vivienne pictured it and squirmed in her seat.

"And then we'd get a late lunch, walk around the city for a while, then go back to the hotel, where I would make sure you're dressed with the appropriate toy before taking you out to dinner. Then, if you were so inclined, I would take you to a private, invite-only club where there are other like-minded people, or we could go somewhere else to have sex."

Vivienne was filled with heat. "Pull over."

"Pardon?" Selene asked innocently.

They were still five minutes outside of town.

"Pull over," Vivienne said again, looking at her pointedly.

Selene obeyed, grinning as she pulled off the road.

Vivienne unbuckled her seat belt, but Selene was already on her lap, kissing her as though the world were ending.

Vivienne pulled Selene against her, sliding her hands up her waist, tugging off her jacket, and pulling up her skirt.

Selene's mouth was hot against her shoulder, and she nipped Vivienne's skin as she palmed her breast through her dress. Then she stroked between her thighs, kissing her again and again as she slid her fingers under Vivienne's panties.

If this continued, it would be over as fast as it began, but there was no use holding back. Selene's finger was already stroking her sex.

Vivienne lifted her hips, wanting her inside, but Selene only teased her more. Vivienne pressed her nails into Selene's back, moaning urgently.

Selene slid her fingers inside, pressing her thumb against her clit, and Vivienne gasped, then sighed, dropping her head onto Selene's shoulder and squeezing her thighs as she rocked her hips.

"You should have come to bed with me last night," Selene whispered in her ear as Vivienne shuddered. "I would have fucked you like you really wanted."

"I should have," she agreed between gasps.

"I have all sorts of lovely implements. But I know what you really want."

"And what would that be?" Vivienne asked, rocking against her hand.

"You want to see me climax. I could have tied you up and made you watch." Selene leaned forward, pressing her lips against Vivienne's ear. "I spent most of the night masturbating, waiting for you. I hoped you would interrupt me. All the things I would have done at your mercy…"

Vivienne sucked in a breath, digging her nails into Selene's thighs. She was on the brink of another orgasm. She squeezed hard against the other woman's fingers.

"Don't you wonder how your name sounds on my lips? Do you wonder how I would sound if you slid inside me?"

Vivienne pushed her hands higher up Selene's skirt. "Yes," she breathed.

"Hands still. You missed your opportunity, and now you're mine."

Vivienne held her breath. She wanted Selene, wanted to make her shiver as she had, to feel her clench around her fingers and moan in her ear.

"Say it. Say you're mine," Selene said and kissed along her neck gently. Vivienne didn't know what would happen if she refused, and she found herself nodding. "I'm yours."

"Good girl," she purred and kissed her neck again as her fingers pressed inside her at just the right spots, massaging her clit with her thumb.

All of a sudden, dizziness washed over her as she realized where she was and what she was doing. Selene pulled back to look at her, her hand still buried in Vivienne's underwear. With the other, she stroked Vivienne's cheek, soothing her, calming her. "You're okay," Selene said. "Don't slip away from me now."

It was a tender moment, and Vivienne shivered. It was a lot, almost too much, as though Selene could love her—but that was impossible. She couldn't love her. She couldn't.

But it was more than that. Vivienne hated how much she wanted Selene, craved her kisses, her touch. Was this what people wanted from the Girlfriend Experience? The feeling of a person's hands on yours, as if they could hold you together?

"Look at me," Selene commanded, summoning Vivienne from her thoughts. But her voice was gentle. Then she kissed her again, softly, and the noise in Vivienne's head stopped.

And then Selene was pushing into her again, thrusting deep. Vivienne came, clenching around Selene's fingers, digging her nails into Selene's thighs. The orgasm was not as intense this time, and it left her wanting more.

Selene pulled her fingers out, then pressed her lips to Vivienne's mouth again.

And right then, Vivienne knew she couldn't do this. Maybe she needed to see a therapist because sex didn't used to make her feel as if she might break, and yet this woman shattered every defense she had built and then coaxed her back together again.

"Are you all right?" Selene stroked her cheek.

Vivienne nodded, leaning into Selene's hand. It was true. She felt nice, although she still couldn't say what she really wanted. Selene had made her acutely aware of how lonely she was and how much she missed the affection of another person. But she wasn't ready to say that she actually cared for her. It wasn't something she could allow. After all, she had engaged Selene's services to avoid having to care for someone.

She pressed down the pain, pressed it down deep, and brushed her thoughts away. "Last night you said you hadn't barred me from your services. Is that true?"

"It is. We can still negotiate. You'll need to tell me what you want."

"I want you to do what you did last night."

"Caning or discipline?"

"All of it."

Selene studied her carefully. "I need to know exactly what you want from this."

"I want relief. The very first time I engaged you, you made me feel relaxed. I want that. I don't care what I have to do to get that feeling again."

Selene smiled. "How about next Sunday? I'll book you for two hours, and we can talk in detail about what you want in a scene."

"I would like that."

"Of course you would." Selene dismounted from Vivienne's thigh, kicking her leg high enough to show that she wasn't wearing any underwear, and dropped back into the driver's seat.

Vivienne was filled with desire again. "May I—"

"No." Selene clicked her seat belt, then turned and looked at her. "I told you. You missed your chance. Now you have to suffer the consequences."

Vivienne sighed and adjusted her clothes. "I'll have you know, I'm quite good in bed."

"Oh, I don't doubt that, but if you want to hear me moan your name in the throes of ecstasy, then you have to work for that privilege."

Vivienne crossed her arms petulantly, trying to ignore the growing wetness between her thighs. She didn't know how Selene shifted her moods so quickly, but now she was in the same state she'd been in before they pulled over. And she was sure Selene knew it.

They drove into town, and Vivienne directed her to her house. Selene stopped at the bottom of the driveway. "Did you want me to drop you off at the top?"

Vivienne sighed. "No. The last thing I need is Claudia asking questions."

Selene reached into the backseat and retrieved the umbrella. "Take this. You can give it back to me next week."

Vivienne took the umbrella, brushing her fingers over Selene's. "Thank you."

"My pleasure."

Vivienne resisted the urge to lean in and kiss Selene again. Instead, she unbuckled her seat belt and climbed out of the car, opening the umbrella. The rain had tapered off to a drizzle. She made her way up the driveway, turning to watch as Selene pulled away.

———◆———

Vivienne shook the water off the umbrella and opened the front door. She could still smell Selene's perfume and wondered if her family would notice.

On her way upstairs, Hattie came out of her bedroom, closing the door behind her. She startled when she saw Vivienne, and she pulled her robe closer around her. "Viv!"

"Hattie," she said, looking her over. "Do you have a guest over?"

"Ah, yes," she admitted, her face flushing. "Jonathan couldn't get home because of the roads and…I invited him back here for dinner and a place to sleep."

Vivienne raised her eyebrows.

Hattie diverted further questioning. "And where were you last night? You got off the phone rather quickly when I asked."

"As I told you, the river flooded, and my car got stuck on the other side of town."

"And that's why you have a love bite on your collarbone?"

Now it was Vivienne's turn to startle. Her sister laughed. "Oh, Viv, don't look so worried. You know we love you. It's been a while since you looked so happy."

"Happy?" She scoffed. "I don't know what you think is going on, but I assure you it's nothing like you think."

"If you say so. I'm going to make breakfast for Jonathan. You should get some sleep. It looks like you didn't get much."

There was no point in Vivienne defending herself. Hattie wasn't far off the mark, and she'd rather her family suspect a relationship than be concerned about what she was really doing.

She decided to follow her sister's advice and went to bed for an hour or so, then showered and went downstairs. The rain had stopped, but the skies remained gray, and the air was pleasantly cool. She headed out to the veranda with a cigarette and cup of coffee. Hattie was sitting in a rocking chair wrapped in a blanket, reading a book.

"Jonathan left?" Vivienne asked.

"To check on the store," Hattie said, studying her.

At that moment, a car pulled up in the driveway. Claudia jumped out and waved goodbye to whomever was in the car. She greeted Vivienne cheerfully as she stepped onto the porch.

Vivienne narrowed her eyes suspiciously.

Claudia looked down and adjusted her bag on her shoulder.

"I take it you were safe from last night's rain?"

"I was. Aunt Hattie said you got caught on the other side of the river. Did you have to stay the night at the office?"

Vivienne lit a cigarette. She could lie, but that would only make it harder to explain why her car had got stuck. "No," she answered. "I tried to come through on the forest roads and got stuck. I'll need to ask someone with a truck for a favor."

"You should ask Luca's father. He has a thing for you, you know." Claudia smiled sweetly.

Vivienne snuffed out her cigarette. Luca's father did *not* have a thing for her. Not anymore. "Maybe I will. Could you check with Luca?"

Claudia nodded and ran inside.

Vivienne waited until her steps had receded. "Was Claudia home last night?"

"No. She called to say she was stuck at a friend's." Hattie paused, then asked, "If you were stuck on the forest road, where did you spend the night?"

Vivienne picked up her mug of coffee. "And why are you so curious? For all you know, I slept in my car."

Hattie smiled knowingly and returned to her book.

Vivienne was more amused than annoyed by her sister's inquiry. She went back in the house and made her way to the office. Setting her mug on the desk, she switched on her computer.

She rolled her shoulders, still feeling like she hadn't had enough sleep. The nap had helped, but not much. And despite the shower, she could still smell Selene's perfume, and every muscle ached where the cane had struck her. Everything reminded her of Selene telling her she had waited for Vivienne to come upstairs.

Shaking off her regret, she reviewed her emails. There was nothing of real interest: students begging for extensions, staff requesting help to locate missing items, and a few status updates from Elijah and the dean about other departments.

Vivienne clicked through them, then returned to working on her lesson plans.

She hadn't got far before she was interrupted by Claudia knocking on the doorframe. "Aunt Vi? I called Luca, and he asked his dad for help. They'll be around later this afternoon with the truck."

"Thank you, Claudia. Did Luca mention what his father would like as thanks?"

"Perhaps a date," she said. "I might have mentioned that you're not seeing anyone right now."

Vivienne glanced at her niece over the monitor. "That may be true, but it does not mean I have time to date."

Claudia shrugged. "Doesn't have to be dating. You could go out for a few drinks. Maybe you'll like each other." She giggled, and Vivienne wondered if Claudia was conspiring to set her up with Luca's father. That would explain her suspicious behavior over the last few weeks.

Vivienne sighed. "I'll think about it," she said, not planning to even consider it. She had no intention to start dating when her current needs were being met quite well.

Just as Claudia turned to leave, Vivienne remembered something and called her back.

Her niece ducked her head around the corner. "Yes, Auntie?"

"Do you need help writing your résumé?"

"Already done. I got a job at the bookshop with Aunt Hattie."

"Oh?"

"Just for a few days each week. I promise it won't interfere with everything else."

"Excellent. I'm pleased you'll be working."

Vivienne considered what that meant. If Claudia was working with Hattie, she suspected that very little work would get done. Claudia's friends would likely visit, and Claudia would spend all of her time hanging out with them. Her duties would take a back seat.

Vivienne sighed. She shouldn't think so harshly of her niece. After all, it was still a job, an opportunity for responsibility. And if she were fired from this one, all the better. Claudia would learn that she couldn't coast through life, hoping her charm would save her.

She returned to building her lessons for the next few weeks. The coming week would be extremely busy with classes and meetings, not to mention Claudia's sports events and the appointment with Selene, which she'd penned in as a meeting for fundraising.

She closed her eyes, feeling a wave of nausea roll over her. She was exhausted, utterly exhausted, and now her coffee was cold. Maybe she needed to eat. It was past lunchtime.

She went down to the kitchen to scrounge through the cupboards and discovered that Hattie had made cookies. As she was brewing a fresh pot of coffee, she heard a truck pull up the driveway.

She stepped out to the living room and peered through the window. She cringed. Seeing Luca and his father made her feel awkward, as if she were doing something wrong. She and Joseph hadn't dated since Vivienne was in her late teens, but they had a history that became more complicated after their children became friends.

She gobbled her cookie and made her way outside just as Luca and Joseph got out of the car.

Luca was dressed like a petite version of his father. He dug his hands into his pockets awkwardly. A cut was still healing on his cheek and lip, but he looked well otherwise. He smiled brightly. "Hello, Ms. Carter."

"Luca. How's school?"

Luca shrugged the same way Claudia did, and Vivienne worried that the bullying was getting worse, despite the punishment.

"Claudia mentioned your car got stuck on the forest road," Luca said as his father came up behind him.

She nodded at Joseph Fitzgerald in greeting, then addressed them both. "I tried to brave the old roads when I realized the river had flooded across the highway, but I hit a hole and ended up getting stuck."

"As I recall, you used to brave those roads when you were young too."

Vivienne laughed at the old memory. "I did," she said. "But never through a storm until last night."

"Do you know which road?"

"I do. I'll show you the way."

"Can Claudia come?" Luca asked. "We've never pulled out a stuck car."

Vivienne nodded, and Luca ran inside to look for Claudia, leaving her alone with Joe. She invited him inside and poured him a cup of coffee.

He grinned at her. "You look nice, Vivienne."

"Thank you. As do you," she said sincerely. His clothes were ironed and his hair was combed. He looked far better than he had right to after his wife died. "How's the business going?"

"As well as it can. Most of my money comes from weddings and other social events these days. People want to rent out the land for the view."

Their conversation was interrupted when Claudia came down the stairs wearing her favorite red jacket. She was followed by Luca. They both looked mischievous, confirming Vivienne's suspicion that they were trying to set her up with Joseph. That would explain their giggles and secret glances.

They finished their coffee. Vivienne followed Joe outside to his truck and climbed inside. Claudia and Luca climbed in the bed. The floorboard was a little dirty, but the seats had been freshly cleaned.

The truck bounced along the road as Vivienne directed him to where her car was. They passed numerous potholes where she might have gotten stuck again if she had managed to get unstuck from the first hole on her own.

When they arrived, Vivienne got out to confirm that her belongings were still in place, then stepped aside to listen as Joe explained to Claudia and Luca what to do if they ever found themselves stuck in the mud. Then he pulled out a piece of flat wood and pushed it under the dug-in tire as far as he could.

Vivienne got in the car and started the engine, then stepped on the gas. The car did not move. She tried again, then put it back in park and got out.

Joe frowned. "You got it in there pretty deep." He adjusted the plank and directed her to try it again.

And again it didn't work.

Joe dug through the back of his truck and pulled out chains. He hooked up one end to the front of Vivienne's car and the other end to the back of his truck. Then he told Vivienne to put the car into neutral. That done, Joe's truck pulled the car out with ease. Vivienne sighed in relief. She would still need to be careful driving home on the muddy roads.

Claudia and Luca were still whispering between them. There was a time when Vivienne might have considered dating Joe again. But a lot of time had passed, and she doubted either one of them wanted to dig up old history. Even if they were willing to, she didn't have time. She didn't particularly want to make time either, preferring to drown herself in work.

Vivienne got back in her car. Claudia got in on the passenger side and buckled her seat belt. "That was very helpful of Mr. Fitzgerald," Claudia said. "And it was good that he came prepared."

"Yes, it was," Vivienne said, pulling onto the road behind Joe's truck.

Claudia found a local station on the radio, then sat back. "You know, Mr. Fitzgerald's brother passed recently."

"I am aware."

"He's been pretty lonely since that happened."

"Perhaps he should find someone to date who shares that emotional grief." She glanced at Claudia. "I don't know why you've decided that he and I are a match, but I assure you, we are not."

"You would be," she insisted. "He's a nice man, he works hard, and he likes his own company, so you two would be perfect for each other."

"Claudia, Joe and I are well acquainted. We knew each other when I was a teenager living in Oakdale." Claudia must know that. Maybe she thought she was reuniting two long-lost loves.

"Why did you break up?"

"It was complicated," Vivienne said. "I was busy and had no interest in pursuing anything serious. We grew apart, and then he met someone with time for him."

"Have you ever pursued something serious?"

Vivienne thought back to her previous partners. She'd been in a few serious relationships and was even engaged once. Inevitably, they broke up for one reason or another. She had begun to think she was cursed until it dawned on her that she wasn't always pleasant to be around. She was cold and withdrawn, preferred her own company, placed her work over everything else, and considered things like romantic anniversaries unimportant.

"No," she said at last.

"Did you ever want your own children?"

"I have you."

"But I'm not *yours*," Claudia said bluntly. She probably hadn't meant to be unkind, but the pain struck Vivienne's heart all the same. She had provided for her, soothed her fevers, and kissed her scrapes and bruises since Claudia was a toddler. But she was right; Vivienne would never be her mother, no matter what she did.

"No," she lied. "I didn't want my own children."

"But I overheard you tell—"

"What is with the questions, Claudia?" she snapped. "What are you getting at?"

"You're not happy," Claudia explained. "You're not happy with me or Hattie or the house. You don't like your job. And for a while, it seemed like maybe you'd found someone, but you say you haven't, so…" She sighed. "I don't know. I just want you to be happy."

"Having someone in your life doesn't necessarily make you happy. Have you considered that I've chosen to be single because that's what I want?"

"But Mr. Fitzgerald is a nice man, and he said—"

"He may say a great many things, but that doesn't mean I want to share his life. We parted ways before you were born for reasons that have long since ceased to matter. I went to college and came back, and by then he was married. I didn't care, Claudia. If I had cared for him, him being married would have mattered."

Claudia was quiet as they left the forest road and turned onto the highway. Then she said, "You're both lonely, so I thought…"

"I understand your intentions, but I will say this only once: Do not interfere with my love life. I am happy to be where I am. I have a family and a good job, and that's all I need."

"What about friends?"

Vivienne considered. "I have colleagues I consider friends."

"Florence?"

Vivienne sighed. "Yes, Florence and I are friends."

"Then why doesn't she come over anymore?"

"Because she's busy with her own work and family."

They were quiet the rest of the way home.

Vivienne pulled her car up the driveway. Joe parked his truck in front of the house, and he and Luca got out. Vivienne smiled at them. She had missed Joe in some ways, but seeing Luca and Claudia grow to be best friends felt right, as if in some other life she and Joe could have gotten it right.

"Do you want to stay for dinner?" Claudia asked Luca, then turned and looked at Vivienne mischievously.

"If we aren't intruding," Joe said.

"Of course not," Vivienne said. "Luca and Claudia can help Hattie."

They headed up the walkway. Joe removed his muddy boots at the door and set them aside. Luca and Claudia followed his example. Vivienne always kept a pair of house shoes by the front door, and she slipped them on after taking off her own muddy shoes.

She sent Luca and Claudia to wash up, then led Joe to the dining room to wait while she made a pot of coffee, arranged some of Hattie's cookies on a plate, set out everything on a tray, and took it to the dining room. "Did you make these?" he asked.

"No, Hattie did."

He smiled. "She always did like to bake. Even when she could barely reach the counter, she used to bake with your grandmother."

Vivienne nodded, although she didn't really remember Hattie baking that much. "How do you know so much about Hattie?"

"I got to know her when I was waiting for you. Whenever I went to pick you up, you wouldn't turn up for at least an hour."

Joe had always been a good and kind man, even when he was younger. And she had probably used him for her own gain, taking advantage of his interest in her.

They nibbled on cookies and drank their coffee. Then Joe broke the silence. "Luca and Claudia have been more than obvious."

"I've noticed. Claudia especially seems quite insistent." Setting her mug of coffee down, she said, "I don't want to mislead you. I'm not interested in a relationship."

"I know. You never were."

Vivienne startled. "What on earth does that mean?"

He set his mug down on the table. "Just that you were always independent. You preferred your own company. It's not a critique, it's just who you are. You're—"

Cold. Vivienne mentally finished his thought. It was the same word that other partners had thrown at her.

"—unbound by that desire."

Vivienne laughed. "I suppose that's true," she said, but the conversation was reopening wounds she thought long ago healed, wounds not unlike her recent welts.

She pushed aside her thoughts of Selene and returned her attention to Joe. "And what about you?" she asked. "Have you dated anyone since you lost your wife?"

He smiled sadly, and in that moment, he looked tired, truly tired. Angelina, Joe's wife and Luca's mother, had been from out of town. She was a lovely, round-faced woman who always looked like she was about to burst into laughter. Joe had looked at her like she was the whole world.

"I don't know," he said. "Too old for the theatrics of it all, and anyway, I know most of the town's occupants."

PRINCIPLE DECISIONS

"It's difficult," Vivienne agreed. "And it's not easy to meet anyone out where you live."

"No," he said. "Mitch was ill for so long…" He trailed off, grief overtaking him.

As much as Vivienne wanted to reach out and comfort him, they weren't really friends anymore. They were barely acquaintances now. It was their children who were friends.

"Do you remember when Mitch would chase after us when we went to the river?" Vivienne asked.

"He could never take a hint. Always wanted to involve himself."

"He taught me to fish better than you did."

Joe smiled at the memory, and Vivienne had a rush of nostalgia, remembering how, when she snagged a fish, both men had offered to help. They were completely surprised when she not only unhooked it but also gutted it.

"You give him too much credit," Joe said. "You were always better at those things than any of the boys."

Vivienne smiled, remembering the times she'd date someone who assumed she was like other girls. It was fun to pretend she had no idea how to do something before demonstrating that she was a better shot, better at fishing, better at any number of things than they were.

"I've been meaning to speak to you," he said. "Claudia's been standing up for Luca ever since he came out. She did lots of research and shared it with his friends, teachers, and our family. It means a lot to see that she loves him so much."

Vivienne smiled. "She has a good heart. She's kinder than I ever was."

"You are kind in your own way. You never let anyone hurt Hattie. Remember when Sarah pushed her into the river?"

Vivienne laughed. "Oh yes. And I remember getting her back for that."

"She was jealous of you. Her boyfriend was wrapped around your finger."

Joe drained the last of the coffee from his mug, set it down on the table, and looked pointedly at Vivienne. "Are you happy, Vivienne?"

"Happy?" She flinched. "Of course I am. I have everything I want."

"I'm glad."

Before Joe could get at what he might be digging at, Vivienne suggested they go check on Hattie and the status of dinner. They found her in the greenhouse with Luca and Claudia. She looked at them suspiciously. "What are you up to?"

Luca looked down guiltily.

"Just looking over the garden," Hattie said. "Luca's got a science project coming up, and I was just suggesting—"

"That perhaps it's time to start dinner?" Vivienne said, interrupting. "I'm sure whatever you're suggesting can wait until we've eaten."

Claudia glared.

"Of course," Hattie said. "I was going to make a casserole, if that's all right with you."

"Sounds good," she said, though she would have preferred something quicker to make.

She and Joe passed the time chatting politely, but she was exhausted, and the coffee had not revived her at all.

At dinner, she listened with half an ear as Hattie and Joe discussed classes with Luca and Claudia.

Vivienne pricked up her ears when she heard "Principal Rothschild." She looked at Luca, trying to trace what the conversation was about.

"She's standing firm on Oakdale High's zero-tolerance policy on fighting," Claudia said, "but I don't know if it was fair about the charity service. They're bullies, and they got the same punishment as us when they're the ones who started it." She huffed. "And it wasn't like they were going to learn anything. They volunteered at the senior center while we worked with little kids. And we were supposed to be working together."

"What I find funny," Joe said, "is that when the other parents and I spoke to her, she had decided on a week's suspension for everyone. And then you spoke with her in private. The next thing we hear is no suspensions at all."

Vivienne pushed her plate away. "It was hardly fair that Claudia was going to be suspended."

"Well, she still punished us all equally," Claudia protested.

Vivienne felt her face heating up. "I couldn't allow a suspension on your record. It's unfortunate that they didn't face a harsher penalty, but I did my best for you."

Joe looked at her curiously. "So you negotiated her down?"

"I did. I agreed with her that fighting should not be tolerated, but there was some justification for what happened. Though I understand that one of the boys was hospitalized, and I'm not sure what Claudia had to do with that."

"He broke his leg," Claudia said, "and that wasn't our fault. After the fight started, one of his friends accidentally knocked him down the stairs. We stopped fighting after that."

"Anyway, the matter's resolved," Vivienne said. "Your charity service is nearly complete."

Claudia shrugged and exchanged glances with Luca.

"Well," Hattie said, changing the subject, "Principal Rothschild certainly has the PTA under her thumb. She completely cut them off when they tried to raise complaints about girls wearing inappropriate outfits to school. She asked if they should start measuring clothes on the boys too."

Vivienne listened with interest. Selene seemed determined to make enemies everywhere. If she continued challenging the PTA, soon she would look like a tyrant, and they would zero in on her.

Or maybe she welcomed the challenge. She seemed unfazed by anything. Still, she hadn't been principal very long, and Vivienne doubted that her position was so set in stone that, if a group of teachers and parents complained, she would get out unscathed. At best, she might be asked to leave her post. At worst, someone would dig into her personal life.

Vivienne shifted in her seat. If someone wanted to find dirt on Selene, Vivienne might be caught in the middle. That was something to be considered. She and Selene had assured each other that they were making no promises. And after Selene had fucked her in the car, Vivienne was deeply aware of how much she craved intimacy with someone.

But it couldn't be Selene, no matter how much she wanted her. Selene was someone she could love, which meant the pain of hurting her would be unbearable. She couldn't go through such heartbreak again.

And yet the thought of walking away made her heart feel like it was tearing apart.

Her own company, her work, and her family had to be enough for now. There was no room for anything else.

CHAPTER 11
LIGHTHEADED

Vivienne stood in front of her class, hoping her students did not see how exhausted she was, despite the copious amounts of coffee she had drunk. Saturday had been lost to recovering her car and unplanned socializing, so she had spent the entire day and most of the night Sunday grading papers and planning lessons.

She turned unsteadily to the whiteboard and wrote out the main points of the lecture. Then, returning to the lectern, she leaned on it heavily to steady herself until she felt her blood flow returning.

She asked for someone to explain the roots of each language structure. Matthew stumbled over his words but managed to state four of the five points she was hoping for. Maddison filled in the missing point.

The rest of the class was a blur, and she was thankful when the students left. She dropped into a chair and waited for the dizziness to pass.

Perhaps she should have eaten something more substantial than a granola bar for breakfast.

Vivienne wanted to attribute her constant nausea to menopause, but the truth was she hadn't felt well lately. Although she had seen her gynecologist not too long ago—thanks to Selene's request for a clean bill of health—she had put off seeing her family doctor for some time. During her last visit, he had lectured her about the long-term effects of stress and smoking.

"Professor Carter?"

She looked up, blinking in the fluorescent lighting, then turned to the doorway.

"Are you okay?" Abigail asked.

"I'm fine." Vivienne picked up her bag and stood up. She did feel better after sitting down for a few minutes. Maybe that was all she needed. Maybe she could squeeze in a power nap on her lunch break.

"We were scheduled to meet. Do you want to do it here?"

Vivienne sighed. Her office was just down the hall. "No, let's go to my office."

She walked with Abigail to her office, unlocked the door, and booted up her laptop. Then she looked at Abigail, who had pulled out her paperwork.

"I graded the language class assignments for the first-year students, but I can't do the religious studies. I don't understand enough of the subject matter. I'm sorry."

Vivienne nodded. She'd expected as much. "Thank you, Abigail. You're doing far more than I expected of a TA."

"I know you're going over everything I grade to make sure it's okay, and I don't know if it's because you don't trust me or—"

"It's not that I don't trust you," Vivienne said, waving her hand. "It's because if I'm going to sign off on your grading, I need to make sure that I agree. There's never been anything I'm concerned about. If you decide to choose academia as a career, I will be happy to provide you with a reference."

Abigail blushed. "Thank you," she said. "But you still have a massive workload. Is there nothing that any of the other professors can do?"

"No," Vivienne said, though it was probably only a matter of asking. She just wasn't sure she could manage that.

Abigail offered to create some lesson plans for the first-years, and Vivienne relented. Abigail's help would provide some relief from the overwhelming pressure.

But lately, real relief came from only one place, and she didn't want to end up hurting herself any further. It was easier to end the relationship where they had left it, no matter how much Vivienne wanted otherwise, no matter how much she had fallen for her.

PRINCIPLE DECISIONS

But she couldn't get the woman out of her thoughts.

Vivienne watched as Hattie and Claudia decorated the Christmas tree. They had chosen it from the Fitzgeralds' farm, and Henry had brought it over. The bright lights warmed the room. Hattie had insisted that Vivienne take it easy over the holidays, and she had to admit that it was nice to sit on the couch, hot chocolate in hand, and watch as Claudia draped tinsel on the tree limbs.

When Claudia was younger, they would all decorate the tree together; it had been far too many years. She was filled with both nostalgia and an awareness that she had missed out on a lot.

"Claudia!" Hattie said, holding out an ornament. "I remember when you made this." Claudia had just turned three when her day care had the children make ornaments from clay. She had squished the clay into a blob with arms that she had assured Vivienne was an angel.

Claudia turned the ornament around in her hands, frowning. "We don't need to keep this anymore."

"We certainly do." Vivienne got up and snatched it away before Claudia could dump it in the trash. "This was the first decoration you made. We're keeping it." She set it up high on the tree, looping it so it wouldn't fall. "Now, what are we choosing for the top of the tree this year?"

"Last year was the snowman," Hattie said. "And goodness, what a nuisance. It ended up falling off half a dozen times."

"We could go with the star." Claudia dug it out from the box.

The star was still in its glory, having been carefully looked after. It was an old family heirloom, but Vivienne wouldn't mind if it disappeared. She took it from Claudia and placed it on top of the tree amidst fading childhood memories.

It was time for new memories.

She stepped back and admired the tree.

After the tree decorating, they baked gingerbread cookies. Claudia iced them all while Hattie began preparing dinner. Vivienne was left to sip her whiskey and bask in a sense of contentment.

She had missed her family. Truly missed them. The past week especially had made her even more aware of everything she had missed.

Claudia's school term still had another two weeks before they broke for Christmas. Vivienne had promised to attend the final football game. She wasn't sure if it was an important game or not and had trouble keeping up with the plays, but Claudia was going, and so would she.

She hadn't heard about Luca playing on the team in some time, and as much as she wanted to assume he had settled in, Vivienne suspected that he had quit, choosing not to be tormented anymore. As much as she hated it, it would be unfair to put Luca through more harassment.

Now that Vivienne was taking a few days off from work, her headaches had begun to ease, and she and Claudia weren't arguing for once. And since Claudia was working now, earning her own spending money to go out on dates with Henry and her friends, Vivienne had lifted her ban and resumed giving her an allowance. She thought Claudia might leave the bookstore, but she seemed to enjoy the work.

And Vivienne found herself…oddly relieved.

Maybe she wasn't failing as Claudia's guardian.

Claudia interrupted her thoughts. "Um, Aunt Vi? Rebecca's family invited me to ski with them for the holidays."

"When?" Vivienne asked.

"From Christmas Eve until January third."

"So you won't be here for Christmas or New Year's Eve?"

"You'll have Aunt Hattie."

Hattie chimed in. "Johnny's hosting a New Year's party at the store. You could come with me, Viv."

"I'll pass," she said, an ache growing in her chest. The last thing she wanted was to go to a party with teenagers. No, she would stay home, watch the fireworks on television, then go to bed. Celebrating the New Year was hardly worth the hangover anymore.

"I can cancel," Claudia said softly.

"Do not even think of canceling. It sounds wonderful. Don't the Walters go every year?"

Claudia smiled and nodded. Vivienne remembered when her niece saw the snow for the first time. They had made snowmen, and Vivienne had shown Claudia how to make snowballs and throw them at Hattie.

And now her niece was off on an adventure with her friends.

"I'll be fine," she assured her, already planning to work through Christmas break. Now she would have more time to catch up. But she knew what she wanted more than anything.

She wanted Selene. She dreamed of her, craved her every moment, with every breath. With Claudia gone and Hattie busy, the holidays would have been a perfect opportunity to see her. Vivienne could spend a few days with Selene, watching her laugh, talk about work and her life. She'd even make breakfast and—

"Viv?" Hattie asked. "Are you all right? You look pale."

"I'm fine." she said, choking back the fantasy.

The truth was, despite everything she had done to stop herself from caring for Selene, it was too late.

She loved her. Loved her with every fiber of her being.

CHAPTER 12
CASUAL INTERACTIONS

Vivienne went to the grocery store to pick up half a dozen last-minute items for the pre-Christmas feast Hattie planned to make before her niece went off to ski. She stepped back into the middle of the aisle to study the different types of flour and bumped smack into the woman she had ghosted not too long ago.

Selene's thick woolen coat was unbuttoned, revealing a patterned button-down shirt and dark pants. Her hair cascaded down her back, and her eyes stood out brightly in contrast.

Vivienne sucked in her breath, pushing down the sudden need to flee while mentally kicking herself for going to the same store where she had run into Selene before. At the same time, she fought back the urge to kiss her, despite how hard she'd worked the past few weeks trying to shove those feelings aside.

She'd been tempted to call Selene—she desperately needed release, given the pressure of her end-of-semester work schedule. She missed the woman's companionship, but she'd pushed aside her desire. Their relationship was too complicated, and Vivienne didn't have the space for it. Selene had not reached out either, but why would she? Vivienne was just her client, after all.

"Vivienne. You look lovely, as usual."

"Thank you," Vivienne said. "I've been busy with papers and exams," she explained awkwardly, the words spilling out on their own. "I haven't…"

"Had time?" Selene asked. "I promise you haven't hurt my feelings."

Her words stung. If Vivienne had wanted to know that she mattered to Selene, had wanted to know she was important to her on some level, her dismissal affirmed that, by not contacting her, she was doing the right thing.

"I see. Well then, I'll let you go," Vivienne said and turned to walk away.

Selene reached out and grabbed her arm. Vivienne turned back, her face set in stone.

"Are you really okay? Selene asked softly.

"I'm fine," she said, shrugging off Selene's hand.

"I'm sure you are. I just thought that perhaps you were upset with me."

"I…that's not…"

Selene's smile faded into a frown. "You *are* upset with me, then."

Vivienne glanced around the store. This was not the place to have the conversation she wanted to have.

Selene nodded understandingly. "How about a drink? On me. Tonight. I don't care if you want to terminate my services, but I am concerned if something between us is unresolved. After all, I am the principal at your niece's school, and I want to avoid unnecessary… awkwardness if there's something I can do to fix it."

Vivienne shook her head. "There's nothing you can do."

"Try me," Selene insisted. "At the very least, let's meet so we can clear the air."

She nodded. "What time?"

"Six? How about Richmond's Bar, the one near the bookstore? It's busy enough that no one will pay attention to us. Or you could come over to my place."

A shiver ran down Vivienne's spine at the thought of going to Selene's house. In fact, even having a drink with her seemed dangerous. She pictured herself at their last meeting—legs spread, ass high, and each hit stinging. She wanted that more than she should. "The bar is fine."

"See you at six. Don't be late," she said sternly, then grinned and walked away.

Vivienne's heart fluttered. Somehow she found the right flour and tossed it into the cart. On the way to check out, she hoped she'd stumble across Selene again, but she didn't. She drove home thinking about the interaction, and despite how much she wanted to talk herself out of the meeting, seeing Selene again had reignited Vivienne's feelings. She was enamored.

Hopelessly so.

After bringing in the groceries, Vivienne went upstairs to shower and dress, selecting a new outfit.

She hesitated over which lingerie to wear.

There was no use trying to convince herself that they were only meeting for one drink at a bar because she knew that if the opportunity arose, she wasn't going to turn it down.

She pulled on a jacket, then told Hattie that she'd run into a friend and was going to meet them for a few glasses of wine.

She arrived at the bar half an hour early and sat in her car to compose herself, her knuckles turning white on the steering wheel that she couldn't stop gripping. Her heart was pounding, and her mouth was dry as she thought about Selene's laughter in her ear and wondering if she could make her laugh and moan in the same breath.

Closing her eyes, she tried to shake off the fantasy.

She picked up her purse, headed into the bar, and looked around. It was still early, and Selene hadn't arrived yet.

Vivienne found a booth near the back and ordered a glass of wine. She looked around. The bar seemed to be filled with mostly middle-aged men and women who looked like they wanted to hit something or cry.

She was beginning to regret meeting here.

The server brought her glass of wine. She had barely taken a sip when the door opened again and Selene entered. She slipped off her jacket, her face flushed from the cold. She was wearing the same clothes she had had on in the grocery store. She looked around the room, and when she saw Vivienne, she smiled, filling Vivienne's chest with a familiar flutter.

"Vivienne," she said, sliding in on the opposite side of the booth. "Don't you look lovely?"

"As do you," Vivienne said and looked away, asking herself why she had changed her clothes and applied fresh makeup. She may as well have worn a sign that said *Fuck Me.*

The server appeared and Selene ordered, then looked at her intently, her eyes twinkling in the light of the table candle. "Why haven't you been coming to see me?"

"In part because I've been busy with the end of the semester."

"And the other part?"

Vivienne sipped her wine. She had considered what she might say to that very question as she had dressed for the evening. She could say that she couldn't afford the sessions anymore, but that was hardly true. Or say that she was seeing someone, also not true. She discarded each lie as it presented itself, leaving her to either tell the truth or fabricate a story that would shift blame on Selene.

And she didn't want to do that.

"I don't know," she said. "I think whatever this is"—she waved her hand across the table—"is blending into something more complicated, and I'm not sure how I feel about that."

"That's fair. We can set clearer boundaries, if you like. I admit I've been rather…unethical in my approach to this, with the football game encounter and the day you stumbled across my home."

Vivienne looked down.

"Do you want to keep playing with me?" Selene asked.

Vivienne looked up to meet her gaze. "I do," she admitted. "I want…everything we had before."

"Everything?" Selene asked. "Or would you like more?"

Vivienne felt her cheeks heat up, grateful that Selene couldn't see her blush in the dim light.

Selene filled the silence. "I want more," she said. "I enjoy playing with you, Vivienne. Quite a fair bit more than I enjoy playing with my other clients. And I wanted to ask you for more a while ago, but I was…worried that you didn't feel the same."

Vivienne allowed herself to smile. "I feel the same."

"If you like, we could make an arrangement," Selene said. "It doesn't have to be romantic, if you're not ready for that, but something more...in-between."

"And what would that arrangement look like?"

"Well, simply stated, I could be your mistress, and you would be my..." She paused, as if considering the right word.

"Pet?" Vivienne finished for her, and she raised her eyebrows.

Selene shrugged. "There must be a better word; not that I wouldn't enjoy collaring you."

Vivienne sucked in her breath and stared at Selene, wondering how it would feel to have her put a collar around her throat.

"You're far too insubordinate to be a slave," she said, and Vivienne felt the woman's foot stroking up her calf. "Servant, perhaps. Or maybe..." She grinned, and Vivienne jumped as the foot reached her crotch. "Handmaiden."

Handmaiden. Her blush deepened. "And what sort of...duties would such a position require?"

"Oh, we'd have to negotiate that. But sex...kink...anything you want, anytime you need it, wherever you want."

Vivienne looked away. "And what would I need to pay for such a privilege?"

"This arrangement would be entirely about mutual satisfaction."

So Selene was asking her to engage in a dom/sub relationship. She should consider how that might affect her life, but the truth was she didn't want to think about any of that. She just wanted what was offered, plain and simple.

"I want to play with you," Selene continued. "I want to fuck you, if you will have me. I like you, Vivienne. And if you don't want any of this at all, I would still like to be friends."

And Selene liked her too, truly liked her. Her heart raced. "I want those things too," she admitted. She sipped her wine, trying to keep her hand steady. "What would this involve?"

"Are you asking, or are you *asking*?" Selene said and slid around the U-shaped booth until she was pressing her body against Vivienne's.

She stared at her mouth. "Because we can talk, if that's what you want, but I need to know right now what you want."

They should talk, but all Vivienne wanted at that moment was to feel Selene's fingers down her underwear.

But not here.

"We should…go," Vivienne said. "Somewhere else."

"Where?"

"Anywhere."

Selene pulled some bills out of her wallet and threw them on the table, then pushed Vivienne gently out of the booth and led her outside. They had barely made it into the alley behind the bar when Selene shoved her against the side of the building and pressed her mouth on hers as she pushed up the hem of her dress.

"Open your legs for me," Selene whispered in her ear, and with her free hand raised Vivienne's thigh.

Vivienne obeyed, and the woman slipped her fingers under the band of lace and slid them over her center in a slow, firm stroke that made her roll her head against the wall.

"Someone could see us," Vivienne gasped, but she rocked her hips against Selene's hand and clutched the lapels of her jacket tighter. "Shouldn't we—"

"Shh. No one will see us if you're quiet."

Vivienne moaned softly as Selene kissed and nipped down her neck. She opened her eyes and looked up. It was dark but still early, too early for this. People might see them, yet the thought of getting caught thrilled her.

She closed her eyes again and rocked against Selene's hand, biting down on her bottom lip to keep from crying out.

The bricks scraped against her scalp and caught on her clothes. The air was cold against her legs, but Selene's breath was hot on her throat.

"You are a divine calling, Vivienne. I'm so glad we ran into each other," Selene said and pressed her mouth hard against Vivienne's.

Vivienne moaned, a shudder building low in her belly, and then Selene was moving her hand faster and running a finger over her clit. "*Shit*," Vivienne hissed, and then she was coming in an alley behind some bar with a woman who used to be her paid dominatrix, who was now her mistress, and all Vivienne could think about was how beautiful Selene looked with smudged lipstick and the streetlight haloing her head.

And then it was over. Vivienne pulled up her underwear and smoothed down her dress.

"Come home with me," Selene said.

"I drove."

"Pick up your car tomorrow. I'm not done with you yet."

Vivienne nodded. Selene laced her fingers through Vivienne's hands and led her to her black sedan, opening the passenger door, then shutting her in. And then Selene was in the driver's seat, smiling at her as if she couldn't believe her eyes.

Vivienne had only drunk half a glass of wine, yet she felt as though she'd finished a bottle. She wondered briefly if this was a good decision, then Selene started the car and she no longer cared.

When they didn't move, she looked at Selene and found her queen looking back at her.

"Take off your underwear."

"I beg your pardon?"

"I'll let you know when you need to beg." She pulled the car out of the parking lot. "Take off your underwear. I won't tell you again."

Vivienne reached under her dress, pushed her hips off the seat, and slid her underwear down her legs and off.

"That's my girl."

As they began the fifteen-minute drive, Vivienne wondered what would happen after they arrived, imagining different scenarios until she was wet between her thighs.

But Selene had other plans. Keeping one hand on the steering wheel, she slipped the other under Vivienne's thigh, drawing it up.

"Move forward for me," Selene ordered.

Vivienne obeyed without hesitation because Selene was her queen.

Keeping her eyes on the road, Selene slid her hand up Vivienne's inner thigh, and as Vivienne moved forward on the seat, Selene stroked her again.

"Don't hold back," Selene said, working between Vivienne's legs. "There's no one here but you and me."

Vivienne moaned.

Selene's hand was slow and steady, and when she slid her fingers in, Vivienne raised a foot onto the console to spread her legs wider, pushing further forward on the seat so Selene could be deeper inside her. She pressed her head back against the leather headrest and pressed her hips up in rhythm with Selene's hands.

She glanced at Selene, who was focused on the road, a curl of amusement at the corner of her mouth.

And then Selene pulled over, her fingers sliding out of Vivienne to put the car in park. Before Vivienne could react, Selene had unbuckled her seat belt and was on top of her, burying her fingers deep again as she straddled her thigh, moving urgently, like they were running out of time.

Vivienne pressed her heel against the car's console. As small as the sedan was, Selene showed no sign of being encumbered. She was fucking Vivienne as if her life depended on it—and Vivienne's life depended on her getting fucked right now.

"Selene," she whispered as she teetered on the edge of another orgasm.

The other woman nipped at her mouth, and Vivienne, unable to focus on either kissing or fucking, panted like a dog. She squeezed her muscles tighter and tighter around Selene's fingers until there was nothing else she wanted but to be in that moment for all eternity.

"Look at you," Selene said and kissed her again slowly, as if savoring the sounds Vivienne was making. "You're all mine, Vivienne."

"Yours," she panted.

And then Selene was hitting just the right spot in her strokes, pressing her thumb on Vivienne's clit until her foot slipped, and with that sudden movement, she was coming again, harder than before.

Selene stopped moving her hand. "I hope you don't have plans for tomorrow because I plan to fuck you until you use your safe word."

Vivienne shuddered. "How can I argue with that?"

Selene smiled, then without warning, pushed her fingers deep inside her again.

Reflexively, she pulled back from the intensity of the touch. "I…" But Selene kissed and nipped at her neck, and Vivienne sighed, melting against her as she stroked her fingers in deeper until Vivienne came again. It was a small orgasm, but it made her ache. She almost asked for another one, but she held back the words.

Selene climbed back into the driver's seat, licking her fingers with more arrogance than she had any right to.

Vivienne dropped her leg onto the floorboard. Despite being fucked multiple times in half an hour, she was still wet and aching for Selene's touch.

She wasn't sure what time it was, but at this stage, she doubted that minutes or hours would mean much if Selene played with her as much as she promised.

They drove in silence. Lost in the aftermath of multiple orgasms, Vivienne barely noticed the passing landscape. She spread her knees apart a little to allow the air conditioning to cool her heated skin. Only when Selene parked did she realize they'd arrived.

Selene led her up the wooden stairs and opened the front door, flipping on the foyer light. After setting her keys in a bowl by the door, she turned to Vivienne, scanning her face, down her body, and back up again. Then she issued a single command: "Get undressed."

"Here? Really?"

"Here," Selene confirmed. "Now."

It wasn't as cold inside as it was outside, but there was a chill in the air, as if the heat had been left off all day.

Vivienne flushed but pulled off her jacket, then unzipped her dress, allowing it to fall to the floor at her feet. She stepped out of it, slipping out of her heels at the same time. Then she unclasped her bra. Selene watched, her arms folded, her lips pressed together, the edges curled up in a smile.

Naked and ready, she stood in front of Selene, burning with excitement.

Selene stepped closer and placed her hands on Vivienne's hips. In her heels, she towered over her. Vivienne lifted her chin and parted her mouth expectantly.

Selene leaned down and pressed a gentle kiss onto Vivienne's lips, and Vivienne melted into it, a cold shiver running across her. Around her waist, Selene's hand held her steady.

Too soon, Selene pulled away. "Stay here," she said, then turned and walked up the stairs. Vivienne watched Selene's hips sway at each step, her hand trailing up the banister. Then she disappeared, leaving Vivienne standing alone in the front room, She heard rustling upstairs and resisted the urge to follow her to see what she was doing; Selene had told her to stay where she was. Her clothes at her feet, she shifted excitedly from one foot to another, imagining what Selene might be planning.

But when Selene returned, her hands were empty. "Be a dear and light the fire," she said.

Vivienne wasn't sure what game they were playing, but she obeyed, kneeling before the hearth, stacking the wood, then lighting the kindling. The fire caught within a few moments, and Vivienne closed the glass fireplace doors, stood up, and turned around to see Selene reclining comfortably in the armchair with a satisfied expression.

Vivienne stepped toward her, her naked body casting a shadow from the firelight.

Selene grasped Vivienne's waist and tugged her onto her lap. Vivienne had no choice but to place one leg on either side until she straddled her. When she rested her weight, she discovered what Selene had brought from upstairs. She gasped.

"Go on," Selene said.

Vivienne tugged down the zipper of Selene's pants. Reaching inside, she pulled out the silicone toy.

Vivienne wanted to slap Selene's grin off her face at the same time as she wanted to kiss it. The strap-on pressed against her thigh. Selene maneuvered her hips until Vivienne felt the toy press first against her clit, then at the opening of her sex.

"Selene," she pleaded.

"Ask me nicely," Selene said.

Vivienne flushed with embarrassment.

"You can ask me," Selene coaxed.

"Please," Vivienne whispered.

"Please, what?" she teased.

"Please, will you fuck me with your cock?"

The words sounded filthy and terrible, and Vivienne felt awkward saying them, but the embarrassment dissolved when Selene looked at her as if she were starving and Vivienne was a feast.

Selene nodded, and for once she seemed to be at a loss for words. Then she lifted her chin, and Vivienne leaned toward her mouth. "Yes," she whispered, running her hand through Vivienne's hair.

Gasping as the toy slid deeply inside her, she sank onto Selene's lap. Vivienne moaned against Selene's mouth as she rocked her hips, and the toy filled her again and again. "*Oh*."

Vivienne grasped Selene's shoulders as she rode the strap-on, squeezing her muscles around it. She moaned, and Selene gripped her hips tighter, forcing Vivienne to grind down on the toy.

She opened her eyes to see Selene's face relax into the moment, and she flushed; she was doing that to her.

"*Fuck*," Selene said sharply, seeming to remember that she was supposed to be in control, but Vivienne saw her command slipping whenever Vivienne raised herself high and dropped down again and again and again.

Selene's nails were digging into Vivienne's hips as she tried to hold her in place. Vivienne stopped moving, leaning in closer until their noses were almost touching. "I want you to fuck me on every surface of this house so you can't go anywhere without thinking how good I look riding you."

"Vivienne."

"Don't you want to fuck me on that lovely kitchen table?"

"I'm enjoying the current show," she said, her voice trembling, and Vivienne knew she wanted to fuck her, really fuck her.

"You can do whatever you want to me. No hard limits tonight." It was a dangerous thing to say, but Vivienne knew that whatever interested Selene interested her as well. There were many things she would happily explore under Selene's guiding hand.

She began to thrust her hips up and down again, kissing Selene hard until she felt nails scrape down her thighs.

"I bet you wish you could feel this," Vivienne said between kisses.

Selene groaned. "You have no idea."

And now it was Vivienne's turn to laugh. For the past few months, Selene had been in control, but now she was in Vivienne's, and Selene was hers to play with.

She rode the shaft until Selene forced her to hold still. "Enough," she said, panting. "Stop."

The climax that had been building slipped away, but Vivienne reluctantly obeyed.

"Get off," Selene ordered. "On your hands and knees."

"Which is it? Get off, or get on my hands and knees?"

Selene set her jaw. "Get on your hands and knees before I change my mind."

Vivienne climbed off, pushing down the urge to laugh. She dropped to her knees but didn't bend over. If Selene wanted to regain control, she would have to work for it.

Selene got up and zipped her pants. The dildo disappeared into them. She slipped off her jacket and undid the buttons on her sleeves, then rolled them up.

Reaching into the jacket pockets, she pulled out a pair of leather gloves.

"Disobedience will be punished," she said. "Last chance. Bend over now, and your punishment won't be so severe."

Vivienne fought the urge to obey. She wanted to see what would happen.

Selene smirked. "I was so hoping you'd make this difficult." She stepped behind Vivienne and stroked her hair, smoothing it back, then grabbed hold and gently pulled her head back. "Do you remember your safe word?" By now, it was a familiar question, reminding her that what was to come was just a play scene. Selene would be right there if she needed her.

"I do."

And then Selene was facing her, one hand still gripping her hair, the other parting her lips. She slid two gloved fingers into Vivienne's mouth, pushing her jaw open.

"I know what you want is for me to spank you, but that would only encourage you to act like a brat." She moved closer until all Vivienne could see was the bulge in the pants. Then she nudged Vivienne's knees apart with the toe of her boot. Vivienne tried to sit up taller on her knees at the same time as she spread them. Her hands hung at her side, closing into fists.

Selene looked down at her, the firelight casting a shadow over her face. She withdrew her fingers from Vivienne's mouth, and Vivienne relaxed her jaw. Selene tugged sharply at her hair. "Did I say you could shut your mouth?"

"No."

"No, what?"

"No, my queen."

"Open up, then."

Holding Selene's gaze, she opened her mouth.

And then Selene unzipped the pants again and pulled out the toy until it was at Vivienne's eye level. "Be a good girl and clean up the mess you made."

Selene pulled her head closer to the dildo, and Vivienne took the toy into her mouth, making it as much of a show for Selene as possible, despite the embarrassment flushing her body.

She drew her lips over it and pushed her mouth forward. Selene pushed her head gently, coaxing her deeper onto it before allowing her to pull back.

And then the toy was pulled away. She looked up at Selene.

Selene smiled down at her, but it was not the smile rewarding her for a job well done. She wasn't through punishing her yet. With a quick movement, Selene released her hair. "On your hands and knees."

This time Vivienne obeyed immediately and bent over. She was drenched to the point that her wetness was sliding down her thighs.

Selene drew a gloved finger between Vivienne's legs where the wetness had dripped down her thigh.

"Whatever am I going to do with you?" Selene said with a sigh. "Ever my darling masochist, aren't you, Vivienne?"

Vivienne dropped her head and stared at the rug on the floor. Nothing seemed to be happening, and she ached for Selene even though she had been inside her more than three times already this evening.

And then gloved fingers slid inside her, the fingers pressing against her insides before they slipped out again. The gloves felt strange—wrong—inside her. And she wanted Selene to do it again.

"Do you want me to fuck you?" Selene asked.

"Yes."

Selene slapped her ass. Vivienne gasped.

"Let's try that again. Do you want me to fuck you?"

"Yes, my queen."

"Good girl."

One of the gloves Selene had been wearing dropped next to her head. And then the head of the strap-on was pressing against her center, pressing against her opening. Vivienne closed her eyes and moaned.

Selene laughed, and Vivienne opened her eyes again, realizing what she planned to do.

What happened next was going to be entirely about Selene.

She pressed into Vivienne until the cock filled her completely. Selene thrust her hips back and forth rhythmically. Vivienne responded, pushing her backside in time with her thrusts, feeling the metal of Selene's pants bite into her rear end.

"Spread your legs wider," Selene said between thrusts.

Vivienne spread herself as wide as she could even though her muscles ached.

And then Selene's gloved hand was pressing high on her back, pushing her head down until her face was against the rug, her nipples rubbing against it. The friction only increased the aching, the wanting. She braced herself with her forearms in an effort to keep her ass up.

It was a fucking meant to remind her of her place as handmaiden, and Vivienne was lost in the moment. But as the tension in her grew, she wanted to reach between her legs and stroke her clit just enough to get herself off. She knew if she did, Selene would quickly slide out of her, and the orgasm close to erupting inside her would die away, leaving her empty.

"Selene," she moaned, her muscles squeezing around the shaft. "Selene, *please*."

Without breaking rhythm and still pounding deep into her, Selene spoke in a voice that was both a question and a reminder that she was in her care. "What do you need?"

Selene stopped thrusting long enough to toss the remaining glove to the floor. Then she reached down and entwined her fingers with one of Vivienne's hands on the carpet to let her know she was right there.

Vivienne squeezed her fingers around Selene's hands to let her know she understood. What they were doing was a scene, a game, and she could make it stop if she wanted to.

But she didn't want it to stop.

She pressed her hips against Selene's again, rocking harder as she gasped for breath.

Selene pressed her mouth against Vivienne's shoulder blade, kissing it gently before sinking her teeth in.

Vivienne gasped, but the pain grounded her.

Selene, still thrusting, dropped one hand from Vivienne's hips to between her legs, stroking her clit.

She started gently, then sped up the movement, and Vivienne gasped. *"Don't stop."* And then she came in a gush, crying out, and pushed against the shaft as her muscles released. Selene caught her before she collapsed on the rug and, withdrawing from her, laid her down gently. She pulled Vivienne onto her side and lay down facing her. "Hey," she whispered.

"Hi," Vivienne whispered back.

"You are incredible, Vivienne."

"I've been told that before." She smiled when Selene laughed, her heart fluttering. "Tell me, my queen, what else do you have planned?"

"Are you not satisfied yet?" Selene asked. "And here I thought I'd thoroughly fucked you."

"I don't believe I said my safe word," Vivienne said teasingly as she pulled Selene closer. "Unless…you need to rest?"

"Insatiable." Selene leaned forward and kissed her. "I'm so very pleased that I bumped into you today."

"As am I," Vivienne said.

She'd been running from what she wanted for far too long. She didn't know if what she had with Selene was a romantic relationship or if it was only sex and kink in personal quarters. Whatever it was, Vivienne wanted it. She wanted Selene. Entirely, completely. However she would have her.

And then Selene kissed her again, and Vivienne sighed with contentment.

She'd worry about what to call this tomorrow. Tonight was about them. The details didn't matter. As long as Selene looked at her like she was looking at her now, she would stay in this sex bubble a little longer. She'd worry about her family and whether this was a good idea in the morning.

But tonight, she was giving herself permission to be selfish.

CHAPTER 13
PHOTOGRAPHY

Vivienne panted, pushing up onto her hands and knees. Selene grabbed her. "Careful," she said.

"I'm being careful!" Vivienne snapped, and then dropped down to the mattress with a groan. Her muscles were sore from holding herself at different angles.

"I told you: be careful."

"I'm fine," she huffed, then pushed herself up again, feeling the ache in her limbs. She rolled off the bed and stood up unsteadily, but as she righted herself, the discomfort shifted.

Selene was lying on her side seductively. Her hair was a mess, but her brown skin glowed through the lipstick marks. How did Selene emerge from hours of sex and kink looking like an empress who had been satisfied by her harem, whereas Vivienne mostly felt *spent*?

Maybe that was because Selene did all the fucking.

"I'm sure you remember the way to the bathroom," Selene teased.

She would have to drag herself downstairs, Vivienne realized with a groan. There were welts on her ass, thighs, and lower back, and walking down the steps would make her painfully aware of each mark.

"Do you need some help?"

"Of course not," Vivienne said. "I'm perfectly capable of walking down the stairs."

"You took a lot," Selene reminded her, and moved some of the toys on the bed, drawing Vivienne's attention to them.

They had been…zealous in their adventures, and Vivienne had only used her safe word once—as a panted plea that she could not take another orgasm. And Selene had slid out of her.

They had been playing with sex, pain, and bondage—and then more sex, pain, and bondage. Now Vivienne had rope burns on her wrist from when she'd twisted back to snark at Selene while she was tying her up. Selene had lectured her for over five minutes about how to move in ropes; it was the worst punishment of the night.

She made her way carefully down the stairs to the bathroom, biting back whimpers, then filled the bathtub with hot water and climbed in, her fatigued muscles relaxing in the warmth.

She rested her head against the tub's edge, succumbing to the bone-deep exhaustion. Then she closed her eyes.

Vivienne woke up when Selene turned off the taps. Water sloshed over the sides of the tub when she sat up. "Try not to flood my bathroom," Selene chastised and lifted the plug to let the water drain halfway.

Vivienne leaned back again. "What time is it?"

"Just past three," Selene said. "Now, scoot forward."

Selene dropped her robe and displayed herself to Vivienne. Despite their night's escapades, Vivienne shivered in anticipation. Then Selene stepped into the tub behind her and pulled Vivienne back against her.

She wanted to know how to think about this arrangement, the casual intimacy of it. How did a dom/sub relationship compare to any other type? And if this wasn't a romantic one, even if Vivienne was letting her heart slip into Selene's hands too quickly, she wanted to at least pretend for a few more minutes that this was real.

Selene put her arms around Vivienne's waist and drew patterns with her hands. Her touch was electric against her skin. Vivienne's chest tightened, and she sighed, her fear of intimacy slipping away momentarily with each gentle, loving stroke.

It had been so long since she'd shared intimacy with another person, and she realized that the ache in her chest had been loneliness. She had poured herself into her work to the point that she no longer had close friends, had no real connection with anyone who didn't need something from her. Yet, here was Selene, asking nothing of her except to relax and enjoy the moment.

"Are you still spent, my handmaiden?" Selene asked, her fingers stroking her gently.

"Mm." She was tired, but warmth was growing between her legs. "One more," she said.

"One more," Selene said and kissed her jaw just below her ear.

Vivienne felt Selene's fingers stroke her sex, and then the ache returned and she rolled her head back against Selene's shoulder and panted until she trembled from the orgasm.

Vivienne laughed as the endorphins washed over her. Selene always seemed to know what she needed. She was both a master of sex and its mistress, and Vivienne was in awe.

Only…she had never once serviced Selene. She'd attempted a few times, and every time, the woman had turned it around, binding her and fucking her.

Was it possible that Selene didn't want to be touched? Was *that* too intimate?

Selene interrupted her thoughts. "Let's go to bed," she said and stood up, reaching for a towel and then wrapping them in it together.

The bed had been cleared and all the toys put away. Selene pulled back the covers and helped her into bed. It was another intimate moment, and her chest tightened again, but she batted the thought away, reminding herself that the woman had had her entire tongue in her vagina. They were well past worrying about the implications of sleeping in the same bed.

She watched the lights being clicked off one by one, and then Selene climbed into the bed beside her just as Vivienne fell asleep.

Vivienne woke to sunlight spilling into the room, and for a brief instant she panicked: she was going to be late for classes. Then she recalled that she was on vacation and didn't have to be anywhere. Hattie might wonder where she was, but given that she'd told her she was meeting a friend for drinks, Hattie would probably put two and two together.

She turned on her side. Selene was still asleep next to her. Her hair, wild and disheveled, fell over her face.

Vivienne studied her, gazing from her nose to her mouth, noting the shape of her jaw and cheekbones before her view dropped to where one arm hugged the blankets. Selene's muscles were clearly defined. No wonder she had pinned Vivienne so easily against the wall last night.

And yet Selene looked small in the bed.

"Watching people sleep is rude," Selene murmured and opened her eyes to look at Vivienne.

"You spent an entire minute staring at my labia yesterday."

"Mm." Selene rolled onto her back and yawned. "Are you hungry?"

"Food would be good," she agreed.

Selene shut her eyes, and for a moment, Vivienne thought she was going back to sleep. But then she threw off the covers and sat up, running a hand through her hair as if to comb it into some semblance of control. Then she swung her legs over the bed, stood up, and pulled on her dressing gown. She turned to look at Vivienne. "Are you coming?"

Vivienne pulled on the other dressing gown and followed Selene down the stairs and into the kitchen. As Selene pulled eggs out of the refrigerator, she directed Vivienne to the glasses, plates, and coffeemaker. The whole scene was oddly domestic. When the food was ready, they seated themselves at the table. They sat close enough that Vivienne could feel Selene's warmth.

"Did you enjoy yourself last night?" Selene asked.

"I did," Vivienne answered, cutting into her eggs on toast.

For a few minutes, the only sound was the clatter of flatware on plates. Finally, Vivienne spoke. "Last night, you discussed an arrangement," she said, sipping her coffee. "I was hoping to get clarity about that."

"We did agree to discuss boundaries. And then I suppose I got carried away."

"We were both distracted," Vivienne said.

"Well," Selene said as she pushed her empty plate away, "what do you want out of this?"

Vivienne had hoped Selene would make the first move. Now she had to navigate her own emotions. "What are the options?" she asked.

"We can continue this as a mutually beneficial kink relationship, or we can go back to being a provider and client. Or," she said, raising her eyebrows, "we can discuss having a true romantic relationship."

"Forgive my ignorance, but what is the difference between kink and romantic?"

"In a kink relationship, I wouldn't be your emotional support, and you wouldn't be mine. If we're not dating romantically, I can't be the person who supports your emotional needs. For that you would need a partner, family member or—"

"Therapist," Vivienne finished.

Selene nodded. "And I wouldn't expect that from you either. There's also a certain level of honesty you expect from a partner that you don't expect with a kink partner, for example, if we saw each other in public."

Vivienne took a bite of food and chewed thoughtfully. Whatever her feelings, her life was too complicated for a serious relationship. For one thing, she was raising her niece, which was further complicated by the fact that the relationship would be with Claudia's principal. And despite Selene putting it out there, she had said nothing to suggest that *she* wanted a relationship. She might be simply trying to gauge what Vivienne wanted.

No, she didn't want a relationship with someone who wasn't as interested in her as she was in them. It was too risky.

"I think a kink relationship is suitable," Vivienne said, then added, "I assume this is an ongoing discussion?"

Selene nodded. "Anytime you want to go a different route, we could discuss that." For a moment, her face looked tight, and she looked away. Then her smile returned to her face. "May I assume that sex will remain on the table?"

"Yes."

"Wonderful."

"So our relationship will remain a mutually beneficial power exchange?"

"Mm. Pretty much the same thing you had before but without the exchange of money, though if you want to financially dominate me, I won't say no."

Vivienne laughed. "Well, that seems straightforward enough. And outside of the bedroom, we're no more than acquaintances?"

"From my experience, people tend to notice if you're trying to pretend there's nothing going on. We can certainly try it that way, but it might be better to say that we're friends. No one needs to know the specifics."

Friends. That would mean that she could invite Selene over her house as well. "And should I call you Anna, then?"

"My friends all know me as Selene. But you can call me Anna, though I usually reserve that name for the professional workplace."

"Do you prefer Anna?"

"Certainly not."

"Then I'll stick with Selene."

"Or 'my queen.'"

Vivienne rolled her eyes. "I'm not saying that if other people are around."

Selene looked at her thoughtfully.

Vivienne realized too late that she had issued a challenge, and there was nothing she could do to take it back. Now Selene would make her say it in a public setting at some point.

"Principal Rothschild would work too," Selene continued. "I like the idea of you squirming on my desk."

Vivienne sucked in her breath at the image, then said, "Is there anything else?"

"There is, but I'll reserve it as a surprise for later," Selene said. "Oh, one other question: are you planning to engage in romantic relationships with other people? It's fine if you are. I just need to know if you'll be having sex with other people."

"I…don't know," she admitted. "I don't usually have time to date anyone, much less be in *two* sexual relationships."

"Well, it's up to you. If it comes up, it'll be a negotiation, just like everything else. How about if we leave it as is for now, and if anything changes, we can discuss it further?"

Vivienne frowned. "What about your clients?"

"I don't have sex with any of my clients." Selene sipped her coffee.

"But you had sex with me."

"Because I wanted to have sex with you."

"Is that standard?"

"If I don't like the person, I won't offer. But you were so lovely when you showed up on my doorstep with your wide-eyed stare, trying to show bravado in a situation that terrified you."

"I was not terrified."

"Oh, but you were. You were so nervous and excited, I thought you were going to combust."

Vivienne scowled. "Hardly. I may have been…nervous"—she pushed her plate away, arranging and rearranging the dirty flatware on it—"but I was hardly terrified."

"At any rate, the decision was as much mine as it was yours."

Vivienne smiled. Perhaps Selene liked her more than she'd originally thought.

"Now that that's out of the way," Selene said, "let's move on to other things."

"What other things?"

Selene smiled, and Vivienne felt her foot stroking her calf. "I believe sex on the table was offered."

"You're insatiable."

"Oh, certainly. But you're also looking adorable wrapped in my robe, and there's nothing more I would like than to see you out of it."

Selene was trailing her gaze down to where Vivienne's robe had parted, revealing cleavage.

"May I have another cup of coffee?" Vivienne asked. "Or are you too impatient?"

"You may," Selene said and poured her a fresh cup.

Vivienne drank her coffee, then got up to take the dirty dishes to the kitchen. Selene followed at her heels, and as soon as Vivienne reached the counter, she leaned up against her.

Vivienne leaned back with a sigh, feeling the woman's mouth on her neck at the same time that the belt was plucked off from around her waist and dropped to the floor.

Selene pressed against her, kissing her throat and stroking between her legs.

Vivienne rolled her head back, her hips rocking as she clutched at the counter. She glimpsed Selene watching, but then the climax took hold and she convulsed, almost slipping from her grip.

Vivienne breathed in and out slowly, trying to ease her pounding heart. When she had recovered a little, she asked, "What time is it?"

"A little past seven. I'll need to get ready for school. Do you want me to drop you off at home?"

Vivienne considered. "No. I should pick up my car from the bar before someone tries to steal it."

"I'll go wash up." And she walked away, licking her fingers seductively. Vivienne fought the urge to grab her wrist and suck her fingers clean, just to watch the lust return to Selene's eyes with no time to satisfy it.

Vivienne retrieved her clothes from the front room and slipped on her dress, then made her way to the nearest mirror to fix her hair. When she picked up her hair to pin it, she noticed the uncovered marks on her neck and shoulders. Not only that, but the rope burns on her wrists were obvious. Although Selene had stopped binding her after the burns became too painful to clean, the welts were still red and raw.

Vivienne sighed and pulled up the collar of her dress, then pulled her coat on. She'd be stuck wearing high necklines until the bruises faded.

Selene came out of the bathroom. Vivienne followed her to the bedroom and sat on the bed, watching Selene apply her makeup.

"Will you be late to school?"

"A little, but I called Mrs. Lewis and let her know I'm having car trouble." She glanced at Vivienne in the mirror. "I'm sure the teachers can handle the children for a few minutes."

"Claudia mentioned that Luca quit the football team."

"Unfortunately, yes. I directed him to the Oakdale Community Center. They have some organized sports there. It won't be as competitive as the high school, but it's better than the toxic environment he was in before."

"And the players' parents?"

"Oh, unhappy as always. But what else do they have to do with their miserable lives? Bullies raise bullies, and I so enjoy breaking them." She picked up a lipstick and applied it. "But if you're asking indirectly how Claudia's doing, she's doing well. Her grades are steady, she has a nice social circle, and her teachers think highly of her."

"Of course they do."

Selene arranged her hair, fixing it into place with her fingers. Vivienne was surprised at how quickly she had gone from being half asleep to looking professionally done up. It made Vivienne want to return home to clean up herself.

"Have everything you need?" Selene asked, spinning around on the vanity stool and getting to her feet.

"I do."

Selene walked over and kissed Vivienne's cheek. She pulled back, cupping her face with her hand and tilting it upward to study the mark she left. "Perfect," she said.

Vivienne sighed and wiped off the lipstick, then followed Selene out.

They were quiet on the drive back to town. Vivienne fidgeted, trying to find a comfortable way to sit before realizing it would be impossible with all the welts. She leaned her head back and exhaled.

Selene laughed. "You'll be thinking about me all day."

"And plotting my revenge."

"Careful. I might call in sick if you keep talking like that."

Vivienne considered calling her bluff but decided against it. They couldn't let this arrangement affect their work.

Selene pulled up next to Vivienne's car, and as Vivienne turned to get out, she felt a tug on her jacket sleeve. "Don't forget these," Selene said, holding up the lace underwear from the night before.

Vivienne felt the blood rush to her face. She snatched at the panties and quickly stuffed them in her purse with a terse "thank you."

"Enjoy your day, Vivienne."

Vivienne hesitated, then impulsively leaned back into the car and kissed her. "You too," she said, then got out and shut the door.

When Vivienne arrived home, Hattie greeted her with a rush of questions. Vivienne glared at her, but that only prompted Hattie to ask who the friend was that she'd stayed with.

"It's none of your business."

"Well, if you have met someone new, they're more than welcome to come over for Christmas dinner," Hattie said.

Not likely. First there would be fallout from Claudia, who would melt down over Selene being in their house. Second, Hattie would grill Selene nonstop. Not to mention Selene, who would take every opportunity to make Vivienne as uncomfortable as possible by toeing the line of boundaries they had put in place.

Though she probably didn't mind the last part.

"Thank you, but I'm sure they've already made plans."

"Oh, well, let me know—I can stop at the grocery store after work."

She brushed past her sister, making her way upstairs to change her clothes. Then she went down to her home office to work on her paper.

By lunchtime, Vivienne had written a thousand new words, so she took a break and went to the kitchen for a bite to eat. When she got back, her phone was blinking with a new notification. It was a text message from Selene. Or rather a demand.

Stuck in a meeting. Send me a picture.

She twitched with annoyance. If she sent a picture, there was a chance someone besides Selene would see it.

I don't think so.

There. A simple, sharp response. She turned back to her work, but her phone buzzed again.

Take off your underwear.

Vivienne glared at the screen. She was halfway through explaining why she didn't have time to do such things when a new message arrived.

Do as you are told.

Damn her.

She glanced at the office door to make sure it was shut, pulled off her underwear, and stuffed them in her desk drawer, but not before taking a picture and sending it. Then she deleted the image from her phone. She would have to delete the entire conversation later.

She imagined Selene sitting at her desk, her legs crossed, as she contemplated a response that was likely to make Vivienne squirm.

The image made her suck in a breath. She slowed her breathing, trying to calm her pounding heart, and returned to her work. She had barely typed a single word when the phone buzzed again.

Masturbate for me.

Vivienne considered. Selene would never know if she had or hadn't. She could lie, say she had, and finish her work…

Except Selene *would* know, and Vivienne would know too. In fact, she was already worked up from the messages.

Hiking up her skirt, she leaned back in the chair and began stroking herself. She shivered at the touch, knowing she was doing this because of Selene, and she imagined the woman watching her.

Vivienne was close to relief when her phone rang. Selene's number lit up the screen. Annoyed at the interruption, she picked up the phone. "Yes?"

"Someone sounds wound up," Selene said.

"Aren't you in a meeting?"

"It finished early. What are you up to?" Selene asked innocently.

Vivienne flushed. "You know perfectly well."

"I do, but I want to hear you say it."

Vivienne squirmed. It wasn't a dirty thing. It wasn't a terrible thing. Before Selene, masturbation had been something she did often to burn off steam on long nights.

But saying it to the woman who'd had her fingers in the same place only a few hours ago was another thing entirely.

"Cat got your tongue?"

"No," she said, "and I'm masturbating at your request."

The other woman laughed. "Right now?"

"Well, no. Right now I'm on the phone with you."

"And why would that make you stop? Be a good girl and let me hear you."

Vivienne closed her eyes. Selene was under her skin, making her to do whatever she wanted, and yet Vivienne couldn't help herself. She parted her legs again and, holding the phone to her shoulder, slipped her fingers under her skirt and between her thighs, stroking herself. She bit her lip to hold back the whimpers. On the other end of the line was silence. Vivienne wasn't sure if that was good or bad.

Finally Selene spoke. "Don't hold back," she said, her voice low.

Vivienne shivered. "Selene," she gasped.

She heard Selene suck in her breath. "Where are you?" she asked hoarsely.

"Home office."

"At your desk?"

"Mm," Vivienne managed.

"Legs spread wide in your chair? What would you do if someone walked in?"

"You could find out." Vivienne had one leg on her desk, pushing with her heel against the wood. "Find out how wet I am for you." Growing bolder, Vivienne added, "You could clean it up and watch me squirm."

There was silence on the other end of the line, and just as Vivienne was about to ask if that had been too much, the other woman spoke, her voice thick with arousal. "Vivienne."

Just that one word. It was practically a plea. Then she said, breathing out the words, "You have no idea what effect you have on me," and her voice pulled Vivienne closer to climax, her gasps increasing as the orgasm built from deep within her.

"Selene, I—"

"Don't finish!"

Vivienne froze. "What?"

"What are you doing in two hours?"

Vivienne had planned to spend the afternoon working on her journal article or reviewing her class materials again or reading other academic journals, but she said, "I don't have any plans."

"Come to my office."

"What time?"

Selene paused, and Vivienne heard the sound of shuffling papers. "Four," she said.

"I'll be there."

"Good." Then she repeated, her voice firm, "Don't finish." And the line went dead.

Vivienne collapsed back in her chair as the anticipated relief slipped away and frustration built. She needed Selene, needed her desperately, needed to bend over her desk and be fucked until she pushed her away—then invited her back again.

She thought about stroking quickly between her thighs to finish, but she didn't. Her queen had commanded her, and she would obey.

She got up from her desk, dropped her drenched underwear in the laundry basket, then washed her hands, returned to her desk. and tried to focus on her article. After several attempts to push Selene out of her head, she finally managed to punch out a few hundred more words before closing her laptop.

Vivienne left a note, promising her sister she would be out for a few hours but would return in time for dinner. She intended to keep that promise; if she spent another night at Selene's, it would raise too many questions.

Vivienne drove to the high school and hurried to the principal's office. Walking past the empty desk in the outer room, she knocked sharply on the closed door, then let herself into the room.

Selene looked up from her paperwork. "Vivienne."

Vivienne flushed. Selene seemed genuinely pleased to see her.

She closed the office door behind her, making sure it locked, then sat across the desk from Selene as she had done not so long ago.

Selene set down her pen. "So lovely to see you."

"And you," she said and waited, not knowing what would happen next. Would Selene throw her onto the desk and fuck her, or would she tease her? She would be happy either way.

"I enjoyed our conversation earlier."

"As did I."

And then Selene pushed back her chair and moved around to the front of the desk. She scanned Vivienne from top to bottom and back again, as if to contemplate what she wanted to do.

"I had a plan," she said, "but now that you're here, I have half a mind to just…" She trailed off.

"What was the plan?"

Selene held out her hand. Vivienne allowed herself to be led to the other side of the desk, where Selene unzipped her skirt and tugged it to the ground.

"No underwear? How naughty." Selene pushed Vivienne into the desk chair and nudged her legs apart. Then she stood back, leaning against the edge of the desk, and smiled at Vivienne, waiting for her to start.

Keeping her gaze steady on Selene, Vivienne began to masturbate, and as soon as she touched herself, Selene's expression changed from mischievous to hungry. She watched Vivienne like nothing else in the world mattered.

Vivienne stroked, gently at first, her nervousness making her more sensitive, but soon, encouraged by the hunger in Selene's eyes, she lifted one leg to press against the desk and spread her thighs farther apart to allow a clear visual.

She panted softly at first, and then she moaned and squeezed her eyes shut as she rocked closer and closer to climax.

Just as she was about to explode, Selene pulled her hands away. Vivienne opened her eyes. Selene was kneeling between her legs.

"I thought I could just watch," she said, pushing Vivienne's thighs apart, "But the show you put on is better than I realized."

"I've had experience," Vivienne said, still trying to catch her breath.

Selene leaned in and licked Vivienne's pussy from the bottom to the top, slipping her tongue over the labia and around the clit. And then Selene slid her fingers into her.

"Oh, I do love fucking you."

"Selene," she moaned. If this kept up, she would come hard enough to squirt.

She clutched the arms of the chair, gasping for breath as Selene sucked and nipped at her. Then her legs squeezed, and she cried out, feeling a gush of wetness. She tried to pull away, but Selene held her firmly, her tongue drawing over her without letup until Vivienne whimpered again. Only after a second climax did Selene pull back, rising to her feet like a vision emerging from the clouds.

Vivienne fell back into the chair with a sigh. Ripples of the double climax trembled down her spine as her clit pulsed.

Selene stared at the wet spot between Vivienne's legs. "What a lovely mess."

Vivienne opened her mouth to respond but was interrupted by a knock at the door.

"Principal Rothschild?"

Selene set her mouth. "I'll deal with it," she told Vivienne in a whisper.

Vivienne, panicking when she realized her skirt was out of reach on the floor, pulled herself forward until she was as close to the desk as possible.

Selene opened the door, but not before wiping Vivienne's wet from her mouth. She positioned herself to block the person from seeing inside the room. "Yes?"

"I heard a scream."

"Ah, yes. We seem to have a mouse problem, Mrs. Lewis. I need you to call the exterminator tomorrow."

"I can do it now—"

"No, no. You've finished for the day. Go home and enjoy dinner with your family," Selene said. "It's nothing that can't wait."

"We should get on top of it as quickly as possible."

"I agree, but one day won't make a difference."

"Okay. Well, as long as you're all right."

"I am. Thank you for your concern. Now, if you don't mind, I have some office work to finish up. Enjoy your evening." And then she shut and locked the door.

"That could have gone worse," Vivienne said.

Selene smiled. "You worry too much. Besides, you like the danger of it."

The woman knew her so well. "Well, as fun as this has been," she said, pushing away from the desk to reach for her skirt, "I should get back to my family before they wonder where I've been."

"If you don't want them to know we're having sex, why don't you introduce us as friends? That way, if we run into each other during school events, we won't have to pretend. Unless you're embarrassed."

"No, it's not that. I...prefer my family not be a part of this," she admitted. "It's ours."

"I'm not going to become their friends just because we're friends, Vivienne."

"You don't know my family."

"Well, I'm somewhat familiar with them. Introducing me as your friend would just be a formality. Not to mention, your home probably has many secluded areas for us to continue our sexual adventures."

Vivienne flushed. She imagined Selene on her knees in her home office or naked under her desk as Vivienne spread her legs.

"Fine," she said, relenting. "You can come over for dinner."

Selene smiled. "Wonderful. Pick a night, and I'll make sure I'm available."

Vivienne closed her eyes, already half regretting her decision. She had probably agreed because of her orgasmic stupor, but when Selene smiled at her like that, she couldn't say no.

"How about Saturday night next week?" Vivienne asked. "I could arrange a small dinner party."

"I can do Saturday," Selene said, then leaned forward and kissed her, sliding one hand up her thigh and unbuttoning her blouse with the other. "Meanwhile, I have one small favor to ask." She nibbled

Vivienne's neck as she slipped off her blouse and bra, leaving her naked on the chair. She stepped back and surveyed her handiwork.

"What favor?"

Selene reached into her handbag and pulled something out, concealing it in her hand. "Would you mind if I indulged in a brief fantasy?" She opened her hand to reveal what looked like two tiny pairs of pliers connected with a jewelry chain.

Vivienne felt her face flush. "Nipple clamps?"

"Oh yes," Selene said.

"You just happen to have those in your handbag?"

"Doesn't everyone? May I?"

Vivienne shrugged, more amused than anything.

Taking the shrug as agreement, Selene took one clamp and attached it to a nipple.

Vivienne sucked in a breath. Her nipples were still sensitive from the orgasm, and although it was a pleasant sensation, it was still pain.

Selene fixed the second clamp to her other nipple.

"Is that all?" Vivienne asked.

"No," Selene said, blushing. "But it's enough for now."

"You can tell me," Vivienne said. "The worst that could happen is I'll say no."

Selene smiled shyly. "I want to photograph you with the nipple clamps on while you're masturbating. You can delete the photos afterwards. My fantasy is that I've caught you in my office playing with yourself, but then you…ask me to record you."

Vivienne felt herself getting aroused again. Had Selene asked her to do this only a day ago, she would have flatly refused. But watching the effect that masturbating in front of her had caused and seeing Selene's control slip—the idea was tantalizing.

"And if I agree, I can delete them if I want?" Vivienne asked.

"You can."

"Use my phone," Vivienne said. It would give her a sense of control.

Selene grinned. "I'll consider this an early holiday gift." She reached into Vivienne's discarded jacket and pulled out her phone from the pocket. She moved around the desk, trying different angles until she found one that satisfied her.

Vivienne propped her legs up on the desk and, sinking low in the chair, reached down between her legs. This time, she put on more of a show, and when she came, she bit her lower lip as her orgasm rocked through her.

Exhausted, she pulled her hand away.

Selene pulled Vivienne to her feet and took her place in the chair, then pulled Vivienne onto her lap and opened up the camera roll.

There were over three dozen photos. They studied them together, then Selene returned to one in particular and edited the image to a black-and-white photo. "I like this one," she said, showing her the photo. "If I could, I'd have it framed and mounted in my bedroom."

Selene had captured her face melting into a smile at the moment of orgasm as she looked at Selene. The camera angle did not show her genitals, but there was no mistaking what she was doing.

"I'm sure you would," Vivienne said, taking the phone from her hand. "But you better get me a necklace for Christmas."

"Anything you desire," Selene murmured and pressed her lips against Vivienne's mouth.

CHAPTER 14
DINNER PARTY

Vivienne peeked around the newspaper at Claudia. Her niece was happily devouring a stack of pancakes.

She knew she should tell Claudia that she was friends with her principal, yet all Vivienne had managed to say so far was that she was having a few people over for dinner and the family was welcome to join them.

In order to fill the slate of guests, she invited Florence over, and then, at Florence's request, she invited Janice, who was Florence's friend. Vivienne didn't want to refuse her request, despite her dislike of the woman, especially since Janice had been so kind to her after her mother's funeral.

Now she had three guests and three family members. Then Claudia asked if she could invite Henry, which made it seven, and then Hattie asked to bring Jonathan. So now they were up to eight.

Vivienne had to plan the menu, buy groceries and wine—then get her sister and Claudia to help, or Vivienne would end up doing all of the cooking herself.

Eight people. And all because she wanted people to see that she and Selene—no, Anna—were friends.

On Saturday morning, Vivienne and Hattie began prepping the food, and by four, the house smelled of lamb, roasted potatoes, and grilled vegetables. Vivienne had just enough time to shower and dress. She fiddled with her jewelry before deciding on an emerald set that complemented her dress. Then she hurried downstairs to make sure the white wine was in the fridge and the red wine was set out to decant.

When the first guest arrived, Claudia answered the door. Henry stood frozen, looking wide-eyed at the adults. Then he held out a bouquet of flowers. "Um, I didn't know what to bring."

"Thank you, Henry," Vivienne said, accepting the flowers. She took them into the kitchen, put them in a vase with water, and placed them in the center of the dining room table.

The doorbell rang again. Vivienne turned to open the door, but Claudia beat her to it.

"Ms. Rothschild?"

"Claudia," Selene said and held out a bottle of wine. "Hattie, lovely to see you."

"Anna!" Hattie said, then quickly recovered from her surprise and smiled. "It's lovely to see you. Viv didn't tell us that you were her mystery friend."

Selene glanced at Vivienne. "Didn't she?"

Vivienne felt her face grow warm. "Well, now that you're here, there's no need for introductions."

"When did you and Ms. Rothschild become friends?" Claudia asked.

Vivienne hesitated. She'd prepared an answer, but now it felt flimsy.

"Your aunt and I keep running into each other," Selene said. "She thought I was a parent until we met to discuss the fight."

"Oh," Claudia said. She furrowed her brow as if she wasn't happy with the situation.

Vivienne couldn't blame her. It was one thing for your aunt to know people in town because she taught them. It was another thing for her to be good enough friends with your principal that she invited her for dinner.

"I brought wine." Selene held out the bottle.

Vivienne accepted the offering and glanced at the label. Not so expensive as to raise questions, but not cheap either. "Thank you. It will go perfectly with dinner."

Florence and Janice were the last to arrive. Florence apologized profusely for being late.

"It's not a problem," Vivienne assured her. "It's good to see you. You're just in time."

They gathered around the table, food was served, and wine passed around.

Vivienne began the conversation by asking Florence and Janice about their plans for the upcoming winter break.

"Elijah and I were planning to travel," Florence said, "but I think it'll be too difficult with the twins, so we might just stay home."

"I had plans with my mother," Janice said, "But that's all gone now. I'm not sure how I'll spend Christmas."

Selene turned toward Janice. "Do you have any siblings?"

"No, I'm an only child."

"It must be hard to lose a parent when you're an only child."

Janice smiled tightly. "You do the best you can. It'll be my first Christmas without my mom."

"But you have the memories of all the previous Christmases with your mother. That won't make it easier, but it might ease the ache."

"Did you lose your mother too?" Florence asked.

"I never really knew my parents," Selene said with a shrug. "They died not long after I was born. But in the end, you make your own family."

"Did you have foster parents?" Vivienne asked.

She nodded. "My parents had only recently immigrated to America from Israel, so there was no one to take me in. I've been on my own since I was sixteen."

"I didn't mean to pry," Florence said. "It's just that you spoke of loss as if you knew what it was like."

Selene looked down at her plate. It was clear to Vivienne that she didn't want to discuss her pain, but no one else at the table seemed to notice. And the way she fidgeted in her seat told Vivienne that she didn't know how to say that.

Vivienne jumped in. "I'm sure we've all lost someone close to us," she said. "Losing my brother and his wife still hurts when the holidays come around. Anna's right. The memories we carry of the people we love and the time we spent together remind us of how precious our time is. And the pain reminds us that we still carry love for them in our hearts." It was a sappy speech, but it broke up the gloomy mood. After that, the conversation drifted to lighter subjects.

As the meal concluded, Vivienne glanced at Selene, who was staring off into the distance. She leaned in and asked just loud enough for everyone to hear, "Would you help me get dessert ready?" And excusing themselves, they picked up their glasses and went into the kitchen.

The dinner party seemed far away. Vivienne studied Selene, who still seemed sad and preoccupied. Vivienne ached for her, but she knew better than to ask. When Selene was ready, she would reach out, and it would be on her own terms.

Selene straightened up and took in a breath, returning to the moment. "I apologize. I didn't mean—"

"There's no reason for you to apologize. You did nothing wrong. Everyone else seemed to forget social decorum and dove into your history as if you were some sacrificial poet."

Vivienne opened the fridge and set the dessert on the counter. Nothing needed to be done with it, but she didn't want to go back to the party just yet.

Selene looked awkward, as if she didn't know quite what to do with herself.

"I did warn you," Vivienne said, trying to lighten the mood. "My family are gossips." She peeked out into the dining room, then smiled at Selene. "You know, it will probably take them a while to notice we're missing. I could show you around my home."

"Show me around?"

"I've seen your office. It's only fair that I show you mine."

Selene brightened. "And just what does Vivienne Carter's office look like?"

Vivienne took her hand and led her to an alcove off from the kitchen, where a large oak door concealed a separate room. She glanced back at Selene before opening the door, as if the room were a secret place reserved for the elite.

In a sense, it was. She didn't normally permit guests into her office, and her family knew better than to enter it when she wasn't there.

She led Selene inside, then stepped aside to let her look around. She closed the door, clicking the lock loudly into place.

Selene turned to face her. "Presumptuous."

"I didn't want any interruptions. But if you want something, we'll need to be quick."

Selene gave a short laugh. "I'm sure there'll be time yet. You're giving me a tour of your house, after all."

"Am I?"

Selene didn't answer but instead studied the books and photos on the shelves. Her back still to Vivienne, she said, "Take off your underwear."

"Is that how we're going to play it?"

"I won't tell you twice." Selene glanced back at her then, and despite the command in her voice, her eyes sparkled.

Vivienne slid her hands up under her dress, sliding the lacy black panties down, then stepped out of them and picked them up. Selene snatched them from her grip.

"You'll need to be quiet," Selene said, stepping in closer. "Can you be quiet for me?"

Vivienne looked at her curiously.

"I ask because you were rather vocal in my office, and I doubt claiming a mouse problem here would be so easily believed."

"I can be quiet."

"Let's see. Otherwise, I might just have to use these," she said, holding up the lacy panties.

"You won't need to."

Selene leaned forward and kissed her greedily, biting and sucking, demanding everything Vivienne had, and Vivienne reveled in it. She caressed Selene's shoulders and ran her fingers through her hair.

Selene gripped Vivienne's hips, pushing her back until she was against the wall. Then she pulled back and, holding Vivienne's gaze, tugged her dress up, then reached down and began slowly sliding her fingers over her folds.

Vivienne closed her eyes and rolled her head back.

"Uh-uh. Eyes on me," Selene said, pulling Vivienne's head away from the wall. "Look at me, Vivienne."

Vivienne obeyed.

"There we go," Selene said, teasing Vivienne with slow, deliberate strokes. Aren't you just delicious." Then she pressed deeply into her, one hand stroking inside as the other held her firmly against the wall.

Vivienne whimpered.

"Be quiet. We don't want anyone to hear."

"I am—"

The last word was choked off as Selene wrapped a hand around her throat, pinning her still. "Open up," she said and pushed the black panties into Vivienne's mouth and held it closed.

Selene's hand on her throat was firm but still allowed for breathing. With each swallow, she felt her muscles pressing against Selene's palm. But if she whimpered, the hand grew tighter, reminding her.

It was painful but erotic to the point that Vivienne pulsated between her legs.

She had engaged in light choking in the past, but with Selene fucking her while holding her throat, Vivienne forgot there was a world outside of this room, outside of Selene. And she never wanted Selene to let her go. She choked back her whimpers and moans as she drew closer and closer to climax until, at last, she squeezed her pussy around Selene's fingers.

When Vivienne had caught her breath, Selene pulled out the gag. She had a strange expression on her face that reminded her of their session a few weeks ago, when Selene had made her climax against a knot on the rope.

Selene stepped back and looked away. Vivienne studied her carefully. "Selene, whatever it is, you can talk to me."

She looked at Vivienne. "I like you a lot," she said. "It's…been awhile since I've been so interested in another person."

Vivienne nodded. "It's been awhile for me too."

And then Selene smiled, but there was a sadness to it, and for a moment, Vivienne thought she might cry. But then Selene blinked, and the mask was back. "I'm sorry for—"

"You have nothing to apologize for." Vivienne reached out and took Selene's hand. "We don't have to go back out there."

"It's your dinner party," Selene reminded her. "What would people think if the hostess disappeared?"

"I don't care what any of them think. I didn't do this for them." Realizing she'd revealed too much, she let go of Selene's hand and glanced away. "What I meant to say was, the whole point of this dinner party was for us to show my family that we were friends."

"Why did you hide it from your family in the first place?" Selene asked.

"I—didn't know how to tell Claudia. But I'd hardly say I hid it. I merely…delayed telling them."

"Are you so worried about whether Claudia approves?"

Vivienne squirmed at the question. The answer was yes. She cared what Claudia thought of her. Deep in her heart, she knew why, but to admit it to herself, let alone Selene, made her feel too vulnerable.

"You're not…ashamed of—"

"No! I'm not ashamed. I…wanted more time of it just being about you and me."

"It still is," Selene said. "Why do you think that will disappear if Claudia and your family know?"

Because things are good as they are now, she wanted to say. And if her family got involved, they would ruin it. Not on purpose, never on purpose, but they always did. "Is it so wrong to want you all to myself?"

A strange expression crossed Selene's face, as if she were looking for deeper meaning in Vivienne's words.

Vivienne flushed. "I only meant—"

"I know what you meant." Selene stepped back and crossed her arms over her chest protectively.

"No, I don't think you do. Selene, I'm a private person. All my life, my family has thought of me as an emotionally repressed, ambitious… hussy," she said, using Hattie's word. "I want one thing separate from them because inevitably they'll show you how…broken I am, and you won't want anything to do with me then."

"Do you think you're broken?"

"Certainly not," she said, "but…" She wasn't sure how to explain it. "They have a way of bringing out the worst in me. When I was younger, I had a reputation for having a very active sex life, and that reputation has followed me my entire life. Even when I began teaching at the university, there were rumors about me sleeping with graduate students. And on top of that, my family thinks I'm selfish, and they're always trying to find out what I'm up to and…" She stopped to take a breath to center herself and remember what she was trying to say. "*This* is good. Whatever this is, it works, and I don't feel ashamed of it. But I don't want other people's perceptions to make it into something it isn't."

"You're worried people will find out and think you're some kind of deviant for engaging my services?"

Vivienne shrugged, unable to explain why she needed to keep this side of herself separate from the rest of her life.

"I'm not going to air your dirty laundry, Vivienne," Selene said. "But I do want to be your friend."

"We are friends."

"Are we?"

Vivienne frowned. "What makes you think we're not?"

Selene smiled. "You're right. Of course we are." She glanced at her watch. "I should go home before it gets late."

"Stay for dessert at least?"

"For dessert," Selene agreed.

Vivienne opened the door and led Selene back to the dining room, then made her way back to the kitchen to prepare dessert service.

When she brought in the dessert tray, Selene was talking about Renaissance art. She was smiling brightly, but the expression didn't quite match her eyes.

The rest of the dinner party passed uneventfully. Vivienne served dessert and coffee, after which Henry and Claudia disappeared upstairs. The grown-ups moved into the living room to discuss recent bestsellers, but Vivienne could barely follow what they were saying with Selene sitting next to her on the sofa, pressing her thigh against hers.

And then the guests left, and the house was empty again.

"So, you and Anna?" Hattie asked.

"Pardon?"

"You and Anna are friends?"

"Oh." Vivienne nodded. "New friends."

Hattie nodded approvingly. "Well, she's all alone here. I'm sure she needs a friend just as much as you do."

Vivienne excused herself and went upstairs. She was tired after entertaining, but that didn't stop her from thinking about how Selene had looked when she pulled away. Vivienne was familiar with that kind of pain, And if Selene wanted to talk about it, she would.

She showered, changed into her pajamas, and climbed into bed, her thoughts still running wild. Just as she was about to turn off the light, her phone flashed with a message.

Thank you for tonight. I enjoyed the evening.

Another message quickly followed.

That Janice woman's a bit strange, though. How did you two end up as friends?

Vivienne quickly wrote back that she was not friends with Janice and had only invited her because Florence asked her to.

While Vivienne waited for Selene to respond, her phone rang. "Selene?"

"I owe you an explanation about my behavior tonight."

"You don't owe me anything."

"I do. Before I moved to Oakdale, I was with someone. We were planning for the rest of our lives when she died in a car accident. Mary—" She choked back a sob. "She was good. She reminded me to ask for what I wanted, and then she was gone. I moved to Oakdale to escape the life we had planned, and I went back to what had once brought me joy. I started up my dominatrix service again, and I met you."

Vivienne waited for Selene to continue. Was she crying?

"I lied to you about a few things when we first started. I do have a few regular clients that I've always had, but there's no one like you,

Vivienne. There's no other client that comes close to what I…permitted with you."

"Oh, Selene," Vivienne said, then something occurred to her. "Did you slip your business card into the book I bought?"

"I did. I was in the bookstore that day and noticed you reading the cover of the latest bestseller. You walked away briefly, and I slid the card in, hoping you'd come back and pick it up. And you did."

"How did you know I would call?"

"I had no idea if you would or wouldn't. I knew nothing about you except you were quite beautiful. I understand if you feel misled."

"I don't. You didn't force me to call you. I did it myself, eagerly."

"And then you came back for a second session," Selene said, all trace of sadness gone.

"Selene…" Vivienne hesitated, not sure for a moment if she should ask what was on her mind. "Why don't you let me touch you?" The words spilled out.

"Sorry?"

"When we're having sex," Vivienne said. "You never let me touch you. You always pull away or distract me with sex and kink. I enjoy those things, but—"

"You don't have to prove anything to me, Vivienne."

"Why do you think I need to prove myself? Should I be proving something?"

"No, I only meant that…I understand if that's not something you *want*," Selene said. "Sex isn't about taking turns. It's about equal pleasure, and I've always preferred giving the pleasure rather than taking it. Believe me, it's a thrill watching someone come undone by your hand. It's a personal preference."

"I'm good at giving pleasure too, you know."

"I have no doubt," Selene said. "But it's been a long time since I let anyone touch me like that. Still, if that's what you want—"

"I only want it if *you* want it."

Selene chuckled. "I'll keep that in mind for next time."

They didn't speak for a moment, then Selene said, "Well, I won't keep you up any later. I'm sure you have things to do with the holidays coming up."

Hattie did most of the Christmas preparations. Only Vivienne's work kept her busy. "Do you have any plans for Christmas?"

"No, I don't celebrate Christmas."

"Hanukkah, then? Doesn't that begin tomorrow?"

"I light the candles for Hanukkah, but that's all. I don't follow religious practices much these days."

"You're not spending the holidays with anyone?"

"No. Why would I?"

"Because it's the holidays. Shouldn't you be spending it with family and friends?"

"I've spent many holidays alone, Vivienne."

"You're coming to my house, then. Claudia is spending the holidays with a friend, so we'll have an extra place at the table."

"But—"

"It wasn't a request," she said, interrupting.

"Well, how can I refuse an order like that?"

"You can't." Vivienne smiled. Tonight might have almost been a disaster, but she would make sure Christmas was not.

"Fine. Then I'll spend Christmas with you."

"Good," Vivienne said. *As it should be.*

CHAPTER 15
CHRISTMAS

Vivienne spent Christmas Eve making sure Claudia had everything she needed. Then she returned home from dropping her off and casually mentioned to Hattie that Selene would be joining them for Christmas dinner, explaining that Anna had been planning on spending Christmas alone. Her sister choked up and promptly agreed.

When Selene arrived around eleven the next morning, Hattie was midway through meal prep. Vivienne took advantage of her absence to press a kiss against Selene's lips the minute she walked in. "Hello."

"Hello," Selene said. "Is this where you excuse yourself to show me around again?"

Vivienne laughed. "Later. I have other things to do first, and you're at the bottom of that list today."

"I'm sure I could find my way on top."

Vivienne rolled her eyes, then took Selene's bag and hung her jacket on a hook. Then she laced their fingers together and led her into the dining room, giving hand a final squeeze before dropping it and entering the kitchen.

"Oh!" Hattie pulled off her oven mitts and kissed Selene on the cheek. "Lovely to see you, Anna."

"Thank you for the invitation."

"You're perfectly welcome. But I can't take credit—that was all Vivienne."

"Indeed." Selene turned to look at Vivienne. "She insisted that I didn't spend Christmas alone."

"No, that would have been dreadful. And we have plenty of food," Hattie said. Shooing them out, she added, "No need to loiter in here. I'm sure you can find other things to do."

If Vivienne didn't know better, she would have suspected that Hattie knew something.

"We'll set the table," Vivienne said, retreating back to the dining room.

"Put some Christmas music on while you're at it."

Vivienne grimaced.

"Not a fan of carols?" Selene asked.

"Certainly not."

"But it's Christmas," Selene said. "You don't want people to think you're a grinch, do you?"

"Does it look like I live in some cave?"

"Oh, my apologies. I should have said a Scrooge."

"Bah! Humbug."

"Well, despite your dislike of Christmas, I hope I get to unwrap something later."

Vivienne smiled. "Careful," she warned, her voice low. "You may be my queen, but this is my domain."

"And what happens in your domain if someone acts up?"

"Do you want to find out?"

"Desperately."

Vivienne selected some CDs of traditional Christmas music, and her heart lifted when she turned to see Selene smiling at her.

"Is there something on my face," Selene asked, "or are you just caught in the rapture of my beauty?"

Yes, she wanted to answer, but instead she said, "Let's go set the table. Then would you like a drink?"

"What do you have?"

"Hattie made apple cider from an old family recipe. Or if you prefer, we can open up a bottle of something."

"Cider sounds nice."

They set the table, then returned to the kitchen, where Vivienne ladled out cider for the three of them. They chatted for a while, then

Hattie said, "Meat's done and the salad's ready. I'll put the pie in the oven to warm."

"Quite a feast," Selene said as they each picked up a dish to carry out.

They adjourned to the dining room. Vivienne sat next to Selene, and Hattie sat across from them. As they ate, they talked about the weather, their work, and Claudia's school as Christmas carols played softly in the background.

After dessert and coffee, Hattie pushed herself away from the table. "I'm stuffed. And tired."

Vivienne knew how hard her sister had worked preparing the meal. "Why don't you go relax in the living room? Se—Anna and I will clean up and put everything away."

"You sure you don't need help?"

"You cooked, Hat. It's the least we can do."

"Oh, well, all right, then," she said. "I'll go set up the movie."

"This was lovely," Selene said after Hattie left the room.

"You're not leaving yet, so don't even think of making an excuse."

"I wouldn't dare."

They began to clear the table. "We usually open Christmas presents after lunch, but since Claudia left yesterday to spend the holidays with friends, we decided to open them early. I have one for you, though."

"I have one for you as well."

Vivienne looked at her slyly. "And what exactly is your present?"

"It's a surprise," Selene said. "And what's yours?"

Vivienne carried a load of plates to the sink. "It's more for myself."

"Is that so? What is it?"

"You'll have to wait and see."

They finished putting the food away, loaded the dishwasher, and wiped down the counter.

"Were your sister not so close," Selene said, "I would bend you over right here."

Vivienne smirked. "And what makes you think I wouldn't have done that to you first? You'd look lovely spread out on the dining room table."

Selene dropped the carving knife she was drying.

Vivienne bent down to pick it up. "You know, I'm very handy with a knife."

"Are you now?" Selene said and glanced at the door. Then she grabbed Vivienne by the hips and kissed her.

Vivienne melted against her in the lingering kiss, then stepped back and laughed. "Be good," she warned.

"And if I'm not?" Selene asked.

"Then I'll find a wooden spoon in one of these drawers and I'll strong-arm you into my office."

"That sounds like encouragement to me."

There were so many things Vivienne wanted to ask her for. Her niece was far away. The island counter would hide them if Hattie came into the kitchen. There was no reason not to make Selene service her here and now.

But that would be wrong.

They returned to drying and putting away the pots and pans, a comfortable silence between them. But when Vivienne peeked at Selene from the corner of her eye, she felt the words rising in her throat, the need to tell Selene that she loved her. She pushed them away. They were happy, she reminded herself. What they had together now was enough. She didn't need to ruin it by telling Selene her feelings.

They finished cleaning up the kitchen and hung the dish towels to dry. And then they were swaying together, Selene resting one hand on Vivienne's hip, the other pulling her into a waltz as Elvis sang "Silver Bells" in the background. Selene was looking at her as if she'd never been so happy.

It had been a while since she'd danced with anyone. "So you thought you'd dance with me for a change of pace?"

"I did," Selene said.

Then Selene was spinning her. Laughing, Vivienne wrapped an arm around her waist.

"Oh, I see," Selene said. "So this is when you lead?"

"My domain," she reminded her, waltzing around the kitchen. "I used to be quite a good dancer."

"Of course you were. You went to boarding school, didn't you?"

"And what do you mean by that?"

"Just that Vivienne Carter never ceases to surprise me about the many things she knows."

"You're not so bad yourself," Vivienne responded, and it was true. Selene was a graceful dancer.

"Mm. Well, we did take some dance classes for our wedding. Mary was a better dancer, though. She took to it naturally."

"You would have been a beautiful bride," Vivienne said. "She was fortunate to have known you."

"Have you ever married?" Selene asked.

"My devotion to work was too much for anyone who might have proposed."

"Their loss," Selene said. "Anyone would be lucky to have you."

Vivienne responded by spinning her around again. "I would say the same about you."

"Mm."

Vivienne was about to say something else when Selene suddenly let go, looking at something behind Vivienne.

Vivienne turned. Her sister was hovering at the entry to the kitchen, a stunned look on her face.

"Don't mind me," Hattie said, recovering from her surprise. Then, making her way to the fridge, she took out a bottle of water and hurried out.

Vivienne waited for panic to set in, but it didn't. If anything, she was relieved. Hattie had seen them, and after an awkward moment, she acted as if nothing was unusual.

And just like that, the moment of intimacy was over. Vivienne poured two glasses of cider, and they made their way to the living room. Hattie was reclined in her usual chair, her legs on the ottoman and a quilt pulled over her lap. She was already nodding off. A movie played at low volume, and the fire had burned down to embers.

Vivienne pulled another quilt from the closet and sat next to Selene on the couch, draping the quilt over them both. Hattie knew anyway, and she no longer cared. It was Christmas, and she was happy. And she wanted a proper relationship with Selene. For the first time in her life, Vivienne was ready to make space for someone else so she could sit next to Selene in the open, hold her hand if she felt like it, and flirt with her openly. She wanted to be able to kiss her, take her out to dinner in public, and fall asleep listening to her heart.

When the movie finished, Hattie stirred. "I'll make some hot chocolate, hmm?" And she got up, stretched, and made her way to the kitchen.

Vivienne stood up, gathered the quilt, and led Selene to the back porch, wrapping the quilt around them against the cold.

"So," Selene said, "I couldn't help but notice how…cozy you were with me."

Vivienne took a moment to steady herself. "May I be honest?"

"Of course."

"I…like you a lot. I don't want whatever this is to be just an arrangement. I want to be in a relationship. With you."

"A relationship?"

Vivienne nodded, turning to look at the sky. Clouds were moving in, and it felt cold enough to snow. "You don't have to agree, but if you do, I need to make sure Claudia is okay with it. Or we can keep it as it is, but I—"

"Vivienne." Her name was a whisper in the night.

She turned to face Selene again and was rewarded with a kiss. Basking in the taste of her, she lost herself for a moment, then pulled away. "Does that mean you also want this?" Vivienne asked.

Selene laughed, her breath a fog in the cool night air. "Yes," she said. "Now, invite me upstairs, and I'll show you the Christmas present I bought you."

"Are you wearing it?" Vivienne asked, scanning Selene's body.

"No, but now I'm intrigued as to what you think it is."

They went upstairs to Vivienne's bedroom and shut the door. Selene looked around the room, and Vivienne wondered if she was going to start rifling through her drawers.

"Don't even think about it."

"Think about what?" Selene asked coyly.

"Touching things."

"And whatever will you do, Professor Carter, if I were to touch things?"

"Try it and find out."

"I need to visit you in your own domain more, if this is how you act."

"Tired of seeing me on my knees?"

"Never," Selene said. She walked over and put her arms around Vivienne's waist. "Do I get to unwrap my present now?"

Vivienne laughed. "You asked me here to give me my gift, or have you forgotten?"

Selene stepped back, pulled out a long, thin box from her pocket, and handed it to Vivienne. The gift was wrapped in emerald paper and tied with a ribbon.

Vivienne removed the ribbon and gently unpeeled the wrapping, taking care not to tear it.

"Oh," Selene said, "you're one of those people."

"Careful, or you won't get your present."

"By the time you finish unwrapping, it'll be morning and no longer Christmas."

Vivienne rolled her eyes. Then setting the wrapping paper aside, she opened the box and gasped.

Inside was a necklace, a chain made up of gold loops the size of nickels. It was long enough to hang between her cleavage. It was beautiful.

"This is known in the kink community as a day collar," Selene said. "I was planning on…officially asking if you would enter into an exclusive relationship with me, but it seems that you asked me first."

"You were going to propose monogamy?"

Vivienne handed Selene the necklace, then turned around and pulled her hair forward over her shoulder. Selene fastened the chain and pressed her lips against Vivienne's skin.

Vivienne turned to face her. "There's something to be said for monogamy," she said. "I won't ask you to give up your work, but I want to be the person you come home to."

Selene smiled. "I should hope you wouldn't ask me to give up my job. It would be rather strange if you asked me to stop being a principal in order to date you."

"No, I meant—"

"Vivienne, I closed my dominatrix service days ago. I only went back into the business because..." She paused, a pained look on her face. "Because I was lonely, and it was a way to feel intimacy without damaging Mary's memory."

"If it hurts, we don't have to do this. We can—"

"You don't listen, do you? I want this. I want you. There's only you, Vivienne."

She looked at Selene, imagining their lives together. Christmas, Hanukkah, Thanksgiving, Valentine's Day. Birthdays and anniversaries. Weekend getaways or travel to other countries.

The thought should have terrified her, but then she leaned forward and pressed her mouth to Selene's, feeling the necklace slide between her breasts.

Selene reached around, grabbed the necklace from behind Vivienne's neck, and gave it a tug, pulling Vivienne away from her. "You want to know my favorite part about this? There are attachments that go right...here," and she tweaked Vivienne's nipples through her clothes.

Vivienne grabbed at her breasts. "How did you do that?"

"I have a gift of always knowing where a woman's nipples are. You wouldn't believe how handy it is."

"I can imagine. Now it's my turn." She turned around and, going to her dresser, picked up an envelope. "I thought about this before I realized how much I"—she paused, not quite ready to say the word *love*—"wanted to be with you," she said.

Selene sat on the end of Vivienne's bed and accepted the envelope. "Did you write me a love letter?" she asked. "Or something filthy?"

Vivienne flushed. "Certainly not."

"Too bad. I've never had any erotic poetry written about me."

"I was thinking about the Girlfriend Experience," Vivienne said, "and I very much wanted to visit an art museum with you. So I looked around, and there's a show on Pre-Raphaelite art that opened in the city last week. I thought you might like to show me around."

Selene grinned. "Did you plan the Girlfriend Experience for New Year's Eve?"

"I did, but I still need to speak to Claudia. I just thought in the meantime—"

"I love it," Selene said. "How many days?"

"We'll leave Thursday, come back Sunday morning. I'll pick up Claudia that night, and…" She trailed off and moved to sit next to Selene on the bed.

Selene opened the envelope. There were tickets to the exhibition, confirmation of the hotel booking, and a printout of a restaurant menu. She looked at Vivienne. "What would you have done if I had said no?"

"Gone by myself," Vivienne said, "or taken Florence. It's…" She coughed, not wanting to admit that she had planned it as a birthday gift to herself. She could always find someone to visit the museum with her and have dinner afterwards. There was no reason either of those things had to be romantic.

But she wanted them to be.

"I like that you printed out your travel plan. I expect you'll take it with you in a folder," Selene said, stuffing the papers back in the envelope.

"Don't be rude," Vivienne said, though she would do exactly that.

"Or what?" Selene asked. "You'll punish me?"

"I just might," Vivienne said, accepting the invitation.

She quickly moved to straddle Selene's lap and kissed her, sliding her hands over her shoulders. Selene moaned and tossed the papers aside.

Vivienne glanced to see where they'd been tossed. "You could treat my present with respect."

"They're only papers," Selene said, kissing Vivienne's neck and throat. "I'll be on my most wicked behavior for you on the weekend." And then she lay back, pulling Vivienne with her as she unzipped her dress.

Vivienne stood up and let her dress fall to the floor, then reached down to undress Selene. When their clothes had been thrown to the floor, she settled again on Selene's lap.

"What do you want?" Selene asked as she stroked Vivienne's thighs. "You could sit on my face."

Vivienne laughed nervously, suddenly shy. "I—" She gulped.

"We can do whatever you want. I'm not judging you."

"I...I want to lead. but only if you want that. Last time you—"

Selene leaned up and kissed her briefly. "I would very much enjoy that, as long as you live up to your boasting."

"I will," Vivienne promised and kissed her deeply. She kissed her jaw, her neck, and down her shoulders. Then, pressing Selene onto the bed, she kissed down her body as if in worship, kissing her breasts and down to her abdomen. She listened to Selene's breath draw in and out, speeding up a little with each beat of her heart.

She wasn't sure if Selene wanted teeth and nails and a passionate romp, but right then, all she wanted was to taste every inch of Selene's body, listen to her breathing, and feel the moans vibrating in her throat. She wanted to see her skin prickle with anticipation. And more than anything else, she wanted to watch her hands dig into the sheets.

So Vivienne went slow, pressing her mouth between Selene's thighs and gripping her hips to hold her steady. She kissed over her center, licking between the folds of her labia, tasting the nectar of her arousal. Selene sighed and reached down to comb through Vivienne's hair.

As Vivienne stroked with her tongue more firmly and eagerly, Selene's hips began to rock in sync, her thighs clenching around Vivienne's head. Soon they moved together in a slow-building tempo.

Vivienne loved Selene, and that made it easy to stroke and kiss her, tasting every inch of her. She ran her hands up her hips and pulled her more firmly onto her tongue. Moaning between her legs, she heard Selene gasp in response.

Vivienne loved her. She'd give her anything she wanted. She would reach out to the skies and pluck the moon if Selene wanted to wear it around her neck. But she couldn't tell her that, so she caressed her over and over with her tongue as Selene's hips rocked against her head and she came with a loud gasp, Vivienne's name on her lips.

Vivienne moved up and kissed her lips once more, then pulled away to look at her, and Selene stroked her face gently. "I see it wasn't empty boasting," she teased.

"I'm not done with you yet," Vivienne said.

"Are you sure? It's getting late?"

"I'm sure. I would like it if you stayed."

"If I stay overnight, your sister will know without a doubt."

"I don't care. I just want you."

"You could steal a girl's heart by saying that."

Vivienne kissed her again, then pulled back to rest on her side. "There's one other thing I want," she said, lazily drawing a pattern on Selene's hip. "After all, you are my queen."

"I am," Selene agreed. "Tell me, handmaiden," she said, tugging on Vivienne's new necklace, "what is it that you desire from your queen?"

"A queen deserves a throne," Vivienne said, "and what better throne than her handmaiden?"

"Are you asking me to sit on your face?"

"I am."

Selene laughed and sat up. "How can I refuse such an offer?" She tilted her head to look at Vivienne. "You don't need to be gentle with me."

"Oh—" Vivienne felt the blood rush to her cheeks.

"Don't get me wrong. I needed gentle for the first time since Mary. But I trust you. And I would very much like to see what you have to offer."

"But you do like it rough?" Vivienne asked to make sure she understood.

"I do."

"And you want that now?"

"Only if you do."

"I'll see what I can do. I might need to work up to being as good as you."

"I won't ever ask you for something you don't want to do. You can always refuse."

"Sit on my face, and we'll discuss after that."

Vivienne lay back on the bed, pushing her hair off her face.

Selene scooted up and cocked one leg to the other side of Vivienne's head. She gripped Vivienne's hands in hers as she settled onto her mouth.

Vivienne worked her tongue eagerly, wanting nothing more than to taste Selene again and again, to make her shake and shiver and cry out.

"Oh, *fuck*," Selene gasped, letting go of Vivienne's hands to grab the headboard.

And still Vivienne licked and probed. The first time was a declaration of love. This time was to prove how wicked her tongue could be, a way to make Selene forget where she was.

As Selene approached orgasm, Vivienne pulled her deeper onto her face, alternately licking her labia and sucking her clit, dragging her teeth dangerously close as if to warn her what she was capable of.

And just as Selene was drawing close, she slid two fingers inside her, pressing in deep.

Selene pulled Vivienne's hair, tugging her head closer, closer, closer, and Vivienne sucked harder, swirling her tongue around her clit as she continued stroking inside. Knowing she could take more, Vivienne slid a third finger inside her.

Selene gasped. "I'm going to get you for this. I'm going to fuck you to within an inch of your life after—" But she couldn't finish, and she tossed her head back and cried out, her body jerking rhythmically.

Vivienne pressed her mouth harder and continued stroking until Selene gasped and cried out again, "Fuck, Vivienne" as a rush of warmth spilled across her tongue and face.

And then Selene fell onto the bed next to Vivienne, breathing heavily. When she could breathe normally, she looked over at Vivienne and said mockingly, "Might be something you need to work up to? You are mine, Vivienne Carter, and you will regret saying that."

"You didn't enjoy it?" Vivienne asked innocently.

"Oh, I did, and now that I know how well you can use your mouth, I'll fuck it until I've dragged out every missed orgasm."

Vivienne grinned, licking the wet around her mouth. "I'm yours to command."

Selene smiled wickedly. "Spread your legs," she ordered.

Vivienne did as she was told. She didn't care if her tongue went numb or if her muscles burned with exhaustion. She would service Selene until dawn, if that's what her queen wanted.

Selene raised herself to her knees over Vivienne. "You've ruined the holidays for me. I hope you know that. I'll expect this from you every year."

Every year. Vivienne sighed happily. It was going to be a long night.

CHAPTER 16
DISAPPROVAL

The day before Vivienne was to leave for her weekend away with Selene, Hattie called to say that Claudia was home early. Apparently, Mrs. Walter had a business emergency, and they had cut short their vacation.

Vivienne ended the call. "Claudia's home," she said, returning to Selene's bed. "I need to go home and see her."

"You could stay for a little while longer," Selene suggested. "Another hour, perhaps?"

It was tempting, but… "I should prepare for tomorrow, and so should you. And I need to speak to Claudia."

"She'll say yes to us. She seems to like me enough. And she knows it's important to you."

Vivienne buttoned her shirt and combed her hair with her fingers. "I'll call you tonight."

"Or you could come around again."

"I need to spend tonight with my family. But if Claudia agrees, maybe you could spend more time with us."

She leaned down to kiss Selene one last time, and Selene responded with decadent passion, making Vivienne want to crawl back to bed. Reluctantly, she pulled away. "Soon," she promised. "I'll see you soon."

"You'd better so I can have my way with you."

Hattie was out when she arrived home. It was a perfect opportunity to have a private conversation with Claudia.

She knocked on her door. Her niece opened it and frowned.

"Claudia. How was your vacation?"

"Fine," she answered, setting her jaw and folding her arms across her chest.

Puzzled at the curt response, Vivienne asked, "Did…something happen?"

"You lied to me. You—" She hesitated, as if considering how much to say. "Aunt Hattie told me you're dating Ms. Rothschild."

Vivienne froze. "We've been seeing each other, and we are looking to…move to the next stage."

"How long have you been seeing each other? Was it just at Christmas"—Claudia scowled—"or longer? Is that why you've been disappearing at night for meetings and drinks? Is that why you invited her to dinner?"

Vivienne paused. Considering all the evidence Claudia had placed before her, it would be hard to deny that they had spent a significant amount of time together since mid-September, when Vivienne had first hired Selene. "Yes."

A look of horror crossed Claudia's face that quickly dissolved into hurt. "Why would you lie to me?"

"Because—" She stopped herself from revealing the full extent of the truth. "Because I didn't know how she felt about me. And I wanted to be sure that she wanted the same thing that I did."

"Which is what? A relationship?"

Vivienne nodded. "Yes."

"No. You can't."

Vivienne blinked. not really believing that Claudia would disapprove. "Claudia, she's a good person. I care for her. I'd appreciate it if you'd at least consider giving us your blessing."

But Claudia was adamant. "No, not her. Ms. Rothschild is my principal. You can date anyone else."

"But Anna is a good person, a kind person. If you need more time, we can—"

"Aunt Vi, please! I've never asked you not to date anyone else, even when I thought they were wrong for you!"

Speechless, Vivienne could only shake her head.

"It's not fair to me! What if you guys break up? What if Ms. Rothschild starts treating me differently? What if the rest of the school finds out?" Her eyes had filled with tears. "You said if I ever had a problem with someone you were dating, you would listen to me! You promised! She's my *principal*. You can be with anyone but her. Please."

She was right. It was a solemn promise she had made. Vivienne didn't care about what people at the school thought, but that wasn't fair to Claudia, who had to be there every day. Students would mock and bully her relentlessly. And if any parents found out, the way Anna treated Claudia, no matter how unbiased, would be seen as favoritism.

Besides, what kind of example would she be setting for her if the one promise Claudia was begging her to keep was the one she broke? And it was true: Claudia had never asked Vivienne not to date someone.

"Okay," she finally agreed, the word a lump in her throat. "I won't…I won't see her anymore."

She felt like she had swallowed a rock. Her throat was raw, and there was a weight in her stomach.

She and Selene were not going to date after all. They were going to break up, and every moment she'd imagined in every possible future was gone before it began.

Less than an hour ago, Vivienne had pulled herself from Selene's warm bed and sweet kisses, promising to return to her soon. And now she dreaded seeing her again, having to say no, she didn't have Claudia's blessing, and she couldn't see her anymore.

She turned to walk away but stopped at Claudia's next words.

"At least it wasn't serious."

She turned to face Claudia. "I beg your pardon?"

"Your relationship. At least it wasn't serious."

Vivienne smiled tightly. She could admit how much she loved Selene but thought better of it. Claudia was headstrong. Vivienne didn't have the energy to get into a fight she could never win without completely overriding Claudia's feelings and self-preservation. "I'll… tell her tonight," she said before turning away.

She made her way downstairs to her car and pulled out of the driveway, but when she reached the next street, she pulled to the curb and burst into tears. She cried until her sobs turned into hiccups. Then, pulling herself together, she fixed her makeup and drove to Selene's house.

What was she going to say? How to tell someone that you love them but can't be with them? She would have given Selene the world if she wanted it. But the only person she loved more than Selene was the girl she considered her daughter.

An hour. That was all it had taken—one hour for her to go from happily in love to heartbroken.

She pulled up to Selene's house and sat in the car for a few minutes to collect her thoughts. She knew that to be fair to both of them, she would have to make it a clean break, but that didn't make it hurt any less.

Sighing heavily, she made her way to the front door. Her heart and hand felt heavy as she knocked.

Selene opened the door, her face lighting up until she saw Vivienne's tear-streaked face. "What happened?" she asked and stepped aside to let her in.

Vivienne hesitated. Maybe she should give her the news right here so she could leave quickly, but Vivienne wanted these last few moments. She stepped in.

Selene shut the door behind her. "Is Claudia okay?"

Vivienne nodded, blinking back fresh tears. Looking up at the ceiling, she tried to remember the words she had rehearsed on the way over.

She had to break off the engagement. She had broken off a half dozen relationships before, and they had all been hard in their own way, but this one felt wrong because, for the first time, she wasn't doing it for herself. She loved Selene and was confident that Selene loved her back.

Finally she choked out the words. "I don't have Claudia's blessing, so we can't..." She swallowed. "I can't see you anymore."

Selene tilted her head, puzzled, then she began to laugh. "That's ridiculous," she said. "Your niece can't—"

"She begged me. *Begged*. She's never—" Selene reached out, but Vivienne stepped back out of reach. "I promised her," she continued. "Many years ago, I said if she said no to someone I was interested in, I would break the relationship off."

"I don't understand. Doesn't she want you to be happy?"

Tears spilled down Vivienne's cheek. When she spoke again, her voice was strangled. "And I am happy, but I promised her."

"I'm sure the promise you made doesn't apply here. Whatever her objections are, she'll get over it."

"No," Vivienne said. "No, Selene. I *promised*."

"But—"

"No."

Selene began pacing the room. "Then I'll talk to her. I'll explain that—"

"You'll do no such thing!" Vivienne snapped. "She would never ask this of me unless she had a good reason. I will honor her request."

"That's ridiculous, Vivienne. Can you hear yourself? You're letting some sixteen-year-old girl decide your happiness. For what?"

"For family! She was an orphan. Her heart was broken when her parents died, and I'm all she has left. Not Hattie, *me*. I'm her family. And if she asks this of me, then so be it. I will keep my promise. She needs to know that promises matter."

"But that's bullshit! I fucking love you. We're happy. I don't understand why that's not enough for her. What more does she want?"

I love you. Vivienne's heart broke all over again at the words she had been waiting to hear.

"There's nothing else she wants," Vivienne said.

"There must be something your niece wants that she can make you give this up."

"No," she said. "Nothing. I made her a promise. It's as simple as that."

Selene shook her head. "It's not fair."

"I know." Vivienne took Selene's hands. "Selene, I lo—"

"Don't. Please." And then she broke into sobs.

Vivienne took her in her arms, kissing her again and again until Selene began undoing the buttons of Vivienne's jacket. Slipping it off her shoulders, she pushed Vivienne against the wall and pulled off the rest of her clothes. She stepped back to pull off her own before pressing against Vivienne and kissing her hard.

But Vivienne pushed her away, and they fell to the ground, bumping a side table and knocking its contents off. A painting fell from its hook, but Vivienne didn't care. All she wanted was Selene.

The sex was hard and rough. If Vivienne bit too hard on Selene's shoulder and Selene's nails dug in too sharply, they simply kept going, marking each other as if they could leave a permanent array of half-moon indents and scratch marks on the skin forever.

And still it didn't feel like enough.

Selene's moans hummed against her, and when she gasped, Vivienne kissed her harder. And then Selene was crying out as she came around Vivenne's fingers, her thighs trembling. And then she did it again, only this time Selene snarled and flipped Vivienne over, working her hand and mouth until Vivienne exploded once, twice, three times. Then she shoved the woman's hands away and tried to catch her breath. She knew if she allowed herself to linger, if she stayed to listen to the woman's heartbeat, she'd never leave. So she kissed Selene for the last time, got up quickly, and dressed.

She pulled on her jacket and opened her mouth to speak, but Selene interrupted. "Don't say it," she said. "It would be cruel to say the words and still choose to leave."

Vivienne turned away and slipped out the door, leaving as fast as she could before she could change her mind.

How was it possible to love another person so much and feel so safe in their arms?

She got into her car, pausing just a moment to study her reflection in the mirror, feeling shame wash over her. Then she started the engine and pulled out of the driveway.

CHAPTER 17
BIRTHDAY

Vivienne took a breath and stared at the calendar. It was her birthday. The word settled over her like a fog. She had expected to wake up in Selene's arms and spend the day tangled in the sheets.

She closed her eyes and tried to push away the rising wave of pain, but the thought of facing her family, today of all days, only magnified her agony.

When she had arrived home last Friday, she'd canceled her vacation, shredding the itinerary in a rage before breaking down into tears again. Her sister looked at her curiously when she told her about the canceled plans but didn't press for details, and Vivienne didn't offer any. She didn't want Hattie to know the truth about Claudia's request.

Hattie had come home from grocery shopping on Saturday to find Vivienne still in her room with the door closed, refusing to speak to anyone. Sunday, she had feigned illness and declined to come down for dinner. Hattie could draw her own conclusions. The last person she wanted prying into her business was her baby sister.

She stayed in bed the entire weekend. She got up on Monday to shower and realized that she still wore Selene's necklace. There was no point in returning it now, even if she could face Selene, so she buried it in her top dresser drawer.

She dressed and ate breakfast before anyone else awoke, then shut herself in her home office to work on next semester's curriculum.

Hattie had planned a family dinner for the three of them at one of Oakdale's nicer restaurants, and Vivienne found herself hoping that

Selene would be there with some excuse and she would get to see her again. But that wouldn't happen.

Her heart ached.

"Viv?" Hattie knocked on her office door and, without waiting for Vivienne to respond, opened the door and walked in. She glanced at her red eyes, then gave her a bright smile. "Happy birthday!" she said.

Vivienne smiled half-heartedly.

"I came in to remind you that we have reservations for your birthday tonight. Are you still up for that?"

She wasn't, but it would only worry her family if she shut herself in her room on her birthday and chain-smoked a pack of cigarettes. "Of course I am."

"And will your friend be joining us?" Hattie asked.

Vivienne clenched her jaw. "No, it will just be the three of us."

"Oh. I thought—"

"I know what you thought," she snapped.

"Oh, Vivienne. Whatever happened, it can be fixed. Even things that are broken can be fixed with time and hard work."

Vivienne shook her head. "Not this," she said, blinking rapidly to hold back her tears.

"But you both seemed so happy at Christmas. I thought—"

"Drop it!"

Hattie flinched.

She turned away guiltily. "Now, if you don't mind, I have some work to do before classes begin next week."

"Of course. I'll...I'll check in with you later."

She spent the rest of the day working until Hattie knocked to remind her that they needed to leave in an hour.

Hattie drove. It was unusually quiet in the car, as if everyone was afraid to touch a nerve. Vivienne stared out the window, trying to bury the hope growing in her chest. If Selene showed up at the restaurant, if she made a case that this was what she wanted, maybe, just maybe, it would be enough to convince Claudia.

They made small talk at dinner. Vivienne tried to engage in the conversation, but she kept glancing at the door. Twice she brightened up when she saw a woman with thick, dark hair enter, and twice she realized her mistake.

She considered reaching out to Selene and suggesting they engage in a quiet affair, but she couldn't betray Claudia like that, and she wouldn't ask Selene to become secretive again. It wasn't fair to either of them. And besides, as much as she wanted to spend her days with Selene, she wanted more to set an example for Claudia about the importance of keeping promises.

Claudia, noticing her distraction, asked, "Are you okay?"

"I'm fine, Claudia," she said. "Behind on work."

"Oh. Is there anything I can do to help?"

It had been some time since Claudia had offered to help. There was once a time when Claudia would help calendar her curriculum, making sure that exams and assessments didn't overlap. "No, I should be caught up soon," she said, "but thank you."

Claudia smiled. "You know, we could go to the market this Sunday."

"I'd like that," Vivienne said.

Her niece was trying. It didn't soothe the heartbreak, but it was nice to think that her relationship with her niece might return to the way it was before the beginning of school.

And then the server was bringing out a cake with sparklers, and her family was singing "Happy Birthday" to her.

She loved her family, but it seemed that they got to live their lives doing what they wanted while Vivienne made all the sacrifices. Realizing that the dam was about to break again, she stood up. "Excuse me."

Hattie, just about to cut the cake, looked up. "But—"

"I need a cigarette," she said and, picking up her jacket from the back of the chair, slipped out of the restaurant. She pulled out a cigarette and lighter out from her jacket pocket, leaned against the restaurant wall, cupped her hand around the cigarette, and inhaled deeply.

She half expected someone to follow her out and check on her, but they left her alone. It would be the perfect time for Selene to appear, as if fate were bringing them together, but that didn't happen either.

She finished the cigarette and ground the butt beneath her shoe. She knew the heartache would lessen over time, but this breakup was wreaking havoc with her emotions. She hadn't cried this much since her high school sweetheart had lied to her friends about his sexual conquest. The lies continued to damage her reputation for years, painting her as a frigid bitch who only spread her legs to climb the social and professional ladder. Over the years, she had trained herself not to care what people said. Selene at least understood her ambition and treated her sexual desires as something to be proud of rather than ashamed of.

Would she ever find anyone else as encouraging and supportive?

Wiping her tears, she looked up at the night sky and tried to find a reason to keep moving forward. In school, she'd had her teacher and her studies. Now she had her family and her career. And yet it didn't seem like enough. Something was missing, and that something was Selene.

She knew that one day her heartache would lessen and she would be able to think about this time without breaking. For now, she would have to pretend.

CHAPTER 18
LOVE

Vivienne spent the rest of the week holed up in her office, preparing for classes. When the semester started up again, she threw herself into her lectures. She was determined to appear as a woman absorbed in her work.

Except it wasn't true. At night, her thoughts of Selene, and what might have been, kept her awake, tormenting her with loneliness. As mid-February approached, Vivienne became painfully aware of advertisements for candy and flowers.

Valentine's day.

It wasn't a day she normally looked forward to, and she was prepared to ignore it until Claudia reminded her one evening that she and Henry would be going to the school dance that day.

"Will your Aunt Hattie will be chaperoning the dance like she did last year?" Vivienne asked.

"If that's all right," Claudia said.

Vivienne felt her stomach clench as she realized why Claudia was asking permission. "I don't see why not. Anyway, Hattie has already agreed, hasn't she?"

"She has, but the school can find someone else if…if you're uncomfortable with…."

"For goodness' sake," she had said. "It's fine. Hattie and…and Anna were friendly before I even met her. They can push past any awkwardness."

She turned back to her computer but had only managed to write a few words when Hattie knocked and bustled in without waiting for a response. "Just thought I'd remind you that Claudia has a cheerleading event this Saturday for the basketball team."

"I won't be able to attend, but I'll try to make the finals."

"What about dinner?" Hattie asked with a hint of sarcasm. "Will you be able to attend that tonight?"

Lately, Vivienne had skipped the family meals. Claudia often stayed at Henry's, which meant that it was usually just her and Hattie. She felt the guilt settle in. Hattie had shown a lot of patience with her lately, and she needed to sit down with her for a meal. "I will."

Hattie beamed. "Wonderful! I'll cook a casserole, then."

Vivienne sighed. There was a reason she was avoiding her sister. More than once, Hattie had asked her about the reason for the breakup, and the last thing she needed was her sister prying into her business, offering advice or, worse, trying to fix it.

It had been over two weeks since she had last seen Selene, two weeks since their breakup—if you could call it that, since they'd never formalized their relationship. At first, Vivienne had checked her phone repeatedly for messages and agonized over whether or not to text her. Then she had searched her room, looking for any excuse to see her before she stopped herself: any contact at this stage would only make things worse.

Yet, when the phone buzzed, Vivienne grabbed it hopefully until she realized that the text message wasn't from Selene but from Abigail, asking if they could meet later that week to discuss her assignments.

Vivienne brushed her feelings aside and responded. She resolved to refocus yet again, taking one step at a time.

Claudia had been in a bad mood all week, and it seemed worse when she returned from the basketball game on Saturday. She stormed through the house, stomped up the stairs, and slammed the door to her room.

Vivienne exchanged glances with Hattie, who had come in behind Claudia. "What happened?" she asked.

PRINCIPLE DECISIONS

The basketball team played a prank at the game. It made the school look very, very bad. Anna was furious and canceled the game, defaulting to the other team what would have been an easy win for Oakdale High."

Vivienne's heart fluttered at the mention of Selene's formal name. "How bad was it?"

"Bad." Hattie grimaced. "They targeted the trans and gay students."

She pushed down the wave of nausea that rolled through her. "And Luca? How is he?"

"He took it better than I did. He only went to the game to support Claudia, but I doubt he'll do that again." Hattie paused. "It looked like the cheerleaders were involved. There's no way Claudia or Rebecca would have been, but the others..."

Vivienne glanced up the stairs.

"I'll go check on her," Hattie said weakly.

"No, I will," she said. "I imagine you've already said your piece."

She knocked softly on her niece's door. "Claudia?" When there was no response, she opened the door.

Her niece sat on the bed with her arms wrapped around her legs. Her eyes were puffy. Her cheerleading uniform was in a pile on the floor.

Vivienne sat on the bed next to her.

"It was awful," she said, her eyes filling with tears again. "It was a targeted attack, and Luca thinks I was involved. But it was the other cheerleaders! They made up a routine when Rebecca and I weren't there about balls belonging on the court and not on gays, and..." She stopped to blow her nose. "But I didn't know, I swear! I had no idea. When they started the chanting, Bec and I had no idea what they were doing."

"I know," Vivienne said. "You would never target your friends like that."

"I'm so angry, and Luca thinks I'm part of it, and I don't know what to do. How...how can I convince him I wasn't?"

"I think with time, he'll realize that you weren't a part of it. But right now, he's hurt, and he's reacting to what happened."

"But I would never—"

"And deep down, he knows that. All you can do is give him some time before you reach out to him."

Claudia wiped her eyes, then nodded. "I hate this," she said. "I don't want to be a cheerleader anymore. I know you said—"

"Quitting may be a good option if the other cheerleaders are doing things like this. You could look at joining the LGBTQIA+ Alliance, or perhaps start your own group. I know these issues can be difficult to navigate."

"You said I should look at extracurricular activities for college. Or maybe I should just join a study group."

She kissed her niece's head. "You don't have to do anything you don't want to. But sometimes the best way to take action is by showing those who were targeted that you don't stand with the bullies."

Claudia nodded.

"Now, how about you come downstairs? We'll have some hot chocolate and watch a movie together. As a family."

"Don't you have work to do, though?" Claudia asked.

"It can wait."

Claudia turned to Vivienne for a hug. "Thank you."

Vivienne lifted her arms and held her niece tight.

―――○―――

Less than a week after the cheerleading incident, the school called Vivienne.

"Ms. Carter? It's Mrs. Lewis."

"Yes?"

"Principal Rothschild would like to see you. There's been an incident at the school with Claudia."

"What happened?"

"It's better if you discuss this with Principal Rothschild."

Vivienne's heart flipped. It would be the first time seeing Selene since the breakup, and from the phone call, it sounded like it wasn't for anything good.

When Vivienne arrived at the school, it was immediately apparent what had happened. The hallways were strewn with toilet paper, and pro-LGBT graffiti covered the walls.

She made her way down to the principal's office and pushed the door open.

Her niece sat outside Selene's door with her head bowed. A bruise was forming on one cheek. She looked up at Vivienne with reddened eyes and then glanced away.

Vivienne looked at Mrs. Lewis. "May I go in?"

The woman nodded.

Vivienne took a deep breath and tried to steady herself. Then she pushed the door open and stepped into the room, shutting it behind her.

Selene looked up unsmiling from her desk. Her eyes flashed. She gestured for Vivienne to take the chair across from the desk.

Vivienne was struck with a sense of déjà vu. She took the seat, setting her handbag down beside her, and clasped her hands in her lap to wait.

"Thank you for coming," Selene said without warmth.

Vivienne nodded. "I saw the mess. I take it Claudia was involved with whoever caused it."

"Clearly."

Vivienne swallowed, unsettled. She'd never seen Selene this angry. Usually, she would have her own harsh words, but sitting before Selene like a chastised schoolgirl, she felt as if she were the one who had wreaked havoc in the school.

"It seems Claudia has…become a ringleader in a protest movement. Just this past week, she organized a walkout of students. Then she called for all sporting events to be canceled, which resulted in her friends getting into a fight with other students."

Vivienne took a deep breath. This behavior was entirely on-brand for Claudia.

"Multiple witnesses agree that Claudia was the one who started the worst fistfight, and given everything else and her own confession, I believe that the only good option is expulsion."

"Expulsion?"

"What other choice do I have? She organized a school walkout that disrupted classes, then instigated a school-wide fight. Would you allow this to stand if it were another student?"

"You can't expel her. She was standing up for her friends, fighting to defend them after that horrendous chant on Saturday."

"And Claudia taking matters into her own hands has made it all the more difficult to deal with that. Before this incident, students had agreed to come forward, which might have led to the expulsion of whoever organized the chant, but now they've all decided they don't know anything. So the students who participated will walk away with a slap on the wrist."

"You cannot be serious! There were hundreds of witnesses at the game!"

"There were witnesses to the cheerleaders' chant, but the basketball players claim they had no idea that their jerseys displayed the slur. They claimed someone had switched the jerseys without them knowing. Selene scowled. "I had planned to cancel all sporting events, but now I can't. It would look like I'm giving in to a protest. The most I can do is cancel the school dance, effectively punishing everyone else involved. But Claudia will still be expelled."

"But expulsion isn't fair to Claudia. It will affect her ability to get into college. She thought she was doing the right thing."

"I'm sure she did, but it doesn't excuse the damage she caused. The cleanup will need to be paid for out of the school's budget. Not to mention there's the escalation of tensions in the school. Your niece has thrown gasoline onto a fire."

"I'll pay for it," Vivienne said. "I'll pay for the cleaning. She can be suspended and serve detention for the rest of the year. Please, out of respect for us—"

Selene snarled. "Don't drag *us* into this."

"She could lose everything!" Vivienne pleaded. "Expulsion will affect the rest of her life. You're closing doors that can never be opened for her again, no matter how hard she works."

"She should have thought about that before she did this! Actions have consequences, as you are well aware."

Vivienne's anger flared. "So her life is ruined by one well-meaning screwup? That's not fair, and don't give me some life's-not-fair bullshit. I get that you're angry, but for fuck's sake, can't you take your anger out on me instead? Claudia is *sixteen*!"

Selene stiffened. "You think Claudia's punishment is because you broke up with me? That I'm, what, doing this for revenge?"

Vivienne glared. Like hell she was going to let niece's future be blown away by one screwup. "You tell me," she snapped.

The words landed between them like deadweight. Too late, Vivienne wished she could take them back.

"Are you fucking kidding me? I gave you everything, Vivienne. I waited patiently until you were ready, and if you had told me that you didn't want to continue because you didn't care for me, I would have accepted that. But you broke up with me because some sixteen-year-old was jealous."

"That is not why I broke up with you, and you know it!" Vivienne snapped. "Don't you remember what it was like to be sixteen? How every embarrassment feels like the end of the world? You're her principal! She didn't want fallout from her peers."

"I loved you," Selene said, tears filling her eyes. "And you gave that up on a teenager's whim, but *I'm* the bad guy because I am doing what any principal in their right mind would do?"

"Selene, I'm—"

"Get the hell out of my office! And don't bother trying to contact me."

The words shattered what was left of Vivienne's heart. She picked up her handbag with as much dignity as she could manage and stepped out of Selene's office, closing the door behind her. She blinked to stop her tears. Deep down she had hoped that Claudia would change her mind after a few months and Vivienne could go back to Selene, but now that door had closed.

Stepping into the outer office, Vivienne gestured for Claudia to follow her.

When they got in the car, Vivienne sat for a moment with her hands on the steering wheel, trying to keep them from shaking. The memory of Selene's snarling face was imprinted on her memory. Vivienne wanted to run back and tell her so many things to change the conversation. She wanted to tell her how much she loved her.

"Aunt Vi?"

She blinked and turned to look at her niece. For a moment, she'd forgotten she was there.

"What were you thinking?" Vivienne asked her, remembering her role in Claudia's life. "A protest?"

"You said—"

"I said to join a group and show your support that way."

"I did! I joined the alliance, and we agreed to protest. Then we got other students, and…" She trailed off. "I thought it would help. I thought it would be a peaceful protest, but the other kids were saying awful things, and I got angry. Then it got out of hand."

Vivienne shook her head. "Claudia, there are so many ways to protest without causing damage. I saw the graffiti. Why didn't you speak to me about this?"

"We've been planning it for a while, back when Lucas was first getting bullied," Claudia admitted. "Then he joined the other football team, and he seemed happy, so we dropped it. But after the basketball game, I wanted to show them that they didn't have the loudest voice. And what's wrong with protesting? Lots of people do it!"

"You protest when people aren't listening. Did you even speak to your principal?"

"No, but she wouldn't have listened!"

"You don't know that. She might have suggested other actions that would have gotten the result you were after." Vivienne took a breath. There was some logic to Claudia's plan, however misguided. "Do you understand how you've made things worse?"

Claudia slumped in her seat. "Principal Rothschild could still cancel sporting events for the year."

"No she can't, Claudia, because you made that a demand. If she canceled them now, it would look to parents as if she's caving to a student who caused school damage."

"But—"

"No. She can't. When you're older, you'll understand that politics is complicated."

"She said she was going to expel me."

Vivienne nodded. "She will. It's the only option she has left."

Claudia began to cry. "I'm sorry. I didn't think—"

"And that was your mistake," Vivienne said sharply. "You didn't think. You didn't ask for an adult's help. Instead, you and your friends acted on their own, and people got hurt. There is always a place for protest, but there are other ways to make a change. Your principal might have helped you, but you didn't even try to speak to her." She reached out and touched her niece on the shoulder. "You used to like her. What changed?"

Claudia looked out the car window. "I thought you and Ms. Rothschild weren't serious, but when I heard you yelling in there, it sounded like you liked each other. A lot."

A lot. That was one way to put it. "The relationship was complicated, but it's over now."

"Because of me."

"Because you asked me to end it. It doesn't matter now, though. Anna doesn't want me back. She doesn't want anything to do with me."

Vivienne started the car and pulled out of the parking lot. "I don't want to discuss this again. What's done is done. We can only move forward."

When they arrived home, Claudia jumped out of the car, threw open the front door, and ran up the stairs. Vivienne went to her office, mulling over what needed to happen next.

They would have to find Claudia a new school. The other public schools were not as well-regarded as Oakdale High. Maybe they could get her into a private school.

There was no point in working now. Grabbing her cigarette and lighter, she headed for the back porch. She stopped when she heard whispering.

"I didn't know this one was different," she heard Claudia say. "She seemed like she was just—"

"You weren't here at Christmas," Hattie cut in. "Anna convinced Viv to dance. In our kitchen."

"Aunt Vi doesn't dance."

"I saw it with my own eyes. They were in the kitchen waltzing like the rest of the world didn't exist. They didn't act like two people in the early stages of a relationship. I don't know when it happened."

After a pause, Claudia said: "I think I messed up."

"You didn't think about how what you wanted would affect your aunt. Now you know for the future," Hattie said and, ever the optimist, added, "Maybe they'll be friends again one day, but it's not easy to recover from a heartbreak."

"There has to be some way to fix this."

"Claudia, it sounds like Vivienne made it clear that Principal Rothschild was no longer interested. She'll move on. Your aunt will find someone else."

"But Aunt Vi hadn't dated anyone seriously in years."

"I know."

Vivienne turned back into the house with a sigh. Claudia's acceptance of the relationship had come too late.

She returned to her office and tried to make herself work, but she ached too much. She shouldn't be so hurt. After all, she had her family, her work, and a few friends. What difference would a romantic partner make?

It was no use. She wanted Selene in her life desperately, even as a friend.

CHAPTER 19
GOOD GIRL

Claudia mostly stayed home for the next three days, only leaving to work in the bookstore with Hattie. Vivienne spent the time reviewing different schools and making inquiries.

She could send Claudia to a private school if she paid extra to make it worthwhile. She could also transfer her to another public school. She gave Claudia the options, told her to review everything so they could set up meetings.

At the end of the week, Claudia appeared at her office door, looking sheepish. "I spoke with Principal Rothschild," she said. "She said I could come back—but I would have to pay for the damages myself out of my own money, and I would have to serve detention and donate time to a charity. Which is fine and fair. I also have to make a public apology."

Vivienne raised her eyebrows. "She let you back?"

Claudia nodded. "I set up a meeting through Mrs. Lewis and apologized. You were right. I didn't want to speak to her because I thought she would be biased after you and she had broken up. But she wasn't. She was actually…fair."

Claudia opened her mouth as if to say something more, but then she closed it again and clasped her hands behind her back.

"I'm proud of you," Vivienne said. "You took ownership of your mistake and were willing to accept the punishment."

"Well, I didn't want to be separated from Luca, Rebecca, and Henry. And she is nothing like our old principal."

Vivienne agreed. Principal Mitchells had often been difficult to deal with, and there had been a few occasions when she had wanted to take Claudia out of Oakdale High. But Claudia had insisted on staying.

"Did she really demand you pay for the damages?"

"No. I offered, and I offered to clean up the mess, but it had already been cleaned up. So I offered to pay for the cost from my own money to show that I understood the responsibility and… Well, you know the rest."

"I'm pleased that it worked out. But don't try anything like that again."

"I won't. I'll speak to her next time. Anyway, Rebecca and Luca have already been discussing a few things with her that we could do to change the culture, so I might help with that."

Vivienne smiled. "Your parents would be very proud of you. Perhaps you should consider a career in politics. Like your father."

Claudia beamed. "I just might. I might run for student council next year to see if I like it."

"That sounds like a good focus."

Claudia lingered, as if she had something else to say.

"Yes?" Vivienne asked.

"Could you pick me up after work tomorrow?"

Was Claudia trying to spend some time bonding with her? "If you like."

"It's just this once," she said and bounded from the room.

Vivienne exhaled a long, drawn-out breath. Now she didn't have to worry about getting Claudia into another school, and Hattie would not need to join a different PTA.

All that was left was for her to keep moving forward, one step at a time, one day at a time.

Vivienne pulled up at the bookstore just past five thirty and got out of her car, still mulling over Claudia's success. Maybe Selene had been right. Maybe Vivienne should have put her own happiness first, should have fought for it as much as Claudia had fought to return to school.

She pushed open the door to the store.

"Vivienne."

She blinked. Selene stood in front of her, still dressed in her work clothes.

Vivienne stuffed her hands into her pockets so Selene wouldn't see them shaking. "I'm just here to pick up Claudia. I didn't know you would be here. I'm sorry," she said and moved to step around her.

"Wait!" Selene said, reaching out to take hold of Vivienne's wrist. "Vivienne, I was…rude to you last time we spoke. I was hurt—not that that excuses it—and I may have been harsher than I should have been." She dropped Vivienne's hand and looked away. "What I'm trying to say is that I'm sorry."

Vivienne was close enough to Selene to smell her perfume. The scent made her want to run as far away as possible and at the same time take her in her arms. She smiled through the awkward feeling. "I appreciate that," she said and then added, "For what it's worth, I'm sorry too for how I spoke to you and what I said."

Vivienne stared at Selene, unable to find words. Her heart was pounding. "I…"

Selene shifted her weight. "It was good to see you, Vivienne."

"Wait. Why are you here?" Vivienne asked. It seemed like too much of a coincidence.

"I'm here to pick up a new textbook we're considering for the senior class. Hattie went to check the back to see if it's in."

At that moment, Hattie appeared.

"Anna, the book isn't— Oh, hi, Viv. What are you doing here?"

"Claudia asked me to pick her up."

"Tonight? But I gave her the night off. She's out with Henry for Valentine's Day." She turned back to Selene. "Anna, I checked the order, but the book isn't in yet. Are you sure someone called you?"

"Yes. Claudia said—" Selene looked at Vivienne.

It seemed that Claudia was still meddling in things.

"You know what, I must have been mistaken," Selene said. "I'm sorry to have bothered you."

"Oh, no bother at all. I'm sorry you came all this way for nothing. I can check on the status for you."

"No, it's fine," Selene responded. "I should be on my way, then," and she brushed past Vivienne.

Vivienne glanced at Hattie, then turned to catch up with Selene as the door closed behind her.

"Selene."

Selene stopped and turned around. "Yes?"

"Did you want to get a drink?" Vivienne asked. "Not at the same bar as last time, but maybe…we could go back to your place."

"Mine?"

Vivienne pulled her shoulders back. She may as well double down on what Claudia had started. "I know Claudia said she spoke to you, but I think it's only fair if we do too. Clear the air."

"Clear the air," Selene echoed, then said, "Sure. Will tomorrow work?"

"Tomorrow works. What time?"

"How about if we meet for coffee around ten?" And giving Vivienne a small smile, she turned and walked away.

Vivienne knocked on Selene's door and tucked a loose strand of hair behind her ear. She was as scared now as she had been all those months ago when she first engaged Selene's services.

When Selene opened the door, Vivienne caught her breath at the familiarity of the moment. "Hello," she said softly.

"Hello," Selene replied and stepped aside to let her in. A pot of coffee and cups were already set out on the coffee table. Selene motioned for Vivienne to sit on the couch next to her, leaving space between them, and poured coffee for both of them. Then she sat back. "Your niece came to my office the other day."

"And she apologized and managed to convince you to let her back in school."

"She made some good points, and she offered to fix the damage that had been caused."

"I understand she paid for the cleaning out of her own pocket."

"And she volunteered to do some charity work. I had her speak at assembly about what happened. She was well-spoken and sincere." Selene smiled. "At the end of our meeting, she said she regretted asking you not to see me. I understand you have always kept your word with her, perhaps to a fault." Selene sipped her coffee. "She also told me how much you'd given up since her parents passed."

Vivienne met her eye. "I'm not a martyr. I've only ever tried to give Claudia what she needs and the love she deserves."

"I don't think you give yourself enough credit. I understand better now the position you were in when you promised her what you did. But that doesn't fix the hurt."

"Of course not," Vivienne said, but her heart sank. She had hoped to return to how things were. But at least they were talking. They might never be lovers again, but they might recover something. "I know I hurt you, but I would like to be your friend again. I've… missed you."

"Just friends?" Selene asked and moved closer, wrapping her hands around Vivienne's.

"What else did you have in mind?"

"I want you. I've never stopped wanting you. It will take some time to rebuild trust, but I want to try, at least."

"Is that so?"

"I was awful to you the other day, so I understand if you need more time to consider everything, and I know both of us will need to make amends. But I love you, Vivienne. I want you, and I want to be with you, if you still want—"

Vivienne cut off her words with a kiss, and Selene melted against her. Knowing that Selene wanted her, wanted to try again, made the kiss that much sweeter.

And Vivienne would fight to keep her.

She ran her hands through Selene's hair, then pulled her onto her lap, biting and sucking at her mouth.

Selene moaned.

And then Selene pulled back, laughing. Taking Vivienne's face in her hands, she said, "I take it this means you want to try again?"

"It does," she said. "I thought…that I might have lost my chance with you."

"Nearly," Selene said. "But I understand what it means to have priorities. I won't ask you to put me before Claudia, but I expect you to fight for me as I would for you."

"That's a fair expectation," she said, unbuttoning Selene's blouse. "Is this where we kiss and make up?"

"You tell me."

Vivienne took Selene by the hand and led her to the rug in front of the fireplace. She finished unbuttoning her blouse and slid her clothes off. Then she kissed down her throat until she was kissing her breasts.

"Don't tease," Selene said. "I've missed you."

Vivienne looked up at her and smiled. "I've missed you too," she said and resumed kissing at her belly, moving down to her thighs until at last she pressed her mouth tenderly against her labia and pushed her tongue inside to taste her. Still moving her tongue, Vivienne slid her hand up the back of Selene's thigh and nudged her leg over her shoulder.

They had so much more to talk about, but right now, all Vivienne wanted was to feel Selene's hips rock against her and hear her cry out.

The fire was down to hot coals by the time they finished making love. Selene stretched out before the heat. Vivienne rested on one arm, watching her. "I love you," she said.

"I love you too." Selene reached out to brush Vivienne's hair from her face. "But I'm not done with you yet."

"Is that so?"

"It is." Selene pushed Vivienne onto her back and straddled her.

After they had nearly exhausted themselves, Vivienne called Hattie to let her know that she would not be home that night.

Hattie squealed. "Will you bring Anna home for dinner tomorrow night?"

"She'll be there," Vivienne said, trying to ignore Selene's hands tapping across her back. "I'll see you tomorrow, Hattie."

"She sounded happy," Selene said.

"Ecstatic, I dare say. We may be invited to double date with her and Jonathan."

"That's a scary thought," Selene said, then began kissing Vivienne along her collarbone.

"The worst," Vivienne agreed, her breath quickening as she felt Selene's fingers playing between her thighs. "Selene, stop teasing and fuck me."

"Mm, I don't think so," Selene said and nipped Vivienne's breast until her nipple stood erect. "You're moving far too much for my liking. You need to show some restraint."

"Oh? And what if I don't?"

"Wait and see."

When Selene took her to bed and tied her up, Vivienne remembered how clever Selene was with her tongue. When she had finally finished with her, Selene pulled her into her arms and held her tight.

"It'll take some time," she said, "to get back to how we were. I'm still hurt."

"However long it takes," Vivienne said. "Whatever it takes."

"I deleted all of the photos you sent me. It didn't seem fair to hold on to them."

"Then we'll have to do new ones. Or perhaps I'll learn how to use the video feature," Vivienne teased.

Selene leaned over and kissed her. "You don't happen to have a copy of the one from my office, do you?"

"I don't. But I'm sure we can recreate it. I've still got the necklace you gave me, and that would make a much better photo."

"It would." Then Selene kissed Vivienne's head, and before Vivienne could say another word, she fell asleep against Selene's chest, their breaths rising and falling in time together.

As the days passed, Vivienne spent as many nights at Selene's house as Selene spent at hers. Staying at Selene's meant that they could be as loud as they wanted, while staying at the Carter residence meant acting more demurely. The last thing Vivienne wanted was anyone from her family walking in on them. So they checked to make sure the doors were locked, hushed each other when they started getting boisterous, and even stopped having sex if someone knocked on their door.

They were both busy with work, and they missed being together during the last week of February. Phone sex and suggestive text messages didn't make up for the lack of touch. By the end of the week, Vivienne burned for her.

When Friday rolled around, Vivienne was eager to leave for Selene's. She intended to pin her down and have her way with her the moment she walked through the door.

Except that when she opened her office door to pack her things, Selene was sitting in her chair, her bare legs up on the desk with her ankles crossed. The sight of her bare feet on the wood made Vivienne shiver with excitement.

Selene smiled wickedly. "I wondered how long you were going to take. I believe your class ended…fifteen minutes ago?"

Vivienne quickly stepped inside and locked the door. She turned back to Selene "You're—" She looked Selene over, moving her gaze from the top of the black leather coat to the bare feet resting on the desk. "Are you naked under there?"

"Come over and find out," Selene said.

Vivienne's vision of dinner and drinks by the fire disappeared as Selene gazed suggestively at her. She looked like a queen posing on her throne as she bid her handmaiden to come closer.

Vivienne obeyed her queen as Selene watched her approach to unbuckle Selene's belt and undo her coat.

Selene was nude. In her office.

Vivienne gulped. They had discussed this scene once before. But discussing the idea of sneaking into her office for sex was less fun than the actual situation, especially when she had had no idea that Selene had planned it.

Selene turned in the chair and then pressed her foot against Vivienne's abdomen, keeping her from moving any closer. Then she reached down beside her and picked up her cane. "Would you like to play a game, my love?"

Vivienne shifted her eyes from Selene to the cane, and her body lit up. She didn't move as Selene stood, making no effort to close the jacket.

She stepped in closer to Vivienne and tucked a curl behind her ear. "On the desk, Professor Carter."

"Of course," Vivienne said without hesitating, and bent over her desk with her ass raised and her feet apart.

She heard Selene's footsteps behind her and felt her hands run over her thighs, then raise her skirt up her hips and around her waist. Then she dragged her fingertips back down to where the garter belt attached to her stockings. She flicked them undone, then reached up to pull the band of lace around Vivienne's waist down to her ankles.

"Much better." Selene brushed against her as she drew patterns over Vivienne's ass. "How many lashings can you take, my handmaiden?" she asked.

"Fifteen."

"My, my. Bold number. Are you certain?"

"Yes, my queen."

"That's my girl." Selene stroked across Vivienne's labia.

Vivienne shifted, trying desperately to keep still.

"I want you to count them, and after each one, you're going to say...what, my love?"

"Thank you, my queen." Vivienne said.

"Good girl. And then, when you've said that, you're going to ask for another because you are such a naughty handmaiden. Aren't you, my love?"

This was Vivienne's favorite game to play with Selene. She could lose herself completely in their world.

"Now," Selene said as she pushed Vivienne's legs apart. "Do you remember your safe word?"

"Music box."

"Good." Selene brushed her hands over Vivienne's back as if to soothe her. "I do so love to see you like this."

There was a rush of air, and the cane struck. Vivienne moaned. "One. Thank you, my queen. May I have another?"

"Of course, dear."

Selene struck again, the cane slapping against Vivienne's ass just below the first strike. "Two. Thank you, my queen. May I have another?"

Strike after strike Vivienne counted until she reached seven. Vivienne whimpered, feeling her arousal.

Selene had once promised she could make Vivienne come through spanking alone, and right now, Vivienne believed it. She was close.

But Selene stopped to pass her fingers over the welts on her ass. She pinched one. Vivienne hissed. "Did that hurt?" Selene asked.

"You know very well it did."

"Let me make it up to you," she said and stroked Vivienne's labia.

Vivienne moaned.

"My, my, Professor Carter. Aren't you just delightfully wet and wanton for me?"

"Selene," she sighed.

And then Selene struck with her bare hand, hard and fast, and Vivienne gasped. *Again*, she wanted to say, but she bit back the word as Selene stroked her pussy again, her fingers hovering just at the opening.

"What was that, my love?" Selene asked.

Vivienne corrected herself. "My queen."

"Good girl."

Vivienne strained to look at Selene over her shoulder.

Selene met her gaze. "Eyes forward."

Vivienne obeyed, pushing down on Selene's fingers, losing herself to the pain on her ass and the pleasure between her legs. Just as Vivienne was about to let go, Selene pulled away.

"Were you going to come for me?" she asked.

Vivienne nodded.

"That's not a yes."

"Yes, my queen," Vivienne said, gasping.

Selene struck her ass again, grabbing hold of her flesh. The next cane strike stung against the skin.

Vivienne cried out, then froze, remembering where they were. She looked at the door, trying to remember if she had locked it or not.

"Shall I check for you?" Selene asked, pressing her lips against Vivienne's ear. "It doesn't seem right to make you do it when you're in such a state." She stroked her again.

She was close to orgasm. It wouldn't take much more than another strike or two or a little more pressure against her clit.

"Say pretty please."

"Pretty please."

Selene laughed and let go of Vivienne. She walked over to the door. "Do you remember locking it?"

"No, my queen."

"You were quite distracted…though distraction has become a habit at this point, hasn't it?"

"Yes, my queen." Vivienne stared at Selene. She was naked under the open coat, her dark hair falling across her shoulders. She held a cane in one hand and reached out with the other to check the door.

It was locked.

"Guess you remembered," Selene said. "Now, where were we?"

Selene reached out to cup her hand beneath Vivienne's jaw and tilted her head up. Then she leaned forward and kissed her lips.

Despite her ass throbbing from the caning, the uncomfortable position on her desk, and her neck arching upward, Vivienne felt herself relax. She had to be in heaven because she felt so wonderful.

She wanted Selene to be with her for the rest of her life. She wanted to spend the rest of her days with her, whether it was at the mercy of her cane or asleep in her arms. She wanted mundane days, holidays, good days, hard days, arguments and makeup sex. She wanted to get lost with her in a new city. She wanted to adopt a dog with her. She wanted to sit on the porch and watch the sunset every night. She wanted to grow old with her.

She would ask Selene to move in with her because she couldn't bear the thought of being without her. She wanted every part of her, good and bad.

And to think it had all begun with black lettering on a bright red card:

Selene
Dominatrix

Selene pulled away from the kiss, and Vivienne lost herself in the blue of her eyes, the perfume washing over her senses, her queen's words echoing in her ear:
"Good girl."

OTHER BOOKS FROM YLVA PUBLISHING

www.ylva-publishing.com

THE X INGREDIENT
Roslyn Sinclair

ISBN: 978-3-96324-271-7
Length: 285 pages (103,000 words)

Top Atlanta lawyer, icy Diana Parker, is driven and ruthless, and stuck in a failing marriage. Her new assistant, Laurie, seems all wrong for the job. Yet something seems to be pulling them into a secret, thrilling dance that's far too dangerous for a boss and employee.
How can they resist the irresistible?

A smart, sexy lesbian romance about daring to face the truth about who you are.

LAID BARE
Astrid Ohletz & Jae [Editors]

ISBN: 978-3-96324-214-4
Length: 154 pages (61,000 words)

If you enjoy erotic stories about women loving women, get your hands on this collection of sensual short stories from nine of the most prominent names in lesbian fiction, many of them award-winning authors.
Stories by Jae, Lee Winter, Harper Bliss, KD Williamson, A.L. Brooks, Lola Keeley, Alison Grey, Jess Lea, and Emma Weimann.

NIGHTS OF SILK AND SAPPHIRE
Amber Jacobs

ISBN: 978-3-95533-511-3
Length: 309 pages (113,000 words)

Dae is rescued from desert slavers by the mysterious Zafirah Al'Intisar and placed as a prize in the Scion's harem. At first, Dae struggles with desires she has never before experienced, but as love and lust collide these two women slowly forge a bond.

A woman, rescued from desert slavers and placed as a prize in a harem, struggles with desires she has never before experienced.

THE TASTE OF HER
Jess Lea

ISBN: 978-3-96324-009-6
Length: 174 pages (74,000 words)

In this tantalizing collection of erotic lesbian short stories, strong, beautiful, and fierce women are laid bare.

These ten erotic stories first appeared in the e-book versions of volume one and two of The Taste of Her *and are now available in one sizzling paperback.*

ABOUT THEA BELMONT

Thea grew-up in rural Australia, developing her love of reading and writing from a young age. As a young adult, she left for the city, where she had her first brush with kink and fell in love with a world that balanced devotion and discipline.

She currently enjoys life in Sydney with her partner and cat.

Principle Decisions
© 2023 by Thea Belmont

ISBN: 978-3-96324-832-0

Available in e-book and paperback formats.

Published by Ylva Publishing, legal entity of Ylva Verlag, e.Kfr.

Ylva Verlag, e.Kfr.
Owner: Astrid Ohletz
Am Kirschgarten 2
65830 Kriftel
Germany

www.ylva-publishing.com

First edition: 2023

No part of this book may be reproduced, scanned, or distributed in any printed or electronic form without permission. Please do not participate in or encourage piracy of copyrighted materials in violation of the author's rights. Thank you for respecting the hard work of this author.

This is a work of fiction. Names, characters, places, and incidents either are a product of the author's imagination or are used fictitiously, and any resemblance to locales, events, business establishments, or actual persons—living or dead—is entirely coincidental.

Credits
Edited by Lee Winter, Michelle Aguilar, and Julie Klein
Cover Design and Print Layout by Streetlight Graphics

Printed in Great Britain
by Amazon